McNally's Caper

'You know', Rogoff started, 'I'm beginning to see us as Laurel and Hardy. I'm the fat one who always says, "Here's another fine mess you've got me into." '

'Al,' I said, 'I swear I had nothing to do with it except recommend that the police be notified.

'But you told Griswold Forsythe to hand me the squeal, didn't you?'

'Well, yes,' I admitted. 'But only because I knew he demanded discretion.'

'Discretion?' He honked a bitter laugh. 'It's hard to be discreet, sonny boy, when someone's tried to choke a woman to death.'

'I know you'll try to keep a lid on it,' I said soothingly. 'How did you make out at the Kingdom of Oz?'

'The Forsythe place? As damp inside as it is out. It's a wonder they all don't have webs between their toes . . .'

About the author

Lawrence Sanders, one of the world's most popular novelists, is the author of twenty-seven bestsellers including the *Commandment* and *Deadly Sin* series and the Archy McNally novels, *McNally's Caper* being the most recent. A New Yorker, he now lives in Florida.

McNally's Caper

Lawrence Sanders

CORONET BOOKS
Hodder and Stoughton

Copyright © 1994 by Lawrence A. Sanders Enterprises, Inc.

The right of Lawrence Sanders to be identified as the Author of
the Work has been asserted by him in accordance with the
Copyright, Designs and Patents Act 1988.

First published in 1994 by G. P. Putnam's Sons.
First published in Great Britain in 1994
by Hodder and Stoughton
A division of Hodder Headline PLC
First published in paperback in 1995 by Hodder and Stoughton

A Coronet paperback

10 9 8 7 6 5 4 3 2

British Library Cataloguing in Publication Data

Sanders, Lawrence
McNally's Caper
I. Title
813.54[F]

ISBN 0 340 62879 0

Printed and bound in Great Britain by
Cox & Wyman Ltd, Reading, Berkshire

Hodder and Stoughton
A division of Hodder Headline PLC
338 Euston Road
London NW1 3BH

McNALLY'S CAPER

1

After a great deal of heavy reflection I have come to the conclusion that everyone is nuts. And I mean *everyone*, not just a sprinkling of ding-a-lings.

You think me a misanthrope? Listen to this . . .

I am the chief (and sole member) of the Discreet Inquiries Department of McNally & Son, Attorney-at-Law. (My father is the Attorney, I am the Son.) We represent some very prestigious clients—and a scurvy few—in the Town of Palm Beach. Occasionally they request the services of a private and prudent investigator rather than take their problems to the police and risk seeing their tribulations luridly described in a supermarket tabloid, alongside a story headlined "Elvis Lands in UFO!"

One of our commercial clients is a sinfully luxe jewelry store on Worth Avenue. They had recently been plagued by a shoplifter who was boosting a choice selection of merchandise. Not their most costly baubles, of course; those were locked away in vaults and shown only in private. But they were losing a number of less expensive items—brooches, rings, bracelets, necklaces—that were on public display.

Their concealed video camera soon revealed the miscreant. They were shocked, *shocked* to recognize one of their best customers, a wealthy widow who dropped at least a hundred grand annually in legitimate purchases. I shall not reveal her name because you would immediately recognize it. Not wishing to prosecute such a valued patron, the jewelry store brought its distressing predicament to McNally & Son, and I was given the task of ending the lady's pilfering without enraging her to the extent that she would purchase her diamond tiaras elsewhere, perhaps at Wal-Mart or Home Depot.

It was a nice piece of work and I started by learning all I could about the kleptomaniacal matron. I consulted Consuela Garcia first. Connie is employed as social secretary to Lady Cynthia Horowitz, possibly the wealthiest of our chatelaines. Connie is my inamorata and au courant with all the latest Palm Beach rumors, scandals, and skeletons that have not yet emerged from the closet.

I also phoned Lolly Spindrift, the gossip columnist on one of our local rags. He has an encyclopedic knowledge of the peccadilloes, kinks, and outré personal habits of even our most august residents.

From these two fonts of impropriety, if not of wisdom, I learned that the shoplifter in her younger years (several decades ago) had been an actress. Not a first-magnitude star, but a second-echelon player who had never quite made it to the top. I mean that in films she always lost the hero to the leading lady and in TV sitcoms she invariably played the wisecracking but sympathetic roommate. She did very well financially, I'm sure, but I doubt if sophomores ever Scotch-taped her photo to dormitory walls.

Then, her career in decline, she had the great good sense to marry a moneyed business executive whose corporation reaped satisfying profits by producing plastic place mats imprinted with classic scenes such as the Parthenon and Las Vegas at night. Upon his retirement the childless but apparently happy couple moved to Palm Beach. He died five years later on the tennis court while playing a third set in 104° heat, and his widow inherited a bundle.

Having learned all I needed to know about the lady in question, I had a videocassette made of all the snippets of tape taken by the jewelry store's hidden TV cameras. The subject was easily recognizable and clearly shown slipping glittering items into her capacious handbag. She did it so deftly, so nonchalantly, I could only conclude she had long practiced the craft.

I decided my best strategy was a "cold call," descending upon her suddenly without making an appointment and giving her the opportunity to prepare a defense. And so on a warmish evening in mid-September I tootled my flag-red Miata down the coast to the Via Palma. The lady's home turned out to be a faux Spanish hacienda with the most spectacular landscaping I had ever seen.

The door was opened by a uniformed maid who accepted my business card and advised me to wait—outside. In a few moments the door was reopened and the matron herself stood before me, clad in hostess pajamas of ginger-colored silk.

"Yes, Mr. McNally," she said, pleasantly enough, "what's this all about?"

I mentioned the name of the client represented by my law firm and told her I wished to discuss a personal matter of some importance. She hesitated briefly, then asked me in. She led the way to a small sitting room where a television set was playing. And there, on the screen, was the lady herself, thirty years younger. I wondered if that was how she spent her evenings: watching reruns of ancient sitcoms in which she had performed.

She was a striking woman with a proud posture and complete self-possession. Her features had the tight, glacial look that bespoke a face-lift, and her figure was so trim and youthful that I imagined breast implants, a tummy tuck, and a rump elevation had been included in a package deal.

She switched off the TV and, without asking me to be seated, looked at me inquiringly. There was no way I could pussyfoot, but as gently as I could I explained that her favorite jewelry store was well aware of her shoplifting. If she doubted that, I said, I had brought along a videocassette that showed her in action.

I didn't know what to expect: furious denial, tears, hysteria, perhaps even a physical assault on yrs. truly. What I received was a welcome surprise: a really brilliant smile.

"Hidden TV cameras, I suppose," she said.

I nodded.

"That's not fair," she said with a charming pout. "Would you care for a drink, Mr. McNally?"

"I would indeed, thank you, ma'am."

Five minutes later we were seated on a mauve velvet couch, sipping excellent kir royales, and discussing her criminal career like civilized people. I was immensely relieved.

"I suppose you think me a kleptomaniac," she said easily.

"The thought had occurred to me," I acknowledged.

She shook her head and artfully coiffed white curls bobbed about. "Not so," she said. "I did not have a deprived childhood. I never lacked for a loving mate in my life. I have no feeling of insecurity nor do I desire to seek revenge against a cruel, unfeeling world."

"Then *why?*" I asked, truly perplexed.

"Boredom," she said promptly. "Shoplifting gives me a thrill. It's such a naughty thing to do, you see. And at my age I must battle ennui as vigorously as I do arthritis. Can you understand that?"

I laughed. I *loved* this splendid woman. "Of course I understand," I said. "But I'm afraid your motive, no matter how reasonable it may seem to you and me, would not constitute a convincing legal defense."

"What is it the jewelry store wants?"

"Payment for or return of the items you have stolen. I presume you still have them?"

"I do."

"What they *don't* want," I went on, "what they emphatically do not wish is to lose you as a customer. They value your patronage."

"As well they should," she said. "I spend a mint there. But they are very agreeable people, very eager to please. I should hate to go elsewhere for my trinkets."

We looked at each other.

"You strike me as a very clever young man, Mr. McNally," she said. "Can you suggest a solution?"

"Yes, I can," I said without hesitation. "Continue shopping there. At the same time resume the depredations that relieve your boredom. But grant permission to the store to bill you monthly for the merchandise you steal."

She laughed delightedly. "A wonderful solution!" she cried.

"It won't spoil it for you to know that your thefts are being observed and you will be charged for them?"

11

She lifted her chin. "I am an actress," she said with great dignity. "I know how to pretend."

"Excellent," I said, finishing my drink and rising. "I am sure our client will be delighted with the arrangement."

She escorted me to the door and we clasped hands.

"Do come see me again," she said.

"Thank you," I said. "I certainly shall. It's been a delightful visit."

"Hasn't it?" she said and leaned forward to kiss my cheek.

I drove home in a sportive mood. I was more convinced than ever that goofiness was engulfing the world, but I also admitted that if everyone acted in a sensible, logical fashion there would be little gainful employment for your humble correspondent.

I arrived at the McNally manse at about ten o'clock. I pulled into our three-car garage between my father's black Lexus and mother's antique wood-bodied Ford station wagon. The lights in mon père's study were still ablaze, and when I entered the house through the back door I saw the oak portal to his sanctum was ajar. It was his signal that he deigned to receive visitors. That evening, I knew, he was awaiting a report on my confrontation with the piratical widow.

He was seated behind his magisterial desk and, as usual, there was a glass of port at his elbow. And, as usual, he was smoking one of his silver-banded James Upshall pipes. And, as usual, he was reading one of his leather-bound volumes of Dickens. I admired his perseverance. He was determined to plow his way through that author's entire oeuvre, and I could only hope he survived long enough to succeed.

He looked up when I entered and put his book aside. He invited me to pour myself a glass of port. I respectfully declined, not daring to tell him that I thought the last case he had bought was on the musty side. But I did relax in one of his club chairs and delivered an abbreviated account of my meeting with the bored shoplifter.

He did not laugh aloud but one of his hirsute eyebrows rose a good half-inch and he stroked his guardsman's mustache with a knuckle, a sure sign that he was mightily amused.

"A win-win outcome, Archy," he commented. "Well done."

"Thank you, sir."

Then he was silent and I knew he had slipped into his pondering mode. I have mentioned several times in previous tales that my father is a world-class muller, always meditating before making any meaningful pronouncement or taking any significant action. After all, he is an attorney and knows the dangers of hasty words and decisions. But is it absolutely necessary to ruminate for three minutes before resolving to add a drop of Tabasco to one's deviled egg?

"Archy," he said finally, "are you acquainted with Griswold Forsythe the Second?"

"Yes, sir, I am," I replied. "The all-time champion bore of Palm Beach."

"And his son, Griswold Forsythe the Third?"

"I know him also. A chip off the old blockhead."

Father grimaced. He did not like me to jest about the clients of McNally & Son. He felt that since their fees paid for our steak au poivre we should accord them at least a modicum of respect.

"The senior Forsythe came to the office this afternoon," mein papa continued. "His problem is somewhat akin to the case you have just concluded."

I groaned. "He's so antiquated he remembers the two-pants suit. Don't tell me the old gaffer has become a shop-lifter."

"No, he is not a thief but he suspects someone in his home may be. He claims several items of value have disappeared."

"Such as?"

"A first edition Edgar Allan Poe. A large, unset cushion-cut emerald belonging to his wife. A Georgian silver soup ladle. A small Benin bronze. An original Picasso lithograph. And other things."

"The thief has expensive tastes," I observed.

"Yes," father agreed, "and Forsythe is convinced he or she is a family member or one of the household staff, all live-in servants who have been with him for years."

"But the thefts are a recent development?"

My liege nodded. "Naturally Forsythe doesn't wish to take the matter to the authorities. He would much prefer a discreet investigation."

This time I moaned. "That means I will have to spend a great deal of time prowling about the Forsythe castle, that ugly heap of granite north of Lady Horowitz's estate. How does Mr. Forsythe propose to account for my presence? Does he intend to tell family and staff what I'm up to?"

"Oh no, definitely not. He will be the only one who knows your true purpose. As you may be aware, he has a rather extensive private library. He suggests that he tell the others you have been employed to prepare a catalog of his books."

I considered that a moment. "It might work," I admitted. "But is he absolutely certain the thief is not an outsider? A deliveryman perhaps. The guy who trims his shrubbery."

"I asked him that, but he believes it would be impossible. When workers are allowed inside they are always accompanied by the housekeeper. And some of the missing items were hidden. The Benin bronze, for instance, was not on display but placed far back on a closet shelf in Forsythe's study. And the unset emerald was in a suede pouch tucked into the bottom drawer of his wife's dresser. Family members and staff may have been aware of their existence and site, but strangers could not know and had no opportunity to search. Mr. Forsythe is expecting you tomorrow morning at nine o'clock."

"Nine?" I said indignantly. "Father, I'm not fully awake by then."

"Try," His Majesty said and picked up his Dickens.

I climbed the creaking stairs to my mini-suite on the third floor. It was hardly lavish—small sitting room, bedroom, bathroom—but I had no complaints; it was my cave and I prized it. The rent was particularly attractive. Zip.

I poured myself a wee marc from my liquor supply stored within a battered sea chest at the foot of my bed. Then I lighted an English Oval (only my third of the day) and plopped down behind the ramshackle desk in my sitting room. I donned reading glasses, for although I will not be thirty-seven years old until March of next year, my peepers are about sixty-five and require specs for close-up work.

I keep a journal of my discreet inquiries, jotting down things I have learned, heard, assumed, or imagined. The scribblings, added to almost daily when I am working on a case, serve as a reminder of matters important and matters trivial.

That night I wrote finis to the story of the shoplifting widow and started a fresh page with my latest assignment: discovering who in the ménage of Griswold Forsythe II was swiping all that swell stuff. I thought the inquiry would be as much of a drag as the victim and his tiresome son. I reckoned the chances were good that the allegedly purloined items had simply been misplaced. For instance, I still haven't found my Mickey Mouse beach towel although I am fairly certain it hasn't been stolen.

I went to bed that night still musing on the looniness of the human condition. My investigation of the Forsythe thieveries was to prove how right I was. But the craziness I uncovered turned out to be no ha-ha matter. It was scary and before it was finished I began to believe the entire world was one enormous acorn academy—with no doctors in attendance.

2

"I was a dirty old man at the age of nine," Griswold Forsythe II pronounced in his churchy voice and waited for my laugh.

I obliged, fighting valiantly against an urge to nod off.

"I see these young girls in their short skirts," he droned on. "Tanned legs that start under their chin and go on forever. And I feel a great sadness. Not because I shall never have them but because I know their beauty will wither. Age insists on taking its inevitable toll."

"Mr. Forsythe," I said, "about your missing treasures..."

"But then," he continued to preach, "age does have its compensations. I'll tell you something about death, Archy: one grows into it. I don't mean you begin to die the day you're born; everyone knows that. But as the years dwindle down you gradually come to terms with your own mortality. And, in my case, begin to look forward to dissolution with curiosity and, I must admit, a certain degree of relish."

"How long, O Lord, how long?" I prayed silently. And you know, the odd thing about this garrulous fogy was that he was not all that ancient. Not much older than my father, I reckoned; I knew his son was about my age. Yet the two Forsythes, II and III, had brought codgerism to new heights—or depths. I shall not attempt to reproduce their speech exactly on these pages; the plummy turgidities would give you a sudden attack of the Z's.

And not only in their speech, but both father and son affected a grave and stately demeanor. No sudden bursts of laughter from those two melancholics, no public manifestations of delight, surprise, or almost any other human emotion. I often wondered what might happen if their rusty clockwork slipped a gear.

"Mr. Forsythe," I tried again, desperately this time, "about the stolen items . . ."

"Ah, yes," he said. "Distressing. And we can't let it continue, can we?"

"No, sir."

"Distressing," he repeated. "Most distressing."

We were seated in his library, a gloomy chamber lined with floor-to-ceiling oak cases of books, most of them in matching sets. There was a handsome ladder on wheels that enabled one to reach the upper shelves, but I couldn't believe he or anyone else in his ménage had read even a fraction of those thousands of volumes.

"I suggest you make this room your headquarters," he instructed. "Your combat center, so to speak. Feel free to come and go as you please. Speak to anyone you wish: family members and staff."

"They are not aware of my assignment?"

"They are not," he said firmly. "Not even my wife. So I expect you to conduct your investigation with a high degree of circumspection."

"Naturally," I said, reflecting that I had been called many things in my lifetime but circumspect was not one of them. "Mr. Forsythe, could you give me a brief rundown on your household."

He looked at me, puzzled. "The people, you mean?" he asked.

Did he think I meant the number of salad forks? "Yes, sir," I said. "The persons in residence."

"Myself and my wife Constance, of course. Our unmarried daughter Geraldine. Our son, whom I believe you know, and his wife Sylvia and their young daughter Lucy. The staff consists of Mrs. Nora Bledsoe, our housekeeper and majordomo, so to speak. Her son, Anthony, serves as butler and houseman. Two maids, Sheila and Fern. The chef's name is Zeke Grenough. We also employ a full-time gardener, Rufino Diaz, but he doesn't dwell on the premises."

"Quite an establishment," I commented.

"Is it?" he said, mildly surprised that everyone didn't live so well-attended. "When my parents were alive we had a live-in staff of twelve. But of course they did a great deal of entertaining. I rarely entertain. Dislike it, in fact. Too much chatter."

I was tempted to ask, "You mean you can't get a word in edgewise?" But I didn't, of course.

"I'm sure I'll get them all sorted out," I told him.

"And when may I expect results?"

"No way of telling, Mr. Forsythe. But I'm as eager as you to bring this matter to a speedy conclusion. And now, with your permission, I'd like to take a look around the grounds."

"Of course," he said. "Learn the lay of the land, so to speak, eh?"

I could have made a coarse rejoinder to that but restrained myself. Griswold Forsythe II led me to a back door that allowed exit to the rear acres of the estate.

"When you have completed your inspection," he said, "I

suggest you request Mrs. Bledsoe to give you a tour of the house. There are many hallways, many rooms, many nooks and crannies. We don't want you getting lost, do we?''

"We surely don't," I said, repressing a terrible desire to kick his shins. Because, you see, I suspected he didn't want me strolling unescorted through his home. Which made me wonder what it was he wished to keep hidden.

The Forsythe estate wasn't quite Central Park but it was lavish even by Palm Beach standards. The landscaping was somewhat formal for my taste but I could not deny it was attractive and well-groomed. There was a mini-orchard of orange, grapefruit and lime trees. Birdhouses were everywhere, some seemingly designed to mimic the Forsythe mansion in miniature. I thought that a bit much but apparently the birds approved.

I was examining a curious lichen growing on the trunk of an oak so venerable it was decrepit when a young miss popped out from behind a nearby palm and shouted, "Boo!"

I was not at all startled. "Boo, yourself," I replied. "What is the meaning of this unseemly behavior—leaping out at innocent visitors and yelping, 'Boo!'?''

She giggled.

I am not expert at estimating the age of children. They are all kids to me until they become youngsters. This particular specimen appeared to be about eight years old, with a possible error of plus or minus three. She was an uncommonly fetching child with flaxen hair that tumbled to her shoulders. Heavy braces encircled her upper teeth but she had the self-assurance of a woman quintuple her age.

"What's your name?" she demanded.

"My name is Archibald McNally," I replied. "But it would give me great pleasure if you called me Archy."

Silence. "Don't you want to know my name?" she finally asked.

"I can guess," I said. "You are Lucy Forsythe and you live here."

"How did you know that?"

"I know everything," I told her.

"No, you don't," she said. "Do you want to hear a dirty word?"

I sighed. "All right."

"Mud," she said and laughed like a maniac. I did, too.

"You're very pretty," she said.

"Thank you," I said. "Not as pretty as you."

"Do you have a girlfriend?"

"Sort of," I answered. "Do you have a boyfriend?"

"Sort of."

"Why aren't you in school today, Lucy?"

"I'm sick," she said and giggled again.

"Nothing catching I hope."

"Well, I'm not really sick but I said I was because I didn't feel like going to school today. You won't tell anyone, will you?"

"Not me," I said. "I know how to keep a secret."

"Hey," she said, "want to see my secret place?"

"I'd like that very much."

She was wearing a pink two-piece playsuit and a matching hair ribbon. She was a gangly child with a lovely apricot suntan and a deliciously gawky way of moving, flinging arms and legs about as if she had not yet mastered the art of controlling those elongated appendages.

She took my hand and tugged me along. We stepped off the bricked walk and slipped into a treed area so thickly planted that sunlight cast a dappled pattern onto ground cover sprinkled with small white flowers I could not identify. Then we came into a small open area hardly larger than a bathmat but carpeted with bright green moss.

"This belongs to me," Lucy said proudly. "It's my secret place. Isn't it nice?"

"It is indeed," I agreed. "What do you do here?"

"Mostly I just sit and think. Sometimes I eat a sandwich."

"Do you invite many guests?"

She looked at me shyly. "You're the first."

"I'm honored," I said. "When you come here to think, what do you think about?"

I wasn't trying to pump the child, you know; just making conversation I hoped would interest her. I know she interested me. I thought her alert and knowledgeable beyond her years.

She considered my question. "Well, sometimes I come here when things get noisy at home."

"Noisy?"

She looked away. "They start shouting. That scares me. I'm afraid they'll kill each other."

"I don't think so, Lucy. Grown-ups have different opinions and occasionally they begin arguing and their voices get louder."

"Then they send me out of the room," she said. "They always say, 'Little pitchers have big ears.' I don't think my ears are so big, do you?"

"Of course not. You have beautiful ears. It's just a saying, like 'Children should be seen and not heard.' I bet you've been told that one, too."

She stared at me in astonishment. "How did you know?"

"I told you I know everything. Lucy, I've enjoyed your company and I thank you for showing me your secret place. But I've got to get back to the house and go to work."

"What kind of work?"

"I'm preparing a catalog of your grandfather's library."

"What's a catalog?"

"A list of all the books he owns."

"There's an awful lot of them."

"There certainly are. That's why I've got to begin. Would you like to come back with me?"

"No," she said. "I'll just sit here and think."

I nodded and started away.

"Archy," she called, and I turned back. "Will you be my friend?" she asked.

I said, "That would make me very happy."

"What we could do sometime," she said, suddenly excited, "is have a little picnic here. Zeke will make us some sandwiches."

"That sounds like fun," I said. "Let's do it."

I left her then. Curious child. Lonely child.

I emerged from the wooded area and stood a moment on the back lawn, examining the Forsythe mansion. I had been correct in describing it to my father as a castle. I have never seen such an excess of turrets, battlements, parapets, and embrasures. All that hideous pile of stone lacked was a moat and drawbridge. The whole thing looked as if the architect had expected the Visigoths to descend on the Town of Palm Beach at any moment.

The rear entrance to the Forsythes' granite shack consisted of double doors. The inner was solidly planked and fitted with a stout lock. That portal was wide open. The exterior door, closed, was merely a screen in an aluminum frame.

Although Mr. Forsythe had granted me permission to come and go as I pleased, I thought it best to announce my arrival and so I rapped lightly on the jamb of the screen. No response. I thought that odd since I could hear a muted conversation within. I knocked more vigorously. Still no answer, but I became aware that the volume of the dialogue was rising.

Eavesdropping is one of my minor vices, and I moved closer to the screen in an effort to hear what was being expressed so forcibly. But I could make out no words, only angry voices. One, male, seemed to be supplicating. The other was female, furious and scornful. I recalled what Lucy had just told me of being frightened by the loud arguments of grown-ups.

Then I heard what had to be a violent slap: someone's palm smacked against another's face. This was followed by a woman's gasp and wail. I delayed no longer but opened the screen door and shouted, "Hallo, hallo! Anyone home?"

Silence. And then, a moment later, a woman approached from what appeared to be a tiled corridor. She was sturdily constructed, wide through shoulders, bosom and hips. I could not get a good look at her features for she was holding a hand to her right cheek.

"Good morning!" I said cheerily. "My name is Archibald McNally. I hope Mr. Forsythe informed you that I'll be to-ing and fro-ing while I catalog his library."

She nodded. "Yes, sir," she said in what I can only describe as a strangled voice, "he told us. I am Mrs. Nora Bledsoe, the Forsythes' housekeeper."

"Pleased to make your acquaintance, ma'am," I said and held out my right hand, knowing that to shake it she would have to uncover her face. She hesitated an instant then did what I had hoped. I saw at once that she had been the slapee, for her right cheek was reddened.

"I've been taking a look at your bully greenery," I said

breezily. "Mr. Forsythe suggested you would be willing to give me a tour of the interior."

It took her half a mo to regain her composure. I could understand that; she had just taken a good clop to the jaw and it had rattled her.

"Yes, of course," she said finally. She tried a brave smile but it didn't work. "If you'll follow me, Mr. McNally, I'll show you everything."

I doubted that but I willingly trailed after her. She was remarkably light on her feet for such a heavy woman. She was wearing a flowered shirtwaist dress and I noted her thick, jetty hair was drawn back and held with a silver filigreed pin.

"That's a handsome barrette, Mrs. Bledsoe," I said. "Is it an antique?"

She turned and I could see she was pleased. She reached back to touch it. "Oh yes," she said, "it's Victorian. Mr. and Mrs. Forsythe gave it to me as a birthday gift. I do like nice things."

"Don't we all," I said, and we both laughed. She ceased leading and we walked alongside each other, shoulders touching occasionally in the narrow hallways.

"I think we'll start at the top," she said, "and work our way down. From attic to dungeon."

"Dungeon?"

"That's what we call the basement area. Very dark and damp. Nothing but cobwebs and our wine racks."

"Cellars are rare in South Florida," I commented.

"Ours is supposed to be haunted," she said. "By the ghost of Mr. Forsythe's grandmother."

"Oh?" I said.

"She committed suicide."

"Ah," I said.

25

3

What a mazy mansion that was! As we traipsed from floor to floor, room to room, I became convinced that the architect had been totally deranged. Regal corridors led to naught but cramped window seats; artfully carved walnut doors opened to reveal a shallow linen press; some of the bedchambers were ballrooms and some were walk-in closets.

I had welcomed this inspection as an opportunity to spot a hidey-hole where the purloined works of art might be stashed. But it was hopeless; there were simply too many "nooks and crannies," as Mr. Forsythe had warned. It would take a regiment of snoops a month of Sundays to search that hodgepodge—and even then a cleverly concealed cache could remain hidden.

"An astounding home," I remarked to Mrs. Bledsoe.

"Well, it is a little unusual," she admitted. "I've been with the family for many years, and it took me two to learn where everything was and how to get about. Just last month I discovered a cupboard I didn't know existed. It was behind draperies in one of the guest bedrooms."

"And what was in it?" I asked eagerly.

"Old copies of *Liberty* magazine," she said.

We were on the third floor, or it might have been the

second, when I heard harpsichord music coming from behind a closed door. I stopped to listen. I thought it might be
Scarlatti or perhaps Jelly Roll Morton.

"That's Mrs. Sylvia playing," my guide explained. "The
younger Mr. Forsythe's wife. She's very good."

"Would she mind if we intruded?"

"I'm sure she wouldn't."

She knocked once, pushed the door open, and we entered. It was a mid-sized chamber completely naked of any
furnishings except for the bleached pine harpsichord and
the bench before it. The seated woman stopped playing
and looked up inquiringly.

"Mrs. Sylvia," the housekeeper said, "this gentleman is
Archibald McNally who is preparing a catalog of Mr. Forsythe's library."

"Of course," the young lady said, rose and came sweep-
ing forward, if one may sweep while wearing tight blue
jeans and a snug T-shirt inscribed with Gothic lettering:
Amor vincit omnia. Right on, Sylvia! She had the same
flaxen hair as Lucy; the two could have been sisters instead
of mother and daughter.

"Mr. McNally," she said, giving me a warm hand and an
elfin smile, "welcome to the catacombs."

"A bit overwhelming," I confessed. "Please forgive this
interruption."

"Not at all," she said. "I needed a break. Vivaldi is *so*
difficult."

So much for Scarlatti and Jelly Roll Morton.

"I had the pleasure of meeting your daughter earlier this
morning," I told her. "An entrancing child. We had a nice
chat."

Her smile faded to be replaced—by what? I could not

decipher that expression but I imagined I saw something
cold and stony.

"You mustn't believe everything Lucy says," and her
laugh was as tinny as the harpsichord. "She's quite imagi-
native."

"Children usually are," I agreed. "How long have you
been playing?"

"Years," she said and turned to look at her instrument.
"I made it."

"You didn't!"

"I did," she said, nodding. "Didn't I, Nora? It came in a
kit but I put it together. It took ages."

"Good for you," I said. "I play tenor kazoo with a pickup
jazz combo at my club but that's the extent of my musical
talent."

She looked at me thoughtfully. "I'm sure you underestimate your talents, Mr. McNally. Do stop by again. Whenever you like."

"Thank you," I said. "I shall."

Mrs. Bledsoe and I continued our tour. But I was weary-
ing. In truth, it was a dreary dwelling, a fitting abode for
the Addams Family. I could understand why Lucy yearned
for a sunlit place all her own.

I was given a brief peek into the haunted dungeon and
then we returned to the kitchen, large enough to feed the
1st Marine Division. The entire staff had gathered, preparing for lunch. I was introduced to all, tried to remember
names and faces, and failed miserably. They were pleasant
enough except for Anthony, Mrs. Bledsoe's son, who
seemed somewhat surly. And Fern, one of the maids, was
apparently afflicted with a nonstop giggle.

The chef, Zeke Grenough, a diminutive man who wore

a wire-rimmed pince-nez, was stirring a caldron of what smelled aromatically like squid stew. I hoped I might be invited to share their noontime repast, for I am hopelessly enamored of calamari in any form whatsoever. But no one urged me to remain and so I bid that lucky crew a polite adieu and departed.

I tooled the Miata south on Ocean Boulevard, my salivary glands working overtime as I reflected there was probably red wine in that stew and it would possibly be served over saffron rice. It was enough to make me whimper.

I pulled into the driveway of the lavish estate belonging to Lady Cynthia Horowitz and drove around to the rear. I entered the main house through the unlocked back door and went directly to the office of Consuela Garcia, social secretary and the lady with whom I am intimate and to whom, regrettably, I am inevitably unfaithful.

Connie, as usual, was on the phone but raised her face for a cheek kiss. I was happy to oblige. Then I flopped into the only visitor's chair available and listened with delight as my leman tore the hide off a florist whose last delivery of arrangements to the Horowitz home had wilted and shed petals not in days but within hours.

"In hours!" Connie shouted wrathfully. "Do you understand what I'm saying? Those flowers had rigor mortis when they arrived. Where did you find them—on graves?"

She listened a moment and seemed mollified. "I should think you would," she barked into the phone. "Get the replacements here by three o'clock or we cancel our account—is that clear? And go easy on the daisies. We're paying orchid prices for daisies?"

She slammed down the receiver and grinned at me. "I love to read the riot act to these banditos," she said. "They think that just because Lady C. has zillions she's a patsy. No way! How are you, hon?"

"Tip-top," I said. "Lunch?"

She shook her head. "No can do. We're planning a benefit dinner and I've got to get cracking on it."

"Benefit for what? Or whom?"

"Unwed mothers."

"Don't look at me like that, Connie," I said. "I'm not guilty."

"I wish I could be sure," she said. "Is that why you popped by—to ask me to lunch?"

"That and some information."

"It figures. Who is it this time?"

"The Griswold Forsythes."

"Dull, dull, dull," she said promptly. "Except Sylvia, the daughter-in-law. She's a live one. The others are lumps."

"What about Geraldine, the unmarried daughter?"

Connie thought a moment. "Strange," she said finally. "Bookish. Travels a lot. And brainy—except when it comes to men. A few years ago she had a thing going with a polo player who turned out to be a slime. Not only did he dump her but, according to the gossip, he took her for heavy bucks."

I nodded. It never ceases to amaze me how many seemingly intelligent women grant their favors to absolute rotters. (I myself have been the lucky beneficiary of that phenomenon.)

"But I guess the Forsythes could afford it," Connie went on. "It's old money, isn't it, Archy?"

"So old it goes back to beaver pelts and canal boats," I told her. "All neatly tied up in a trust fund. I don't think the Griswolds Two and Three have done a lick of work in their lifetimes. They keep a small office on Royal Palm Way not far from the McNally Building and they employ a male secretary one year younger than God. A few months ago I had to deliver some documents and the three of them were playing tiddledywinks."

She howled. "You're making that up!"

"Scout's honor. What else have they got to do except clip bond coupons? Well, luv, if you can't have lunch I better toddle along and see what the Chez McNally has to offer. Thanks for the info."

"Call me tonight?" she asked.

"Don't I always?"

"No," she said. "Kissy-kissy?"

So we kissed. Very enjoyable. Almost as good as squid stew.

I arrived home to discover the only inhabitant present was our taciturn houseman, Jamie Olson. He and his wife, our cook and housekeeper Ursi, are the McNallys' live-in staff and manage our home with Scandinavian efficiency and an Italianate delight in good food. They are an elderly couple and a blessing, both of them.

Jamie is also a great source of backstairs gossip currently making the rounds amongst the domestics serving the nabobs of Palm Beach. Butlers, maids, and valets know or can guess who's doing what to whom, and more than once I have depended on Jamie Olson to fill me in on the high and low jinks of our uppercrust citizens.

My mother and Ursi having departed on a shopping expedition, Jamie was preparing a luncheon that consisted of four varieties of herring with warm German potato salad, plus buttered black bread. I saw nothing to object to and the two of us sat at the kitchen table and scarfed contentedly.

"Jamie," I said, "do you know Mrs. Nora Bledsoe, the keeper of the keys for the Griswold Forsythes?"

"Uh-huh," he said.

"Married, divorced—or what?"

"Her mister took off a long time ago."

"Oh?" I said. "Present whereabouts unknown, I suppose."

"Yep."

"So she went to work for the Forsythes. What about her son, Anthony? Butler and houseman, I understand. Do you have any scoop on him?"

"Mean."

"By 'mean' I presume you wish to imply he's a bit on the nasty side."

He nodded.

Jamie really does know things but getting him to divulge them requires infinite patience.

"Anything else you can reveal about the Forsythes' staff—for or against? What about the chef, Zeke Grenough?"

"He's straight."

"And the maids, Sheila and Fern?"

Jamie gave me a gap-toothed grin. He had, I realized, neglected to insert his bridge that morning. "Those two like to party," he reported. "There was some talk that Forsythe junior was making up to Sheila—she's the pretty one—but the old man soon put a stop to that."

"I'll bet he did," I said. "And what about the mistress of the castle, Constance Forsythe. Anything on her?"

"Horsey."

"You mean she looks like a horse?"

"Boards 'em. Got a farm out near Wellington."

"That's interesting. Racehorses? Polo ponies?"

"Show horses. Jumpers."

And that's all he could tell me about the Forsythes. I finished lunch and handed him a tenner. The Olsons drew a generous salary, of course, but I never considered Jamie's confidential assistance was included in their monthly stipend so I always slipped him a pourboire for extra services rendered. My father would be furious if he ever learned of it.

Before I returned to the Forsythe manse I went up to my digs and loaded a Mark Cross attaché case with yellow legal pads, file cards, a small magnifying glass, and a roll of gummed labels. Since I was going to be on stage I figured a few props would help authenticate my role as an earnest cataloger of libraries. I also took along my reading glasses, although I hate to wear them in public. They make me look like a demented owl.

The Forsythes' front door seemed stout enough to withstand a battering ram but was fitted with a rather prissy brass knob in an acanthus design. I pulled it and heard chimes sound within. A moment later the heavy portal was swung open and I was greeted by Sheila, the pretty and nongiggling maid.

"Me again," I said, giving her my 100-watt Supercharmer smile. (I decided to hold the 150-watt Jumbocharmer for a more propitious time.)

"Oh sure," she said, stepping back to allow entrance. "You know your way to the library?"

"If I get lost I'll scream for help," I said. "What's your last name, Sheila?"

"Hayworth," she said. "And no, I'm not related to Rita." Saucy, this one.

"You could have fooled me," I said. "The resemblance is striking."

34

We both laughed because she was a shortish blonde on the zoftig side and looked more like *Klondike Annie* than *The Lady from Shanghai*. She waggled fingers at me and sashayed away. She was, I noted, wearing high heels, which I thought rather odd for the maidservant of a genteel and apparently hidebound family.

After two wrong turnings in those lugubrious corridors I finally located the library. The door was ajar and I blithely strolled into my designated "combat center." Then I stopped, entranced. A woman, perched high on the wheeled ladder, was reaching up to select a volume from the top shelf. She was wearing an extremely short denim skirt.

Her position in that literary setting *forced* me to recall Browning's apt observation: "Ah, but a man's reach should exceed his grasp, or what's a heaven for?"

4

She heard me enter and turned to look down at me coolly. "You must be Archibald McNally," she stated.

I confessed I was.

"I am Geraldine Forsythe. I understand you are to compile a catalog of father's books."

"That is correct, Miss Forsythe, but please don't let me disturb you. I intend to work as quietly as possible with no interruption of the family's daily routine. Your father suggested I make this room my headquarters, but whenever my presence is inconvenient for you, do let me know."

"No," she said, "it'll be no problem."

She began to step down from the ladder and I hastened forward to assist her.

"I can manage," she snapped at me. "I've been doing it for years and haven't fallen yet."

So I stood aside and waited until she was standing on the parquet floor facing me. And we were almost eye-to-eye, for she was quite tall, rangy, with wide shoulders and a proud posture. I guessed her age at forty-plus. She had a coffin-shaped face with remarkable eyes, as astringent as an iced dry martini.

I noted the novel she had selected: *Mansfield Park.*

"You admire Jane Austen?" I asked.

"Not particularly," she said curtly. "But I no longer read books written by men. They don't address my concerns."

That seemed to me an uncommonly harsh judgment. "Have you tried the Bible?" I asked as pleasantly as I could, but she glared at me.

"Are you a trained librarian?" she demanded.

"Unfortunately I am not," I replied, "but I don't believe this project requires philological expertise. It's really just a matter of taking inventory, isn't it?"

"Like a grocery clerk," she said, and there was no mistaking the sneer in her voice.

"Exactly," I said equably. "The only problem I anticipate is locating books borrowed by family members and staffers and not returned to the library."

I was thinking of that missing first edition of Edgar Allan Poe.

I thought Geraldine blushed slightly but I wasn't certain.

"I assure you," she said stiffly, "I shall immediately return all the books I have borrowed and finished reading. And I'll leave you a note of those still in my possession."

"Thank you for your kind cooperation," I said politely.

She stared at me, looking for sarcasm and not finding it. Little did she know that she was facing the King of Dissemblers. She started to move away, then turned back to stare again.

"I have a feeling I've seen you before," she said, and it was almost an accusation.

"That's possible," I replied. "I've lived in Palm Beach most of my adult life, and the town isn't all that big."

"Are you a member of the Pelican Club?" she asked suddenly.

I admitted I was.

"That's where I saw you," she decided. "I went there once. No, twice. It's a dreadful place. So vulgar."

I smiled. "We prefer to think of it as unpretentious, Miss Forsythe."

"Vulgar," she insisted, paused, then said, "If you'd care to invite me there some evening I'd like to confirm my first impressions."

Shocked? My flabber was gasted. I mean we had been clawing at each other's throat for the past several minutes—in a civilized manner, of course—and now the lady was asking for a date. Connie had been right; Geraldine was a strange one.

"It would be a pleasure," I said gravely. "This evening?"

She gave that a moment's serious thought as if she had other social engagements that required her presence.

"Very well," she said finally, "but not for dinner. Later, and only for a drink or two."

"Excellent," I said. "Suppose I stop by around nine o'-clock."

"That will be satisfactory," she said in a schoolmarmish fashion. "I assume informal dress will be suitable?"

"Perfectly," I assured her.

She gave me a chilly nod and stalked from the room. She left me, I must admit, shaken and bewildered. I couldn't even begin to fathom her mercurial temperament nor understand her motives for wanting to revisit a saloon she had decried as vulgar. One possibility, I mournfully concluded, was that Geraldine Forsythe's elevator didn't go to the top floor. More evidence of the basic nuttiness of human behavior.

I actually worked as a cataloger for more than an hour. I started separate pages for each of the north, east, south, and west walls of the library. I then counted the number of bookshelves on each wall and made a note of that. I assigned a key number to each shelf—N-1, E-2, S-3, W-4, and so on—and began counting the number of volumes on each shelf.

I was busily engaged in this donkeywork when my labors were interrupted by the entrance of a stocky woman clad in twill jodhpurs and a khaki riding jacket. She was carrying a crop and brought with her the easily identifiable scent of a stable, but not so strong as to be offensive. I rose to my feet and shook the strong hand she offered.

"Constance Forsythe," she said. "The older Mrs. Forsythe, as I'm sure you've guessed. And you're Archibald McNally?"

"Yes, ma'am. I'm pleased to make your acquaintance. I hope my presence here won't be an inconvenience."

"Not to me," she said with a short laugh. "I'm out at the barn almost every day. Do you ride?"

"No, ma'am, I do not. Horses and I have an agreement: I don't ride them and they don't bite me."

"That's smart," she said. "They can give you a nasty chew if you're not careful. Listing my husband's books, are you?"

She said "my husband's books" not "our books."

"Yes, I'm preparing a catalog," I told her. "I've just started."

"I don't know why Griswold wants a catalog," she said. "Insurance, I suppose, or estate planning. Something like that. Your father is our attorney, is he not?"

"That's correct. Prescott McNally."

"I met him years ago. A gentleman of the old school, as I recall."

"He is that," I agreed.

She wandered about the library flicking her riding crop at the shelves of leather-bound volumes. "I've read damned few of these," she commented. "Not very spicy, are they? Geraldine is the reader of the family. Have you met my daughter, Mr. McNally?"

"Yes, I had that pleasure about an hour ago."

She snorted and it sounded amazingly like a whinny. "I'm glad you found it a pleasure. Most young men are put off by Gerry. She has a tendency to speak her mind. Gets it from me, I imagine." She turned suddenly. "Are you married, Mr. McNally?"

"No, ma'am, I am not."

She nodded. "Who was it that said every woman should marry—and no man?"

"I believe it was Disraeli."

"He was right, you know. If I had been a man I would never, never have married."

I smiled, amused by this forthright woman. She was bulky and had a mastiff face, ruddy and somewhat ravaged. I wondered if she was a heavy drinker as horse-women frequently are. But there was no denying her brusque honesty. I thought of her as the leviathan of the Forsythe Family with all these little sloops bobbing about her.

"You've met everyone in the house?" she asked me.

"I believe so. Of course I already knew your husband and son. Do they ride, Mrs. Forsythe?"

I heard the whinny again. "Not those two," she said. "Unless the horse is wood and bolted to a merry-go-round. I'm the only nag nut in the family. Well, that's not exactly true. Sylvia comes out to the farm occasionally when she gets bored with her harpsichord. She rides very well indeed."

41

"And your grandchild, Lucy?"

"That darling! I'm going to get her up on a pony if it's the last thing I do."

"Mrs. Forsythe," I said, "perhaps you can answer a question that's been puzzling me for years. Why do so many young women—I'm speaking mostly of teenagers—become enamored of horses?"

She gave me a mocking grin. "That's easy," she said. "Because horses are big, strong, handsome, affectionate, and loyal. Everything the lads they know are not."

I laughed. "Now it *does* make sense."

"Usually young girls grow out of it," she continued. "After they realize they can't go to bed with a horse. Then they settle for a man."

"We all must compromise in this life," I said jokingly.

But suddenly Mrs. Forsythe was serious. "I wish Geraldine had learned that." She looked at me speculatively. "Perhaps you can teach her," she added.

Then, apparently feeling she had said enough, she left the library abruptly, leaving a slight odor of eau de equine in her wake.

I sat down again at the desk. But I didn't immediately return to my work. There was no mistaking Mrs. Forsythe's intention, and I spent a few moments recalling all the instances when anxious mommies had attempted to interest me in their unmarried daughters. I am not claiming to be a great catch, mind you, but neither am I an impecunious werewolf, and so I am fair game.

I do not condemn the mothers for trying desperately to ensure their little girls' futures. Nor do I blame the daughters, for they are frequently unaware of mommy's machinations and would be horrified if they did know. Nor do I feel any guilt in slinking away from maternal schemings with as much speed and dignity as I can muster.

I spent an additional hour listing books in the Griswold Forsythe library and meticulously recording title, author, publisher, and copyright. This was all camouflage, you understand—a subterfuge to convince everyone (including the thief) that I was engaged in a legitimate pursuit. My labors were as exciting as tracing the genealogy of the royal family of Ruritania.

Finally I revolted against the tedious task and made preparations to depart. I carefully left my preliminary notes atop the desk where they could easily be examined by any interloper. But first I plucked two sun-bleached hairs from my scalp (when the job demands it, your hero will endure any agony) and placed them on pages 5 and 10 of my manuscript. It was, I thought, an artful method of determining if anyone was interested in inspecting my work.

I then left without encountering any of the residents, although I heard raucous laughter coming from the kitchen area. But when I approached my fiery Miata, parked on the bricked driveway in front of the Forsythe mansion, I found Anthony Bledsoe eyeballing the car. He was clad in a uniform of sedate gray alpaca, but his hands were thrust deep into his trouser pockets—bad form for a properly sniffish butler.

The surliness I had noted early that morning had apparently dissipated, for he greeted me with a small smile. "Nice wheels," he remarked.

"Thank you," I said. "Hardly a Corniche but it suits me."

"Fast?" he inquired.

"Enough," I replied.

He walked slowly around my chariot and I thought I saw longing.

"What do you drive?" I asked him.

"My mother's car," he said dolefully. "An Oldsmobile. Six years old and ready for a trade-in."

"I don't think she'll go for a two-seater like this," I observed.

"No," he said, "but I would."

He gave the car a final admiring glance and turned away. "Anthony," I called, and he looked back. "What time do Mr. Forsythe and his son customarily return from their office?"

"Four o'clock," he said. "Exactly. Every day. You can set your watch by those two characters."

It was not an appropriate demonstration of respect for his employers. I didn't expect him to tug his forelock in their presence, you understand, but he might have spoken of them without scorn. I am somewhat of a traditionalist, y'see. I mean I always remove my hat when a funeral cortege passes by and, at the start of baseball games, I have been known to hum the national anthem.

I drove home reflecting that although Connie Garcia had labeled the Forsythes as "dull, dull, dull," I was finding them a fascinating and perplexing family of crotchety individuals. Eccentrics, I reckoned, and one of them had recently adopted stealing as a hobby. But for what reason this deponent, at the time, kneweth not.

I changed to swimming trunks (in a modest tie-dyed pattern) and went for my daily swim in the Atlantic, one mile north and return in a gently rolling sea as warm as madrilene. I returned to my rookery to shower and dress. Since I was to meet Geraldine Forsythe later that evening I selected my rags with care: a jacket of cranberry silk over

slacks of olive drab. The polo shirt was Sea Island mauve
and my loafers were a pinkish suede.

I thought the final effect was eye-catching without being
garish, but at our preprandial cocktail hour my father took
one look at my costume and exclaimed, "Good God!" But
you must realize his sartorial preferences include balbrig-
gan underwear and wingtip shoes.

Dinner that evening was a delicious feast. Ursi Olson
had located a rack of out-of-season venison somewhere
and, after marinating, served it roasted with a cherry sauce
spiked with cognac and a frosting of slivered almonds.
What a dish that was! It made one believe that human
existence does have a Divine Purpose.

Before my father retired to his port, pipe, and Dickens I
asked if he would provide me with a copy of the list of items
Griswold Forsythe II had reported as missing. He promised to supply it and asked what progress I had made in my
investigation.

"None," I reported cheerfully, and his only reaction was
the arching of one eyebrow, a shtick I've never been able
to master.

I trotted upstairs to the second-floor sitting room, where
mother was watching a rerun of *Singin' in the Rain* on
television. I was terribly tempted to forget about my date
and stay so that once more I could see Gene Kelly perform
that exhilarating dance in a downpour. But duty commanded and so I kissed the mater goodnight and bounded
downstairs to the garage.

Ursi and Jamie Olson were still in the kitchen cleaning
up, and I popped in long enough to filch a single cherry
from the leftovers of the venison roast. Then I was on my
way, thinking life is indeed just a bowl of cherries—if
enough good brandy is added.

5

Geraldine Forsythe had asked if she might dress infor-
mally, and certainly my own raiment would not be unsuit-
able for Bozo the Clown, but when I saw her awaiting me
outside the Forsythe front door I thought I should have
donned dinner jacket and cummerbund. She was wearing
a black satin slip dress, obviously sans bra, held aloft by
spaghetti straps. Draped loosely about her neck was a
white silk scarf so gossamer it seemed ready to waft away
on the next vagrant breeze.

"You call this casual dress?" I asked her.

She shrugged. "I felt like gussying up," she said.

"Well, you look splendid," I assured her, and that was
the truth. Her broad, tanned shoulders were revealed and
although she was no sylph, apparently having inherited her
mother's stockiness, she definitely had a waist, and her
long, bare, rather muscular legs were of centerfold caliber.

She was much amused by my little red runabout and it
took her a moment to solve the problem of how to swing
into the bucket seat without popping a seam. But she was
soon safely ensconced, belt buckled, and we set off for the
Pelican Club.

This private eating and drinking establishment is located
on the mainland in a freestanding building not far from the

47

airport. It is easy to describe what it is *not:* the Pelican Club is not elegant, austere, hushed nor dignified. It is, in fact, rather raffish and the favorite watering hole of young male and female roisterers in the Palm Beach area. I am proud to be one of the founding members and it was my idea to place over the door, in lieu of a neon sign, a bronze plaque inscribed with Merritt's famous limerick anent the capacity of the pelican.

It was Friday night and the joint was noisy, smoky, and beginning to crank up to the riotous behavior for which it was justly infamous. I secured two adjoining stools at the crowded bar, and Geraldine Forsythe looked about with an interested glance that belied her condemnation of the Club as dreadful and vulgar.

"You said you've been here before, Miss Forsythe?" I inquired.

"Yes, Mr. McNally," she answered. "Twice. And it hasn't changed."

I didn't pursue the topic but asked if she would be offended if we became Gerry and Archy in place of Miss Forsythe and Mr. McNally. She readily agreed and I used the diminutive to introduce her to Mr. Simon Pettibone, an elderly gentleman of color who is the Club's manager and bartender. We ordered vodka gimlets that were served on cocktail napkins bearing the Club's crest, a pelican rampant on a field of dead mullet, and our motto: *Non illegitimi carborundum.*

Because of the high decibel rating we found it necessary to lean close to converse. I found that a pleasurable experience. She was wearing "Passion." She was certainly not a great beauty—I thought her jaw too aggressive and, as I have stated, her eyes were flinty—but she was no gorgon, and that evening her frostiness had thawed. She seemed to be making a determined effort to be agreeable and succeeded admirably.

We chatted awhile about her travels (extensive) and mine (limited). We concurred that London was more enjoyable than Paris and the best food in Europe was to be found in the Provence. We also decided that Edith Piaf and Aznavour were marvelous balladeers but couldn't compare with Billie Holiday and Sinatra. In fact, there was so little disagreement between us that our conversation began to flag and I ordered another round of gimlets.

But before they arrived Gerry leaned even closer and put a warm hand on my arm. "Archy," she said, "you're a lawyer, aren't you?"

"No," I said, "regrettably I am not. My father is an attorney; I am a sort of para-paralegal."

She stared into my eyes, all seriousness now. "I've asked around about you," she said, "and I understand you do private investigations."

"Occasionally," I admitted. "Discreet inquiries when requested by our clients."

"Well, the Forsythes are clients, are we not?"

"True enough," I said, wondering what was coming.

We didn't speak while our drinks were being served. Gerry sipped her fresh gimlet and leaned close once again.

"Could you make an investigation for me, Archy? A very confidential investigation?"

Then I understood the reason for her softened attitude; she wanted something from me. And I had fancied her affability was the result of the McNally charm. Are there no limits to the male ego?

I took a gulp of my drink. "Tell me about it," I suggested.

She had removed the silk scarf and held it folded on her lap. Now, as she pressed closer, one of those spaghetti straps slipped off a smooth shoulder and dangled. I replaced it as delicately as I could, fearing that if I did not the lady might lose something she could ill afford.

"Well," she said, almost breathlessly, "lately I've been missing things. Personal things."

"Missing?"

"They've just disappeared. Jewelry mostly. A pearl choker from Tiffany. A cameo brooch I bought in Florence. A silver and turquoise bracelet. And most recently a miniature portrait painted on ivory I inherited from my grandmother. Archy, they are all beautiful things and I loved them. Now they are gone and I'm convinced someone in our house has taken them."

"No possibility of their being misplaced?"

"None whatsoever," she said decisively. "They've been stolen."

"Did all the items disappear at once?"

"No. One at a time, I think. Over a period of several weeks."

"Gerry, have you told your parents about this?"

She shook her head. "They'd immediately think it was someone on the staff, and father would want to call in the police and there'd be a big brouhaha. I want to avoid that if I possibly can. I was hoping that while you're cataloging daddy's books you might poke around, or do whatever investigators do, and see if you can discover who's stealing all my things."

"No sign of a forced entry? I mean it couldn't be an outsider, could it?"

"Not a chance," she said. "We have a very expensive security system. It has to be someone who lives in the house."

"Do you suspect one of the staff?"

"I just hate to. They've all been with us for years and we trust them. Nothing like this has ever happened before. It's so depressing."

"Gerry, I really think you should tell your father."

"No," she said gloomily. "He'd fire everyone. I think the best way is to handle it quietly without anyone knowing you're making—what did you call it?—a discreet inquiry. Will you help me, Archy?"

I sighed. "All right, I'll look into it. With the proviso that if I don't come up with something in, say, a few weeks or a month at most, you'll tell your father about the thefts and let him handle it as he sees fit. Is that satisfactory?"

She nodded. "You'll do your best, won't you?"

"It's a promise."

"You're a sweetheart," she said. "I think we better leave now. The place is getting awfully wild."

I didn't think so; just the normal Friday night insanity. But I signed the tab and we departed, leaving the revelry behind us, which saddened me exceedingly.

We drove directly back to Ocean Boulevard and I pulled into the Forsythe driveway.

"Don't bother getting out," Gerry said. "I'll just pop inside. Archy, thank you so much for the drinks and for listening to my problem. You will help, won't you?"

"I'll do what I can, Gerry. No guarantees."

"Of course. I understand that. But I can't tell you how much better I feel knowing you're going to try."

She twisted awkwardly to kiss me. I held her a brief moment. Her strong body felt slithery under the black satin.

I waited until the front door closed behind her, then I headed homeward. I was in a thoughtful mood, asking a number of questions to which I had no answers, to wit:

Why did she select the Pelican Club as a setting in which to tell me of her missing jewelry? We could have had the same conversation in the privacy of the Forsythe Library.

With whom had she previously visited the Club—her ex-beau, the polo player who allegedly dumped her—but not before clipping her for "heavy bucks"?

Why had she thought it necessary to dress as she had—to help persuade yrs. truly to come to the aid of a damsel in distress?

Why did she believe her father would immediately call in the police if she told him of her stolen gems when he refused to inform the authorities when his own property was snatched?

I fell asleep that night still wrestling with those conundrums. (Naturally I neglected to phone Connie Garcia.) And when I awoke on a rainy Saturday morning I had not solved a blessed one. I began to wonder if Geraldine Forsythe might be a Baroness von Münchhausen with a penchant for spinning wild and improbable tales.

I could understand that. I like to spin them myself.

Usually my father spent Saturdays at his golf club, playing eighteen holes with the same foursome for the past century or two. But that morning was so wet and blowy there was no hope of getting in a game and so he had retired to his study with a copy of *Barron's*—to check the current value of his Treasury bonds no doubt.

Griswold Forsythe II belonged to father's club, an organization with a male membership so long in the tooth it was said you could not hope to be admitted unless you could prove prostate problems. A canard, of course.

I reckoned the same wretched weather keeping Sir McNally indoors was also forcing Mr. Forsythe to remain at home. I felt I needed more information from him regarding his missing geegaws: insured value, location of the items before they disappeared, who amongst family and staff knew where they were kept, and so forth. I phoned the Forsythe home and, after identifying myself, asked to speak to the lord of the manor.

When he came on the line it was obvious he was extremely agitated. "Archy," he said, "can you come over at once?"

"Is anything wrong?" I asked.

"Something dreadful has happened."

"Be right there," I promised.

I pulled on a yellow oilskin and, not wanting to waste time putting the lid on my barouche, I asked mother if I might borrow her ancient Ford station wagon. Within moments I was driving northward along the shore through a squall so violent it threatened to blow me off the road. If I had been in the Miata I suspect I would have ended up in Tampa.

And when I arrived at the Forsythe castle I found the atmosphere as chaotic inside as out. It took me awhile to learn the cause of the disturbance, for everyone insisted on speaking at once and there was a great wringing of hands, tears from the women and curses from the men. Disorder reigned supreme.

I was finally able to extract a semicoherent account of what had occurred. Apparently, during the wee hours of the morning, someone had entered the bedroom of Mrs. Sylvia Forsythe III and attempted to strangle her. She and her husband occupied separate bedchambers, she never locked her door, and the assault was not discovered until she failed to appear at breakfast.

The giggling maid, Fern, was sent to ask if Mrs. Sylvia

wanted something brought up, and it was she who found the victim lying unconscious on the floor, nightclothes in disarray. Fern's screams brought the others running and when the young woman could not be roused the family physician was called.

He arrived within a half-hour and was able to revive Mrs. Sylvia. She was presently in bed and, according to the doctor, had not suffered any life-threatening injury. She was able to speak in a croaky voice but could not identify her assailant. She had been sedated and was in no condition to be questioned further.

Mr. Griswold Forsythe II pulled me into the library and closed the door.

"GD it," he said angrily, and it was, I imagined, the strongest oath he was capable of uttering. "I don't understand what's happening around here. First thievery and now attempted murder. What on earth is going on?"

"Mr. Forsythe," I said as gently as I could, "this matter must be reported to the police."

"No, no!" he shouted. "Absolutely not! The newspapers, television, the tabloids—all that. Can't have it. *Won't* have it."

"Sir," I said with the solemnity the moment required, "you *must* report it. Attempted homicide is a serious crime, and not making a police report might possibly result in your becoming the subject of an official investigation. I strongly urge you to phone the authorities at once. I suggest you speak to Sergeant Al Rogoff. He and I have worked together several times in the past, and I can vouch for his intelligence, competence and, most of all, his discretion."

He gnawed on that a moment, then drew a deep breath. "Yes," he said finally, "you're probably right. I'll call."

He picked up the phone and I left the library. I met a

tearful Fern in the corridor and she directed me to Mrs. Sylvia's bedroom on the second floor. I found Griswold Forsythe III standing guard outside his wife's door. He was wearing a three-piece suit of mud-colored cheviot, almost identical to his father's. I wondered if the male Forsythes patronized the same tailor and ordered two of everything.

"How is she, Griswold?" I asked.

"Dozing," he said distractedly. "The doctor is with her now. He says her respiration and heartbeat are normal and she should make a complete recovery. But I'm worried."

"Of course you are," I said. "Have you any idea who might have committed such a horrible act?"

He stared at me and his eyes seemed slightly out of focus as if his thoughts were elsewhere. "What?" he said. "Oh. No, I have no idea. It has to be someone in the house. That's what makes it so awful. I simply cannot believe this happened."

I was saved from replying when the bedroom door opened and the paunchy doctor came out carrying his black satchel.

"You may go in now, Mr. Forsythe," he said. "But stay only a few minutes and try not to disturb the patient."

Griswold nodded, stepped inside, and closed the door behind him.

"How is Mrs. Forsythe doing, sir?" I asked the physician.

He looked at me. "I am Dr. Cedric P. Pursglove," he said haughtily, and I wondered if that middle P. stood for Popinjay. "And who might you be?" he demanded.

I was tempted to answer that I might be Peter the Great but, sadly, I was not. "Archibald McNally," I told him. "My law firm represents the Forsythes."

Of course he immediately assumed I was an attorney

and I didn't disabuse him. I mean there was no point in confessing I was merely a scullion in the McNally & Son kitchen.

"From a legal point of view," he said in such a pompous manner that I had a terrible urge to goose him, just to see him leap, dignity shattered, "—from a legal point of view this distressing matter should be reported at once to the proper authorities."

"I so advised the senior Mr. Forsythe," I informed him.

"Wise counsel," he said as if pronouncing a benediction. "I further recommend a police physician be called to examine the patient and perhaps take photographs."

I was startled. "Why should that be necessary, sir?"

"The contusions caused by the attempted strangulation are obvious on the neck of the intended victim. But there are other wounds of a superficial nature that might prove significant."

He spoke of his patient as if she were a laboratory specimen. This doctor, I decided, had all the bedside manner of Jack the Ripper.

"What kind of wounds?" I asked him.

"Deep scratches and a few small, open cuts on the neck."

"Have you any idea what caused them?"

"I am not a forensic pathologist," he said crossly, "but it is my firm opinion that they were made by long fingernails."

I stared at him, shocked. "Dr. Pursglove, are you implying that Mrs. Forsythe's assailant was a woman?"

"It is, I think, a reasonable assumption," he said at his pontifical best—or worst. "And there is contributing evidence. It is no simple task to strangle a human being,

56

particularly one as young and vigorous as the patient. It would require considerable physical strength."

"And that is an added indication her attacker was a woman—she was rendered unconscious but not killed?"

He nodded with grim assurance. "It is my belief that if the strangler had been a man Mrs. Forsythe would now be deceased."

6

I reclaimed my yellow slicker and left the Forsythe home without speaking further to any of the inhabitants. Although my name is Archy, let me be frank: I departed in unseemly haste because I did not wish to be on the premises when Sgt. Al Rogoff arrived. His accusations, I well knew, would come later. And better later than sooner.

I arrived home to find my father and mother, Madelaine, in the living room moodily inspecting an inconsequential puddle on the parquet floor. It had been caused by the fierce rain leaking in under French doors to our small flag-stoned terrace. My parents were tsk-tsking in unison.

I told them what had occurred at the Forsythes', and they were both stunned.

"How dreadful," mother said, putting a trembling knuckle to her lips. "Prescott, is there anything we can do?"

"Have the police been notified?" father asked me.

"Yes, sir," I said. "After I persuaded the senior Mr. Forsythe. I do think you should be there during the police investigation and questioning."

"You're quite right, Archy," he said. "I'll go at once. Maddie, where did I leave my umbrella?"

I waited until he had been adequately outfitted in raincoat, rain hat, and rubbers, and equipped with a bumbershoot large enough to shelter four close friends. He departed in his Lexus and I moved into his study to use the phone. I called Connie Garcia.

"Thank you for phoning last night," she said coldly, "as you so sincerely promised."

"Sorry about that, dear," I said. "We had a tremendous flood in the living room—the rain was gushing in under the French doors to the terrace—and I was busy with mop and bucket for hours. Listen, how about lunch at the Pelican?"

"Today?" she said. "Are you mad? It's still pouring and I've just washed my hair and have no intention of taking a step outside."

"Ah, what a disappointment," I said. "Oh, by the way, Connie, you mentioned that Geraldine Forsythe had been blindsided by an unscrupulous polo player. You don't happen to recall his name, do you?"

She was silent a moment. "Sorry," she said finally, "I just can't remember it—if I ever knew."

"Oh, well, it's not important," I lied. "I'll buzz you tomorrow and if the weather has cleared by then perhaps we can have a nosh."

"Sounds good to me, Archy. I could do with a bowl of chili to chase my chilly."

We chatted a few more minutes about this and that, and she was in a sparky mood when we rang off. Connie does have her snits but usually they are not of long duration. Unfortunately while they last they sometimes result in physical assaults on the McNally carcass. But infidelity, like all delights, has its price.

I then tried my favorite chronicler of Palm Beach turpitude. I knew Lolly Spindrift worked on Saturdays preparing his gossip column for the Sunday edition of his paper.

Naturally he would demand a newsworthy disclosure in return for the information I wanted but I thought I could finesse that.

"Hi, darling," he said chirpily. "Don't tell me you called to remark that it's great weather for ducks. If I hear that once more today I'll scream."

"Actually, Lol," I said, "I phoned to invite you to lunch. How about Bice? We'll have a nice salad with a side order of quid pro quo."

"Oh-ho," he said, "it's tattle time, is it? I'd love to, doll, but I just can't. I'm chained to this sadistic word processor and it won't turn me loose until my copy is complete. What have you got for me? I hope it's something juicy. I need a final item that'll cause a splash or my devoted readers will think old Lolly is losing his edge."

"This will cause a splash," I promised, "but you'll have to write it as a question because I don't know the answer."

"All right, all right," he said impatiently. "Half my scoops are phrased as questions. It's a great way to avoid libel suits. Let's have it."

"Quote: 'What were the police doing at the Griswold Forsythe mansion early Saturday morning? Rumor hath it that there have been dark doings in that haunted castle.' Unquote. How does that sound, Lol?"

"A doozy," he said immediately. "A smash finish for the column. But is it for real?"

"Have I ever stiffed you?"

"No, you've been true-blue, sweetie. But why do I have the feeling you're not telling me everything you know?"

"It's everything, Lol," I assured him. "If I learn more you'll be the first to hear about it."

"I better," he warned, "or you'll go on my S-list. You do know what that is, don't you?"

"I can guess," I said. "Now here's what I need: A few years ago Geraldine Forsythe, the unmarried daughter, reportedly had a thing going with a polo player. Apparently he treated her in a most ungentlemanly manner including nicking her for a sizable sum. Question: Do you know the name of the knave?"

Lolly laughed. "I don't even have to consult my private file. It so happens I hoped to start a thing with that hulk myself but it came to naught. It wasn't that he was unwilling to swing, but he was suffering from a severe case of the shorts and was looking for a fatter bankroll than mine. I heard later that he had latched onto Geraldine. His name is Timothy Cussack."

"Cussack?" I said and smote my brow with an open palm. "I should have guessed. He was cashiered from the Pelican Club a year ago for nonpayment of his bar tabs. Is he still playing polo?"

"Heavens, no! He fell off a horse and broke a bone. His fetlock or pastern or something silly like that."

"And what's he doing now, Lol—do you know?"

"The last I heard he was working as a trainer at a horse farm out near Wellington."

"Uh-huh," I said. "Interesting—but not very. Thanks for the poop, Lol, and keep defending the public's inalienable right to know."

"Up yours as well, Priapus," he said, and I hung up laughing. Outrageous man!

My next move might have been to learn the name of Mrs. Constance Forsythe's horse farm out near Wellington and determine if she was employing the man who had betrayed her daughter. But I thought additional research was required first.

I donned my oilskin again and set out for the Pelican

Club in mother's station wagon. The rain had not lessened but at least the wind had lost its intensity and I was able to navigate the flooded roads successfully. The vehicle I was driving, I suddenly realized, was older than I, and I hoped when I was its age I might be as stalwart and dependable.

As I suspected it would be, the Pelican Club was deserted on such an indecent day. Only the staff was present, with Mr. Simon Pettibone behind the bar watching a rerun of "Dynasty" on his little TV set. He looked up with amazement when I entered.

"Mr. McNally," he said, "you braved the elements to honor us with your presence?"

"Thirst will drive a man to desperate measures," I replied, swinging aboard a barstool. "What do you recommend to banish the blues, Mr. Pettibone? I plan to have only one so I suggest it be muscular."

"A negroni will provide needed warmth and nourishment. But only one," he warned. "For it is a potion to be respected."

"As well I know," I said, "from sad experience. Very well, one negroni, Mr. Pettibone. And if I insist on a second I advise you to summon the gendarmes."

I took one sip of the ambrosial concoction he set before me and suddenly the rain ceased, the sun shone, and Joan Blondell and I planned a weekend at Biarritz. Not literally, of course, but that's the effect a negroni can have on an impressionable youth.

"Mr. Pettibone," I said, "do you recall an ex-member named Timothy Cussack?"

"I do indeed," he said promptly. "A welsher."

"Exactly," I said. "I don't believe I ever met him. What kind of a chap was he?"

"Oozy."

"And what precisely did he ooze?"

"Personality," Mr. Pettibone said. "Charm. Too much, and so it oozed."

"Ah," I said, "a trenchant observation. I've heard him described as a hulk. Large, is he?"

"Oh yes. And handsome in a meanish kind of way, as if he might enjoy kicking a dog."

"Doesn't sound like a sterling character."

"No, that he is not."

"A scoundrel?"

Mr. Pettibone considered a moment. "I do believe he's working up to it," he said. "Or down."

"What do you suppose drives him?" I asked.

"Mr. McNally, some people just have a natural talent for meanness. I think that may be true of Timothy Cussack. And also, of course, he was perpetually short of funds."

I nodded. "As Shaw once remarked, 'The lack of money is the root of all evil.' "

"I never had the pleasure of meeting Mr. Shaw," Pettibone said solemnly, "but obviously he was a man of wisdom."

I thanked him for his assistance and finished my drink. (Take note: only one.) I then drove home in a negroni-bemused mood. I was accumulating additional bits and pieces of information but to what purpose I could not have said. The Forsythe saga was beginning to resemble one of those children's puzzles in which numbered dots are connected in sequence to form a picture. But in this case most of the dots were unnumbered—or missing.

At dinner that evening my father commented that the police questioning of the Forsythe family and staff had been brief and inconclusive. Everyone had eagerly cooperated but nothing new had been learned. Sgt. Rogoff had stated that his investigation would continue. I could believe that; tenacity is his middle name. (Not really, of course; it's Irving.)

Later that night I was upstairs making desultory scribblings in my journal when the sergeant phoned, as I knew he inevitably would.

"You know," he started, "I'm beginning to see us as Laurel and Hardy. I'm the fat one who always says, 'Here's another fine mess you've got me into.'"

"Al," I said, "I swear I had nothing to do with it except recommend that the police be notified."

"But you told Griswold Forsythe to hand me the squeal, didn't you?"

"Well, yes," I admitted. "But only because I knew he demanded discretion."

"Discretion?" He honked a bitter laugh. "It's hard to be discreet, sonny boy, when someone's tried to choke a woman to death."

"I know you'll try to keep a lid on it," I said soothingly. "How did you make out at the Kingdom of Oz?"

"The Forsythe place? Hey, that's a creepy joint, isn't it? As damp inside as it is out. It's a wonder they all don't have webs between their toes. Archy, it's another NKN case—nobody knows nothing. And don't tell me that's a double negative; I still like it."

"Did you talk to the family physician, Dr. Pursglove?"

"Oh yeah," Al said. "He's Mr. Congeniality, isn't he? I called in Tom Bunion from the ME's office. He was delighted to come out in this monsoon, as you can well imagine. Anyway, he more or less confirms what Pursglove says: the attacker was probably a woman. So where does that leave us?"

"Well, it certainly narrows the list of suspects to the women who were in the house at the time, doesn't it?"

"Not necessarily," Rogoff argued. "It could have been an outsider."

"Al, they're supposed to have a state-of-the-art security system."

"Doesn't mean a thing," he said. "It can be switched off, can't it? As it is every morning. The control box is in a pantry off the kitchen. Anyone in the place could have thrown the switch and allowed someone to come in without making the balloon go up. By the way, what were you doing there before I was called in?"

"The Forsythes are clients of McNally and Son. The senior Griswold was in a panic this morning after they found Mrs. Sylvia. My father was busy so I went over."

"Uh-huh," Rogoff said. "And what were your notes doing on the library desk? I recognized your scrawly handwriting."

"Oh *that*," I said breezily. "I'm cataloging Mr. Forsythe's books."

"You're doing *what*?"

"Cataloging the Forsythe library. I don't spend all my time nabbing villains, you know."

"Son," the sergeant said heavily, "you've got more crap than a Christmas goose. But I'll let it go—for now. You know all the people in that nuthouse?"

"I've met them all, yes."

"Excluding the injured woman and Lucy, the kid, that leaves Constance Forsythe, the daughter Geraldine, the housekeeper Mrs. Bledsoe, and the two maids, Fern and Sheila. Five females, all with fingernails long enough to make those wounds on the victim's neck. Assuming no outsider was allowed in, who's your pick?"

"Al," I said, "I just don't know and that's the truth. I can't even guess. Too many imponderables."

"I love the way you talk," he said. "You mean it's all shit—right?"

"Something like that."

He sighed. "I hate these domestic violence cases. You can dig for weeks, months, years and never get to the bottom. You know that Fern, one of the maids?"

"Sure. The one who giggles."

"Well, she wasn't giggling this morning. Boo-hooing as a matter of fact. But I guess that's understandable; she found the victim. Anyway, we were making a half-assed search of that loony bin and came across some bloodstained tissues in a wastebasket in Fern's bedroom. She claims she got blood on her hands when she tried to revive Mrs. Sylvia. Could be."

"Of course it could," I agreed. "And that's all you discovered?"

He laughed. "Not quite. Griswold Forsythe the Third, the uptight, upright heir to the throne, has a small but choice collection of nude photos."

"You're kidding!"

"I'm not. They aren't professional. I think he took them himself. Polaroids. Same background, same lighting. We left everything where we found it. Now is that discretion or isn't it?"

I didn't want to ask my next question but I had to. "Did you recognize any of the models?"

"Sure," Rogoff said cheerfully. "The two maids." He paused for dramatic effect. "And Griswold's sister Geraldine. Now do you know why I hate these family messes?"

"Yes," I said dully, "now I know."

We hung up after warm expressions of fealty, some of

which were heartfelt. I like Al and I think—I hope—he likes me. But although we may be friends we are also, during the cases we work together, avid competitors. Nothing wrong with that, is there?

I admit I was shaken by his final revelation. Griswold Forsythe III an eager snapper of nude photos? Including his maidservants and sister? It was mind-boggling. I imagined for one brief moment that it might be just an innocent hobby, somewhat akin to collecting Indian head pennies.

Then I realized how insane that was. My fault was that I had assumed a man who wore mud-colored, three-piece cheviot suits and to whom verbosity was a way of life was incapable of passion, legitimate or illicit. It was obvious that I had underestimated Griswold Three—and probably all the other denizens of the Chez Forsythe as well.

I went to bed that night resolved to practice and exhibit more humility in my relations with others. But I knew in my heart of hearts that this noble resolution, like so many I had made in the past, was doomed to ignominious failure.

7

The rain had stopped by Sunday morning but the sky still had the color and texture of a Pittsburgh sidewalk. I confess I am somewhat phobic about the weather; when the sun doesn't shine I don't either. But my spirits were boosted when I breakfasted with my parents in the dining room. Ursi Olson served us small smoked ham steaks with little yam cubes in a dark molasses sauce. I could almost feel the McNally corpuscles perk up and move onto the dance floor for a merry gavotte.

Mother and father departed for church, and I phoned Connie Garcia. She was in a laid-back Sunday morning mood and didn't seem inclined to make a definite date for lunch or dinner.

"Did you see the paper, Archy?" she asked.

"Not yet."

"Lolly Spindrift says something is going on at the Forsythe home. He says the police were called."

"Good heavens," I said. "I wonder what it could be."

"I thought you might know," she said. "You've been asking a lot of questions about that family lately."

"Well, they *are* our clients, you know. Perhaps I'll take a run up there and see if they require assistance. I'll call you this afternoon, Connie, and maybe we can meet later."

"Sounds good," she said. "I'll try to get my act together by then. Archy, if you learn anything spicy at the Forsythes', will you tell me?"

"Don't I always?"

"No," she said.

We hung up and I meditated, not for the first time, on my romance with that dishy young woman. I had a great affection for her, no doubt about it, but my tender attachment did not prevent my being unfaithful when an opportunity occurred. I could only conclude that infidelity was part of my genetic code, like snoring, and I must learn to live with it. I could only hope that Connie would as well.

I donned a blue nylon jacket, clapped on a white leather cap, and ventured out into a muggy world. I spun the Miata northward along Ocean Boulevard and en route I spotted, coming in the opposite direction, the big, boxy Rolls-Royce belonging to Griswold Forsythe II. I don't know what model it was, but it was aged and seemed high enough to allow a formally attired gentleman to enter without removing his topper.

It was proceeding at a sedate pace and I was able to note that Griswold III, the famous nude photo fiend, was driving while his mother, father, and sister occupied the rear. The family was on its way to church, I reckoned, which gave me the chance of chatting up the stay-at-homes without interference.

I encountered, on the front lawn of the Forsythe estate, a blocky servitor clad in faded overalls and sporting a magnificent walrus mustache. He was raking the grounds of palm fronds and other arboreal debris blown down by the previous day's gusty winds. Assisting him in his labors was my new friend, Lucy, who was striving mightily but futilely to stuff a very large pine branch into a very small plastic garbage bag.

"Hi, Lucy," I called.

"Hi, Archy," she sang out. "Look what the storm did."

"I know," I said. "But everything will dry out eventually."

The gardener glanced at me and tipped his feedlot cap.

"Good morning," I said to him. "My name is Archibald McNally, a friend of the Forsythes. You're Rufino Diaz?"

"Thass right," he said, surprised I knew his name. "I take care of the outside."

"Much damage?"

"Not too bad," he said. "We lost some ficus, and two new orchid trees I had just planted got blown over. But I stuck them back in, tied them up, and I think they'll take. The ground got a good soaking and thass important."

I nodded and turned back to the little girl. "How is your mother, Lucy?"

"She got hurt."

"I know. Is she feeling better now?"

"I guess. She's got a bandage around her neck."

"Perhaps I'll see if she's able to receive visitors."

I started away but Lucy came running after me. She clutched my arm and pulled me down to her level.

"You remember?" she whispered.

"About what?"

"My secret place. You promised you'd come to a picnic there."

"Of course I will—after it dries out."

"And we're still friends?"

"Absolutely," I told her. "Stick with me, kid, and you'll be wearing diamonds."

She sniggered and scampered back to her work. I went to the half-open front door and found Mrs. Bledsoe peering out.

"Good morning, Mr. McNally," she said. "I'm keeping an eye on Lucy. I don't want her to get too wet."

"She's doing fine. How are you, Mrs. Bledsoe, after yesterday's unpleasantness?"

"Bearing up," she said. "This too shall pass."

"I'm sure it shall," I said, not at all certain. "And how is Mrs. Sylvia?"

"Much better, thank you. She is wide-awake and alert and had two poached eggs and a cup of tea for breakfast. No toast because her throat is still sore, you know."

"I can imagine," I said. "Do you think she's in any mood for company?"

"I can ask."

I followed her down the hallway and up the staircase, seeing again what a robust woman she was. Curious, but she and Constance Forsythe were the same physical type: square and resolute. I thought of them both as no-nonsense women who managed that rather giddy household with an iron hand in an iron glove. But I may have been moonbeaming.

I waited outside Mrs. Sylvia's door while Nora Bledsoe went in to confer with the patient. She came out a moment later.

"Yes," she said, "she'll be happy to have company. The doctor has ordered her to stay in bed and rest for another day, and she's bored. Wants to get back to her harpsichord, I expect."

"That's understandable," I said. "Mrs. Bledsoe, do you have any idea who might have done this awful thing?"

"None whatsoever," she said grimly and marched away.

I entered the bedroom and found Sylvia Forsythe lying under a canopy as fanciful as a Persian tent. She was wearing a white gown, her head on two lace-trimmed pillows. A silk sheet was pulled up and tucked beneath her arms. There was a gauze wrapping about her throat, and atop the flowered counterpane was an opened musical score. She smiled brightly as I approached.

"Mr. McNally," she said, "how very nice of you to visit."

Her voice was husky and unexpectedly come-hitherish.

"My pleasure," I said. "I do hope you're feeling better."

"Much," she said. "I want to be up and about but I promised Dr. Pursglove to stay in bed another day. Pull up a chair."

I moved a chintzy number to her bedside and sat down. She reached a hand to me, I clasped it and she did not release my paw.

"I'm delighted to see you looking so well," I told her. "And Mrs. Bledsoe says you had not one but two eggs for breakfast."

She laughed. "And I'm famished. I've been promised pasta alfredo for lunch and I can't wait."

I nodded toward the score. "And meanwhile you're studying Vivaldi."

"Scarlatti," she said, and we smiled at each other.

She was an enormously attractive invalid. Her wheaten hair was splayed out on the pillows in a filmy cloud and her paleness gave her features a translucency revealing an inner glow. And she held my hand in a warm grip. This woman is married, I sternly reminded myself. And she is recovering from a grievous injury. But the McNally id could not be restrained.

She noted me staring and turned her head away. "I feel so helpless," she said in her husky, stirring voice.

How was I to interpret that comment? I didn't even try.

"Mrs. Forsythe," I started, but she looked at me again and shook her head.

"Sylvia will do," she said. "And may I call you Archy?"

"Honored," I said, and gently disengaged my hand from hers. It was a noble act but a moment later I wanted to grab it up again and nibble her knuckles.

"Sylvia," I said, "do you have any idea who attacked you?"

She sighed. "So many people have asked me that: the doctor, that police sergeant, my husband, father-in-law— just everyone. I've told them all the same thing but I'm not sure they believe me. The last thing I remember is being awakened from a sound sleep and becoming aware that someone was choking me. After that I have no memory at all. It's just a total blank. Dr. Pursglove says that sometimes happens: the mind wipes out a painful, traumatic experience to aid healing. Self-protective, you know. But he expects the recollection will slowly return."

She looked at me wide-eyed and I did not believe a word she had said. But "You're lying!" is not something one shouts at a convalescent young female—or at a healthy young male either. I was convinced Sylvia Forsythe knew the identity of her assailant. Why she chose not to reveal it was another unnumbered dot in that picture puzzle I was trying to draw.

It seemed useless to pursue the matter and so I continued my detecting by switching to another subject. "Your mother-in-law tells me you're an expert rider," I remarked.

"Not expert," she said, "but I do enjoy it. I'm proud to say I've been thrown only once."

"I understand Mrs. Forsythe operates a horse farm and trains jumpers," I went on. "Do you ever compete?"

"Oh no," she said, "I'm not that good. I just like to ride around and gallop occasionally. That's exciting."

"What is the farm called?" I asked casually. "It sounds like an interesting place."

"Oh, it is. You really should see it, Archy. It's called the Trojan Stables. Isn't that a wonderful name?"

"It surely is."

"It costs a fortune to run. Do you know the price of hay?"

"No," I said, "I haven't been eating much lately."

She grinned at me. "Well, I suspect the function of Trojan Stables is to train jumpers and serve as a tax loss. I hope this conversation is confidential, Archy."

"Of course it is," I assured her. "I'm a loyal employee, and even if the IRS uses thumbscrews I won't talk. I may blubber but I won't talk."

She laughed and took up my hand again. "I like you, Archy," she said. "You're fun and there's not much of that around here. Perhaps we might go out to Wellington together and I'll show you around the Trojan."

"I'd enjoy that," I said, and wondered what Griswold Forsythe III might think of my squiring Sylvia. But then, I recalled, when Sgt. Rogoff had listed the models in Griswold's nude photos he hadn't mentioned the man's wife.

Then we were silent, but it was a reflective quiet. I imagine most of you ladies and gents have known such a moment—a briefness of balance, a shall-I or shall-I-not choice when you question not if you have the desire (that's a given) but if you have the energy, psychic or physical or both.

And always, of course, there is the problem of logistics. If the union contemplated is to be consummated, then where, when, and how? Sometimes craving remains just that only because to scratch the itch would require planning as complex as that for D-Day.

And so Sylvia Forsythe and I gazed at each other tenderly while all we were thinking remained unspoken. Finally she released my hand and I assumed that was a signal of dismissal. I rose and expressed hope for her quick recovery.

"I'll be fine," she said with a radiant smile. "And thank you again for stopping by. How is your cataloging job coming along?"

"Slowly," I said.

"Good," she said and left it to me to figure out what she meant.

I was retreating down one of those gloomy corridors when suddenly Fern stepped from an alcove and clamped my arm. "What did she tell you, Mr. McNally?" she demanded, sharp face hard with anger.

I was tempted to make a tart reply—"None of your business!"—but thought better of it. "Mrs. Sylvia?" I said softly. "Only that she was feeling better and hoped to be up and about in a day or so."

The maid released my arm and began to gnaw on a thumbnail. "She thinks I did it," she said fiercely, "but I didn't. I couldn't do something like that. I hate and detest violence in any way, shape, or form."

Then I was thoroughly convinced I had blundered into a haunt of boobies.

"I don't believe Mrs. Sylvia believes you did it," I said. "She remembers almost nothing about the attack and can't identify the perpetrator."

"Well, I didn't do it," she repeated, still chewing at her

thumb. "And anyone who says I did is a double-damned liar."

"Fern," I said, hoping to calm her, "I must confess I don't know your last name. You know mine but I don't know yours. That's not fair."

"Fern Bancroft," she said glumly, and I thought how odd it was that both maids had the surnames of movie stars. But then my own name is similar to that of a famous mapmaker and during my undergraduate days I was known as Randy McNally.

"Well, you mustn't worry about this unfortunate incident," I told her. "To my knowledge no one has accused you of anything. Try to put it from your mind."

"You know I'm innocent, don't you?"

What a question! She was referring to the attempted strangling of Mrs. Sylvia, of course, but it was difficult to attest to the complete innocence of a young woman who had posed for nude Polaroids.

"I believe you," I said simply, thinking that might suffice.

"I just don't know what's happening around here," she wailed. "Everything is so mixed up."

"It will all settle down," I said soothingly.

"I don't think so," she said and leaned closer, still munching on her thumbnail. "There are things going on," she added in direful tones.

I began to get a new take on Fern Bancroft. When we had first been introduced I had thought her something of a linthead, only because of her chronic giggle. But now I suspected that habit might have a neurasthenic origin. She was not giggling because she found life amusing but because she found it close to unendurable, and a constant laugh was her guard against hysteria.

Thank you, Dr. McNally.

"Fern," I said, "what exactly is going on that upsets you so?"

"Things," she said and darted away. I was left in a state of utter confusion and a lesser lad might have been staggered by it. But I have learned to live with muddle—e.g.: my relations with the feminine gender—and so I was more fascinated than daunted by the hugger-mugger in the Forsythe household. It merely confirmed my belief, previously propounded, that the world is a nuthouse run by the inmates.

I hoped to make a quiet and unobserved departure but I was doomed to another slice of fruitcake that Sunday morning. Sheila Hayworth, maid No. 2, was in the entrance hall busily wielding a feather duster with no apparent purpose or effect.

"Hi, Mr. McNally," she said cheerily. "Aren't you glad the rain stopped?"

"Delighted," I said. "People always say the farmers need it, but truthfully I don't much care what the farmers need—do you?"

"Not me," she said forthrightly. "I grew up on a farm and never want to see another one as long as I live."

"A farmer's daughter," I marveled. "I wouldn't have guessed."

"Now don't tell me you're a traveling salesman," she said coquettishly. "I've heard all those old jokes."

What a flirt she was!

"I may travel occasionally," I said, "but I have nothing to sell."

She gave me a bold glance. "I wouldn't say that. Tuesday is my day off."

Her impudence was impressive. "I'll keep that in mind," I told her.

"You do that," she said. "You can always leave a message for me with Rufino."

"The gardener?"

"Uh-huh," she said, staring at me. "He has a cute little apartment in West Palm."

Her brazenness was amazing and, I must admit, engendered a slight weakening of the joints between femur and tibia. I mean I'm as eager for a romantic lark as the next johnny but I like to play a role in its creation. But in this drama (comedy? farce?) Ms. Hayworth seemed to be playwright, director, set designer, and female star. It was a trifle humbling to be reduced to a walk-on.

Naturally I didn't wish to offend the lady by a brusque rejection, but neither did I wish to flop upon the floor and wait to have my tummy scratched.

"It's something to think about," I said, a spineless remark if ever I heard one.

She gave me a mocking glance. "Do you require references?" she inquired archly.

I realized I had met my match with this one and a hasty escape would be prudent. But then she added, "I could provide them, you know. From men whose opinion I'm sure you trust."

I was aware that my smile was glassy as I fled without saying another word. Rufino Diaz was still raking the lawn and gave me a half-wave of farewell as I drove away. I headed homeward, thoughts jangled, trying to guess the identities of those men whose opinions I would trust.

I had to conclude she was referring obliquely to the Griswold Forsythes, II and III. And perhaps Anthony

Bledsoe, the butler. And perhaps Zeke Grenough, the chef. And perhaps Count Dracula and Friar Tuck.

I realized I was now making no sense whatsoever. I blamed the fogging of my keen, cool, and lucid mind on a morning spent at the Forsythe asylum. I seemed to have been contaminated by whatever was afflicting the residents. I decided a good dose of normalcy was needed as an antidote. And so the moment I arrived home I built myself a vodka gimlet.

Purely for medicinal purposes, you understand.

8

The remainder of that Sunday was blessedly uneventful. I stayed inside all afternoon and the quiet ordinariness of the McNally household was a comfort. We had a fine rack of lamb for dinner, I took a nap, worked on my journal, ate cold corned beef and cheese sausage as a late supper, and forgot to phone Connie Garcia. Everything seemed refreshingly sane and orderly.

Of course Ms. Garcia called me later that night to read me the riot act for neglecting her. It required twenty minutes to beg forgiveness and squirm my way back into her graces. But even my performance was a relief because I had done it so many times before and routine was welcome after that confused morning at the Forsythes'.

Monday brought genuine sunshine and a concurrent return of the McNally brio. My father supplied me with a list of the items of value reported as missing by Griswold Forsythe II, and to that I added the articles of jewelry Geraldine Forsythe told me she had lost. It made an impressive inventory. Obviously someone was looting the family manse—but for what purpose? Was the thief fencing the swag or merely assembling his or her own collection of objets d'art?

By the time I arrived at my miniature office in the

McNally Building I had decided I needed to know more about the finances of that seemingly dysfunctional Forsythe clan. I phoned Mrs. Trelawney, my father's private secretary, and asked if His Majesty might spare me a few moments.

"Fat chance," she scoffed.

"Try," I urged. "The fate of the civilized world hangs in the balance."

"That's a good one," she said. "You've never used that before. Okay, I'll give it a go."

She came back on the line a moment later and announced I would be granted an audience of ten minutes if I arrived instanter. I went charging up the back stairs to the boss's sanctum, not wanting to wait for our lazy automatic elevator. I found the padrone standing before his antique rolltop desk. He did not appear to be overjoyed by my visit.

"Yes, yes, Archy," he said testily, "what is it now?"

"The Forsythe investigation," I said. "Father, it would help if I knew a little more about the family's finances. To be specific, who controls the exchequer?"

Of course he immediately lapsed into his mulling mode, trying to determine how much information he might ethically reveal. Finally he decided to trust his bubbleheaded sprout—to a limited degree.

"There is a grantor trust in existence," he said briefly. "The elder Forsythe is the trustee."

"Wife and children have no independent income?"

"They are given rather meager allowances for their personal expenses."

"Meager, sir?" I said. "As in skimpy, paltry, and stingy?"

"That is correct," he said with a wintry smile. "But he is

also responsible for the taxes and upkeep of the Forsythe properties, including salaries of staff. It is not an inconsiderable sum, I assure you."

I persisted. "In other words, spouse and children are totally dependent upon Mr. Forsythe's largesse."

"Yes," he said irritably, "if you wish to put it that way."

"And in the event of the trustee's demise?"

"The estate is then distributed to the named beneficiaries. After payment of taxes, of course."

"And wife, son, and daughter are the named beneficiaries?"

He nodded. "The granddaughter's legacy will be held in trust by her father until she comes of age. There are additional bequests to members of the domestic staff."

"I don't suppose you'd care to reveal the value of the individual bequests."

"You don't suppose correctly," he said frostily.

"Considerable?" I suggested.

"Yes," he said, "I think that's a fair assumption."

I knew I'd get nothing more, thanked him for his assistance, and returned to my office. What had I learned? Little more than I had already guessed. The one mild surprise was that Mrs. Constance Forsythe was not independently wealthy. In Palm Beach, as elsewhere in the world, money usually marries money—which is why the rich get richer and the poor get bupkes.

I spent the next several minutes consulting telephone directories—more valuable to the amateur sleuth than a deerstalker cap and meerschaum pipe. I looked up the address and phone number of Rufino Diaz, the Forsythes' gardener. My purpose? No purpose. But during an investigation I am an inveterate collector of facts. Most of them inevitably turn out to be the drossiest of dross—but one never knows, do one? I also found the address and phone number of the Trojan Stables in Wellington.

I scrawled notes on both locations and tucked them into my wallet. I then bounced downstairs to our underground garage, boarded the Miata, and set out to explore.

On that morning, I recall, I was wearing an awning-striped sport jacket with fawny slacks, pinkish mocs (no socks, naturally), and my favorite fedora of white straw. The sun was beaming, the humidity mercifully low, and I felt it quite possible that I might live forever. The denoue-ment of the Forsythe affair was to demolish that illusion.

I found the home of Rufino Diaz with little trouble. I was not amazed to discover he lived in a motel—many South Florida motels are happy to have year-round tenants—but I was surprised by the prosperous appearance of the place. I don't wish to imply it was the Taj Mahal, but it did seem to be more elegant and expensive than one might expect of the residence of a man who raked lawns for a living. I realized that Sheila Bancroft had probably spoken the truth when she said Rufino had a "cute little apartment." With Jacuzzi and ceiling mirrors, no doubt.

The Trojan Stables required a more lengthy search but was well worth the effort. It was a handsome spread—twenty acres at least, I estimated—with a smallish office building and a barn that looked large enough to accommo-date twenty horses. The grounds were well groomed, with a practice ring, bridle paths, hurdles, and a water jump. The entire layout was encircled by a picket fence of weath-ered barn wood. Very attractive.

I cruised slowly, eyeballing the site. I thought I spotted Constance Forsythe standing firmly planted, hands on hips, observing a rider putting a young bay over the hurdles. But

I did not stop to say howdy. Instead I drove back to the beach, pausing en route at a small deli in a strip mall to scarf a roast beef on white (mayo) and bologna on rye (mustard) with a bottle of Whitbread ale. I make no apology for this prodigal consumption of calories. After all, I'm a growing boy—and especially around the midriff.

I arrived at the Forsythe mansion and was admitted by Sheila Hayworth. She blinked twice when she saw my attire but made no comment, pro or con. Occasionally I am forced to endure the sneers of philistines who believe wrongfully that my flamboyant dress indicates color blindness or a sad lack of taste. I point out to them that I am merely following the laws of natural selection. All biologists know that the peacock with the most extravagant tail wins the peahen.

I used the phone on the library desk to call the Trojan Stables. A man answered and I asked to speak to Mr. Timothy Cussack. I was informed that Cussack did not work Mondays but was expected on the morrow. I hung up having confirmed that the former polo player who had treated Geraldine Forsythe so shabbily was now employed by her mother. A curious situation, wouldn't you say?

I then leafed through the stack of notes I had left atop the desk. The hairs I had carefully placed on pages 5 and 10 had disappeared. But that, I admitted ruefully, did not prove a family or staff member had been prying; it might have happened during Sgt. Al Rogoff's search. My dilemma reminded me of President Truman's anguished plea for a one-armed economist, someone incapable of saying, "On the other hand . . ."

I went looking for Mrs. Nora Bledsoe and found her seated at a small desk in the pantry, a room larger than the McNally kitchen. She was wearing horn-rimmed specs and appeared to be working on household accounts, entering bills and invoices into a ledger. She gave me a smile of welcome, a very nice smile that softened her somewhat imperious features.

"May I help you, Mr. McNally?" she asked.

"I hope you can," I said. "Mrs. Bledsoe, I notice that in a few of Mr. Forsythe's matched sets of leather-bound books a single volume is missing. It may have been borrowed by a member of the family or staff and I intend to ask everyone to provide a list of books temporarily removed from the library. My concern is that outsiders may have had access to the shelves. Is that possible? For instance, who handles the dusting chores?"

"My son and I and the two maids do the day-to-day straightening up," she replied. "And once a week we have a commercial cleaning service that takes care of vacuuming, washing windows, waxing the paneling and things like that. But they are never left alone. Never! We accompany them wherever they go. In addition, I make certain no bags or packages are taken from the house. I'm not saying it's utterly impossible for one of the cleaning crew to steal something small, slip it into his pocket, and walk out with it. We don't search them, you know. But we've been using the same company for years and to my knowledge we've never lost a thing. As for removing one or more of Mr. Forsythe's books, I'd say that was highly unlikely."

"Thank you, Mrs. Bledsoe," I said. "You've been very helpful. By the way, is your son around?"

"Not today. Anthony is off on Mondays."

"Well, I'll catch him another time. Perhaps he's borrowed a book or two."

"I doubt that," she said dourly. "Very much."

I started out but she called, "Mr. McNally," and I turned back.

"I have a book in my bedroom from Mr. Forsythe's library," she said with a weak laugh.

"Oh?" I said. "Could you tell me the title, please. I'll make a note of it."

"The Love Song of J. Alfred Prufrock," she said, blushing slightly.

"Excellent choice," I told her and left. I returned to the library, musing on the vagaries of us all. I mean, who could have guessed the formidable housekeeper read Eliot? But then who would guess I enjoy listening to barbershop quartets?

I went back to my drudgery for the nonce, having nothing better to do. You know, the surprising thing was that most of the books showed evidence of having been read. The pages were cut, some were dog-eared, and a few bore lightly penciled comments in the margins—such profound judgments as "Well put!" and "Rubbish!"

I simply could not believe the Griswold Forsythes II and III had read all that much. But most of the volumes had been published at least a century ago, and I could only conclude the dog-earing and notations had been made by Forsythe forebears, perhaps including the lady who had committed suicide and whose ghost was said to haunt the dungeon.

I was laboring at my cataloging chores when the library door was opened. Geraldine Forsythe entered, and I rose to receive her.

"Good afternoon, Archy," she said.

"Good afternoon, Gerry. You're looking perky today."

"I feel perky," she said. "It's the sunshine I suppose. I

brought you a list of books I've borrowed from the library."

"Thank you," I said, wondering how much longer I'd have to continue this masquerade. "It will be a big help."

She lowered herself into the leather armchair alongside the desk. She was wearing a poet's shirt, tails dangling over rather scanty white twill shorts. She lolled back and hooked one long, tanned leg over the arm of the chair. I am not an expert on body language but even an amateur might rightfully term that pose provocative.

"How is your sister-in-law feeling?" I inquired.

"Sylvia? Oh, she's up and about. Playing that stupid piano of hers, I expect."

"Harpsichord," I said gently.

"Is that what it is?" she said indifferently. "Well, she's recovered. You haven't seen her?"

"Today? No, I have not."

"That's a surprise," she said. "Our Sylvia is not a shy one."

I didn't quite know how to interpret that and made no reply. The sandaled foot hanging over the chair arm began bobbing up and down which indicated, I reckoned, a certain amount of emotional perturbation.

"Archy," she said, "do you know a man named Timothy Cussack?"

I frowned with concentration. "Cussack?" I repeated. "Sounds familiar but I don't believe I've ever met him."

"He once belonged to the Pelican Club."

"Perhaps that's where I heard the name. But he's not currently a member?"

"No," she said. "He was booted out for bouncing checks."

"Ah," I said, eager to hear what might be coming.

"Well," she said, not looking at me, "he was a polo

player until he got hurt. I had a thing going with him for a while but then it ended."

I said nothing, waiting to hear how much more she would reveal.

"The reason I bring up his name," she continued, "is that I think he may have something to do with the disappearance of my jewelry. I'm not accusing him, you understand, but Tim was always hurting for money. I just thought you might want to check up on him."

I was silent a moment, thinking how best to handle this. "Gerry," I said, finally, "I'll certainly look into it, but where can I find this Cussack fellow?"

Then she turned to stare at me. "He's working at mother's stables. That's a laugh, isn't it?"

Her stare was at once defiant and challenging, and I knew she expected a reply—or at least a remark.

"Gerry," I said softly, "is your mother aware of your previous relationship with this man?"

"Of course," she said crossly. "Mother likes to come on tough but she's such a softy. She gave the skunk a job because she felt sorry for him. I guess he's a good trainer, but I was furious when I heard about it."

"And now you feel he may be involved in the theft of your jewelry? But would he have the opportunity? Has he ever been a guest in the house? Is he a frequent visitor?"

"No," she said, "not since we broke up. But I'm not accusing him of stealing the stuff himself. I think someone else may be taking it and giving it to Tim."

Was I dumbfounded? You betcha. "Giving it to him?" I said. "As a gift?"

Her short laugh was ugly. "More like a payoff," she said.

It took me half a mo to understand what she was implying.

"Are you suggesting blackmail?" I asked her.

She shrugged. "Could be. I'm just guessing, you understand. I have no evidence."

"Supposing, just supposing, your suspicions are correct, who is the victim of the blackmail and committing the actual theft?"

She leaned forward to scratch a bare ankle. Her head was lowered and I couldn't see her face. "My sister-in-law," she said in a tight voice. "Sylvia goes out to the farm to ride once or twice a week. I think she and Tim have something going and she's paying him off with my jewelry to keep his mouth shut—or maybe just in return for favors granted."

"Gerry," I said, "that's a very, *very* serious accusation."

Then she raised her head and showed me a face twisted with hurt. "It's not an accusation. I told you I have no evidence. But it's what I think is happening. I know Tim Cussack and I know Sylvia, and believe me it's possible. They're not nice people."

"It's a bloomin' soap opera!" I burst out.

"Of course it is," she readily agreed. "That's what life is, isn't it—a soap opera?"

"Sometimes," I said, and then with more prescience than I knew I possessed, I added, "Until it becomes a tragedy."

"There's nothing tragic about this," she said decisively. "It's just a tawdry sitcom and I want it ended. I couldn't care less if Sylvia wants to cheat on my brother. It's their problem, not mine. But I don't want to finance my sister-in-law's fling. You understand?"

I nodded.

"And you'll help me, Archy?"

"I'll do what I can."

She smiled and it made her look ten years younger. She stood up suddenly and before I had time to rise she was at my swivel chair and had slipped a warm arm about my shoulders. She leaned down, lips close to my ear.

"Oh, you're a sweetie," she said. "A sweet, sweet sweetie. Help me, Archy, and I'll make it worth your while. Really I will."

She pressed close and kissed me. Then she straightened and winked—yes, she actually winked!—and strode from the library, tanned legs flashing.

I sat behind the desk a few moments longer, reflecting that two hours spent in the Forsythe home were equivalent to a frontal lobotomy. I felt I was being reduced to their level of craziness. These were people Connie Garcia had called "dull, dull, dull," and they were all turning out to be actors in an amateur production of *Animal Crackers*.

The hell with it. I packed up and went home. The sea was too choppy for my usual afternoon swim, so I trudged upstairs to my lair. I lighted what I hoped was my first cigarette of the day (but wasn't sure) and poured myself a small marc. Then I donned reading glasses and set to work on my journal. I had much to record since the last entry.

After almost an hour of scribbling I read my disjointed notes, observations, and conjectures. Then I read them again. And you know, I realized I had learned something that day that might prove to be extremely significant.

Surely you can guess what it was.

9

I awoke late on Tuesday morning after having enjoyed a good night's sleep and a dream so lubricious I cannot recount it here lest I earn the censor's wrath—and the envy of my No. 1 pal, Binky Watrous, who complains constantly and bitterly that he can dream only of forklift trucks. I think the poor lad needs professional help.

I bounced downstairs to a deserted kitchen and fixed my own breakfast: a glass of chilled Clamato, duck pâté on a toasted bagel, and two cups of black instant. That may sound rather unusual to you but I see nothing bizarre about it. I once ate a whole baked flounder for breakfast—but that's another story.

The weather was splendid, an instant replay of the previous day, and as I headed up the coast in my sparky chariot I felt such a surge of joie de vivre that I broke into song. I wished for an audience so many could enjoy my rendition of "Bill Bailey, Won't You Please Come Home?"

When I pulled up to the front entrance of the Forsythe manse I saw an elegant trio lounging beneath the portico. The Griswold Forsythes, senior and junior, were wearing brass-buttoned navy blazers over white flannel slacks. And between father-in-law and husband stood Mrs. Sylvia Forsythe, obviously dressed for riding: jodhpurs and boots, an open calfskin vest over a white turtleneck sweater.

Those three moneyed people looked so well scrubbed, so insouciant and faintly bored, that I had a sudden onslaught of nostalgia for a time I never knew. I could see them posed negligently for a Pierce-Arrow ad or perhaps debating whether or not to drop in at one of Gatsby's parties. Sleek was the word for them, the men with their hair slicked back and the woman with a cool glow. They made me feel like a lumpen.

I alighted from the Miata and Griswold III came ambling over to offer me an anodyne smile and a languid hand to shake.

"Hullo, Archy," he said. "Ready for another go at father's books? Making progress, are you?"

"Coming along," I answered. "And where are you off to? Not the office surely."

"Not today," he said. "Father and I are going out on some fellow's yacht."

"Sounds like fun," I observed.

The word seemed to offend him. "It's business," he said with such an air of self-importance that I wanted to feed him a knuckle sandwich. "This fellow hopes to sell us his boat. We're considering it. Ah, here's our wagon."

The big Rolls-Royce, driven by Anthony Bledsoe, came purring from the back of the mansion where the five-car garage was located. The houseman parked, hopped out, and held the door open.

"See you around, Archy," Griswold the Lesser said with a casual wave. "You and I must have a proper lunch one of these days."

"Yes," I said, "we must." I was horribly tempted to add, "So we can discuss the proper lighting of nude photos."

He climbed behind the wheel of the Rolls, his father joined him up front, and the tank pulled slowly away. Tony Bledsoe trotted back to the garage again and I joined Sylvia Forsythe.

"Hi, Archy," she said, putting a light hand on my shoulder. "Listen, you don't really want to spend such a scrumptious morning in that depressing library, do you?"

"Not really," I confessed.

"Why don't you follow me out to the stables and I'll show you around."

"Splendid idea," I said.

Bledsoe brought Sylvia's car around. It was a silver-gray Saturn, a very jazzy vehicle. He got out and held the door for her.

"Tailgate," she called to me. "I don't want you getting lost."

I nodded and headed for my roadster.

"Have a good time," Tony said, and I heard the longing in his voice.

Sylvia headed south to take the Flagler Bridge across Lake Worth to the mainland. I must tell you that woman drove as if pursued by Old Nick. I mean we *flew* and I nervously anticipated being stopped by the polizia and dragged off to durance vile.

But we arrived at the Trojan Stables without incident. By the time I dismounted from the Miata, Sylvia was standing near the office building chatting with Mrs. Constance Forsythe, who looked a mite blowsy with stained riding pants and a bush jacket that had spent too much time in the bush. I joined the ladies.

"Mrs. Forsythe," I said, addressing the elder, "I must tell you that your daughter-in-law drives like a maniac."

"I know she does," she agreed. "She'll break her lovely

neck one of these days. If she rode my horses like she drives her car I'd have her gizzard."

Sylvia laughed and touched the other woman's cheek. "Horses are different, darling," she said. "Is Tim busy?"

"Out with a student right now."

"I want to show Archy around. Okay?"

"Of course. See if you can persuade him to muck out a few of the stalls."

"Not me," I protested. "When it comes to pitchforks I'm a complete klutz."

"You might learn to enjoy it," Constance said with a throaty laugh. "All that *Parfum d'Manure.*"

I wanted to say, "That's offal," but it's a written not a spoken pun.

Sylvia and I strolled about the horse farm and there is little I can add to what I have already described. The only surprise was the main barn, which had only half the stalls I had estimated. But the building included a tack room and living quarters for the stable boys—something like a dormitory.

"No drinking or drugs allowed," Sylvia said. "Caught once and out you go."

"Very admirable," I said, thankful I wasn't a stable boy. "Handsome horses," I commented although I know absolutely nothing about horseflesh except that when I place a bet it causes them to run slower.

"Constance doesn't own them. She boards them and feeds them, takes care of their ailments, and provides instruction in riding, jumping, and dressage—things like that. For a hefty fee, of course."

"It's a pricey hobby," I guessed.

"Horse people are nuts," Sylvia said flatly. "Hey, there's Timothy. Tim!" she called, waving. "Over here!"

We were standing on the tanbark outside the barn. The young man turned, waved back, and came sauntering toward us. Something insolent in that gait, I thought.

"Archy," Sylvia said, "meet Timothy Cussack. Tim, this is Archy McNally."

We shook hands, smiling like villains at each other. He was a hunk, no doubt about it. But not heavy or clumpy. More like a fencer or diver: tall and whiplike. Face suntanned almost to cordovan, which made his choppers startingly white. Pale eyes and a wide mouth with faint laugh lines. I could see what had seduced Geraldine Forsythe.

"I've been giving Archy the fifty-cent tour," Sylvia said.

"Yeah?" he said. "You ride?" he asked me.

"Wheels," I said. "Not legs."

He laughed and I heard another clue to his charm. It was a hearty up-from-the-chest laugh and infectious. It was difficult to doubt his sincerity—but I managed.

"Sylvia will convert you," he advised me. "She's becoming one of our best exercise boys—girls, persons, whatever."

"What do I get today?" she asked him.

"How about Lady Macbeth?" he suggested.

"Tim!" she cried. "That's like riding a desk."

"She needs a run. Her owner is still up north and the poor beast hasn't been able to sniff the clover. Give her a break."

"Okay then," Sylvia said. "Lady Macbeth it is."

She went back into the barn; Timothy Cussack and I were left together.

"I keep thinking I've seen you before," I told him. "It couldn't have been the Pelican Club, could it?"

"Might have been," he said peaceably. "I drop by there occasionally. Not often. Dull place."

"It can be," I said, not yet ready to condemn him for this minor fabrication.

"What do you do?" he asked idly.

"I'm a flunky at my father's law firm, McNally and Son."

"Sounds like you got it made," he said.

I thought that was an extraordinary thing to say, expressing contempt and envy simultaneously.

"Well, I don't have a law degree," I informed him. "I just do odd jobs. Investigations and such."

Perhaps I had said more than I should have, because up to then he had been placidly pleasant, not displaying any great interest in our chatter. But suddenly his expression and manner became more animated.

"Investigations?" he said. "Like what?"

I was saved from answering by the reappearance of Sylvia, leading a saddled white mare, undeniably plump.

"We've only had her a few weeks," Cussack explained to me. "She does need thinning down. Right now I doubt if she could step up a curb, let alone take a low hurdle."

I must admit I admired the man, admired the way he talked and the way he carried himself. He leaked self-assurance, but nothing pushy, you understand; just cool confidence and an amused way of looking at things. I thought it possible he was totally amoral.

Sylvia brought Lady Macbeth alongside us. I took a small step backward. That horse looked enormous.

"Timmy," she said, "give me a leg up."

He linked his fingers, she stepped in the cup his hands formed, and he tossed her onto the English saddle. The whole movement was so smooth it was almost balletic. Sylvia waited, erect, while he adjusted the stirrups. Then she walked the horse away.

"No more than a canter," Cussack called after her, then

turned back to me. "Want to try a ride?" he asked. It wasn't quite a jeer but it came close.

"I think not," I said. "But thank you for the offer."

"Listen," he said, serious now, "you mentioned you do investigations. Free-lance?"

"Nope," I said promptly. "Only for clients of McNally and Son. You're in need of a shamus?"

He looked at me a long moment and I saw wariness in those fallow eyes. Then he turned to watch Sylvia Forsythe, who was now trotting Lady Macbeth along one of the bridle paths.

"Maybe," Cussack said. "It depends."

I was dying to ask, "On what?" but decided not to pin him. "Happy to have met you, Tim," I said, departing.

"Likewise," he said absently.

I decided to stop at the Pelican Club on my journey back to the beach and accumulate some nourishment. All that time spent in the bracing air of the Great Outdoors had given me an appetite—and a thirst.

The bar was crowded with the lunchtime mob and I glanced into the dining room. There, seated at our favorite table, was my light-o'-love, Connie Garcia. I scuttled to her side and she looked up.

"May I join you?" I asked.

"Sorry," she said, "I'm waiting for Humphrey Bogart."

"He's been dead for some time," I pointed out.

"So have you," she said. "You don't call, you don't write, you don't fax. What's *with* you?"

"My dear child," I said loftily, sliding onto the chair opposite her, "you must realize that I toil for a living, and frequently at jobs that require long hours and the utmost concentration on the business at hand."

"Which is usually monkey business," she added. "Are you going to feed me or not?"

"You haven't ordered yet?"

"Just got here before you arrived."

I waved at Priscilla Pettibone and she came sashaying to our table.

"Oh my," she said, "how nice it is to see Romeo and Juliet back together again. Or is it Julio and Romiet?"

"We didn't come here for a side order of sass," I told her. "We want food and drink, in reverse order. What's the special today?"

"Me," she said. "But if that doesn't suit you, Leroy is pushing crabmeat salad. Real crab, not that rubbery stuff you get in plastic packages."

"Sounds great," Connie said. "I'll have the crabmeat salad and a glass of chardonnay."

"Double it," I said. "And the sooner the better."

She winked at us and went into the bar area. Connie and I helped ourselves to kosher dill spears placed in Mason jars on each table along with a basket of peppered focaccia wedges.

"All kidding aside," Connie said, "what *have* you been doing?"

"All kidding aside," I answered, "I can't tell you. Client confidentiality and all that rot."

"But it has to do with the Forsythes, doesn't it?"

"Why do you say that?"

"Because you asked me about them and then there was that item in Lolly Spindrift's column."

"Clever lady," I said.

"So your job *does* involve the Forsythes?"

"Wild horses—and I met a few this morning—couldn't drag that information from me."

"Too bad," Connie said, "because just yesterday I heard some hot gossip about the Forsythes."

I'm not sure how one's ears perk up but I think mine did. "That's interesting," I said. "What did you hear?"

But then Priscilla served our wine and salads, and there was a cessation of talk as we began stuffing. An observer might think we had both been on oat bran diets for several weeks.

"So," I said after my hunger pangs had diminished slightly, "what gossip did you hear yesterday?"

She stopped excavating her salad bowl and looked up. "What will you give me?" she demanded.

"Connie," I said, "what you have just asked leaves me totally aghast. I mean I am saddened that after our many years together—intimate years I might add—you should require payment before divulging rumors that might possibly be of assistance and further my career. This is extortion, nothing less than rank extortion, and I refuse to be a party to it."

"How about a dinner at Cafe L'Europe?"

"You've got it," I said eagerly. "What did you hear?"

"Well, I heard it through a friend of a friend of a friend. The original friend was having lunch in the back room of Ta-boo and at a nearby table were the Forsythes, father and son. They weren't exactly shouting at each other, you understand, but there was a king-sized argument going on: red faces, raised voices, some pounding on the table. Very nasty it was, the informant reports."

"And did the informant overhear the subject of the fracas?"

"Afraid not. But apparently it was a first-class squabble. Archy, is that a clue?"

I almost choked on a chunk of crabmeat. "A clue to *what?*"

Connie shrugged. "Whatever it is you're doing."

"Darling, I appreciate your help. Really I do. But I'm not certain of the importance of the Forsythes' brannigan. Perhaps they were arguing about the best way to iron one's shoelaces. They're quite capable of that. But thank you for the report."

"And our dinner is still on?"

"Of course. Give you a call tomorrow."

"No," she said firmly. "I'll call you tonight."

We had lemon sorbet and cappuccino for dessert. Then I signed the tab and we went out to our cars.

"Thanks for the grub, luv," Connie said. "Do I get a goodbye kiss?"

"With mucho pleasure," I said, and so we kissed in the sunbaked parking lot: a delightful kiss tasting faintly of garlic. Connie looked smashing that day—but then she always looks first-class. She is shortish and plumpish but has a glowing suntan that doesn't end, a mane of long, glossy black hair, and burning eyes. All admirable physical attributes, to be sure, but her greatest attractions are her wit and supercharged esprit. What bounce she has! Kissing her is akin to sticking your tongue in a light bulb socket. Then she turns on the switch.

After that fervent parting I drove to the Forsythe estate wondering what might have been the cause of the altercation that made both men, *père et fils*, become red-faced and pound the table. I could not believe it was anything serious simply because I did not take either of them seriously. I thought they were both bloodless prigs. What a mistake that turned out to be!

Anthony Bledsoe opened the front door for me. I had the weirdest feeling that he had been awaiting my return.

"Have a good time?" he asked.

"Very enjoyable," I replied. "Although I'm not all that keen about horses. Do you ride?"

"Occasionally," he said. "I like it. Sometimes, on my day off, I go out to Mrs. Forsythe's farm and she lets me exercise one of the nags."

"Oh?" I said. "Do you know Timothy Cussack?"

"Tim? Sure, I know him. Nice guy."

"Seems to be," I said. "I met him for the first time today. Was he a good polo player?"

Bledsoe laughed. "When he wasn't hung over. Our Timmy likes the sauce."

"Don't we all," I said, tempted to add that bordelaise was my favorite. "Is Lucy home?" I asked him.

"Oh yeah," he said. "The school van dropped her off about fifteen minutes ago. She's out back somewhere."

I nodded and went into the library, thinking I really should do a spot of cataloging. But the dreary chamber depressed me and I fled. I went hunting for Lucy, that lorn child who seemed like an outsider in the disordered Forsythe household.

10

I finally found her in the secret place. She was sitting on the ground, a small pad on her lap. She was chewing the stub of a pencil and her face was twisted with concentration.

"Hi, sweetheart," I said.

She started, then looked up and smiled. Sunlight glinted off the bands on her teeth.

"Am I really your sweetheart?" she asked.

"Of course you are," I told her. "I have several but you are definitely Numero Uno. What are you doing?"

"I'm writing a poem," she said timidly.

"Good for you," I said. "Will you read it to me?"

"It's not finished yet."

"Well, when it's finished may I read it?"

"I don't know," she said doubtfully. "It's very private."

"I thought we were friends, Lucy. Friends can show each other their private poems."

"They can? Do you have any private poems?"

"Many," I assured her.

"Tell me one."

I thought she was a bit immature for "There was a young man from Nantucket," so I recited "I never saw a purple cow." It was an immediate success; she laughed and clapped her hands.

"That's a nice poem," she said. "I like it when they rhyme. My poem rhymes."

"Grand," I said. "Did you go to school today?"

"Uh-huh."

"And what did you teach the teacher?"

She laughed again. "You're silly," she said. "The teacher teaches us. Everyone knows that. Today we learned about George Washington."

"Splendid chap. Never lied."

"Yes, he did," she corrected me. "But only when he had to. He didn't like to lie. Some people do, you know."

Her wisdom was breathtaking.

"I can't believe anyone lies to you, Lucy."

"Oh, yes they do," she said sadly. "My mother, my father—lots of people. They're supposed to love me but they really don't. Leastwise they never say they do and so they're lying, aren't they?"

This was becoming murky and I didn't quite know how to handle it. "I'm sure your parents love you, Lucy," I said, "but sometimes people find it hard to express their love. They just assume you know it."

"Well, if they both love me," she said with the illogic of the very young, "then why are they always fighting?"

"Darling," I said, "perhaps it has nothing to do with you. They may disagree about other things but I'm certain they agree about their love for you."

"I don't know," she said gloomily. "I heard mom say to dad, 'If it wasn't for Lucy I'd be out of here tomorrow.' And he said, 'Don't let the kid stop you.' That doesn't sound like they love me, does it?"

I felt like weeping. She was disclosing things I really didn't want to know. I was acutely uncomfortable listening to these distressing revelations. Most of all I was anguished by the intensity of her unhappiness. No child should be a shuttlecock between gaming parents and, even worse, be aware of it.

"Lucy," I said, "I love you," and the moment I said it I knew it was true. I leaned down to stroke her silken hair. "So don't ever believe no one loves you. Many people do, I'm sure, and I'm one of them."

"That's okay," she said bravely. "I'm not going to cry. I decided I'm never going to cry again."

I had to leave her; I just couldn't take more.

"Listen, dear," I said, "I hope you haven't forgotten about that picnic you and I are going to have."

"Oh no," she said, eyes wide. "I remember."

"Good. Let's make it real soon."

"I love you, too," she said suddenly.

Then I left and stumbled my way back to the main house, sad and shaken. I was ready to return as quickly as possible to the McNally digs and have a wallop to restore my belief in this, the best of all possible worlds. But it was not to be.

As I proceeded down the main hallway to the front door, the Griswold Forsythes, II and III, were just entering in their blazers and flannel bags. We stopped to chat.

"Good voyage?" I asked them.

"Nice cruise," the younger replied. "Fine lunch with bubbly. But I don't think we want to buy that particular yacht, do we, father?"

"We don't want to buy *any* yacht," the older said sharply. "Archy, may I see you in the library for a moment."

Griswold III departed, his crest somewhat droopy, and I followed the II into the library. He took the swivel behind the desk and I sat in the armchair alongside. I imagined, with dread, he was about to report another item of value was missing. It turned out to be worse than that.

"My wife and I occupy separate bedrooms," he said stonily. "Last night I retired shortly before midnight and found this note placed on my pillow."

He reached into his jacket pocket and then handed me a square of paper. It had two straight and two ragged edges as if it had been torn from the corner of a larger sheet of white foolscap.

Written on it in large block letters were two words: YOUR NEXT. The printing was quavery, as if it had been done with the left hand of a right-handed person, or vice versa. There was no way of knowing if it had been inscribed by man or woman.

I studied those two words a moment and naturally, because I have rather pedantic leanings, I immediately noted the absence of an apostrophe. If the first word was intended to be a contraction of YOU ARE, the writer was obviously a dolt. But perhaps the message was meant to be an abbreviated warning that another of Mr. Forsythe's possessions would soon disappear: YOUR (something) NEXT.

I explained this to our client. He listened impatiently and didn't seem impressed.

"I guessed all that myself," he said irritably. "I am not an idiot, you know. I believe it is a misspelled threat against my person—YOU ARE NEXT, without the apostrophe. Do you agree?"

"Yes, sir," I said. "I think that's the correct assumption. And after what happened to Mrs. Sylvia I urge you to report this to Sergeant Rogoff as soon as possible."

He looked at me queerly. "It's a shock," he said, "to

realize that someone in your home plans to do you harm. Strangle you, perhaps."

"You have every right to feel that way, Mr. Forsythe. It's a terrible thing. Who has access to your bedroom, sir?"

"Everyone in the house. The door is never locked."

"All the more reason to call in the police. Would you like me to phone Sergeant Rogoff now?"

He paused a moment. "No," he said, "not yet. I want to make a few inquiries myself this evening."

"Please, Mr. Forsythe," I urged, "don't postpone it. I take this note very seriously. Your life may be in danger."

"I am well aware of that, young man," he said almost angrily. "And this evening I shall lock my bedroom door and prop a chair under the inside knob. I'll survive the night, I assure you." He pondered, pulling at his lower lip. Then: "I suggest you, Sergeant Rogoff, and I meet at my office tomorrow. You know where it is?"

"Yes, sir."

"My son has an appointment with his periodontist at noon. Our clerk"—(He pronounced it 'clark')—"customarily leaves for lunch at twelve fifteen. If you and the sergeant arrive at twelve thirty I believe we'll be able to have a private discussion about this unpleasant matter without interruption. Is that satisfactory?"

"I would prefer the police be notified immediately, Mr. Forsythe, but if that is your wish we'll meet with you tomorrow. You don't want to discuss it here?"

"No," he said shortly. "Not in this house."

"During our talk with Sergeant Rogoff do you intend to inform him about your missing property?"

"No."

"Have I your permission to tell him?"

"No."

The Abominable No-Man.

I sighed. "Very well, sir, we'll do it your way—against my better judgment I might add. May I keep the note?"

"Keep the damned thing," he said roughly. "The writer has made his point."

"Or hers," I said.

He stared at me a sec. "You may be right," he said.

I stuffed the note into my pocket and rose to depart.

"Archy," Griswold Forsythe II said formally, "I wish to thank you for your efforts on my behalf."

It was a gentlemanly thing to say and also, considering the circumstances, rather gallant and touching. He was not lacking in courage. Foolhardy perhaps, but not a craven.

I drove home at a carefully disciplined speed because if I surrendered to my baser instincts I would have broken all local and state laws dealing with the reckless operation of a vehicle. But once inside the McNally kitchen I mixed a vodka and water with such haste that Ursi Olson, preparing our dinner, looked at me with surprise.

"Thirsty?" she asked.

"Parched," I told her.

I took my plasma into father's study and used his phone to call Sgt. Rogoff at his office. He wasn't in, but the desk sergeant who knew me said he was on a forty-eight. I had Al's home phone number and called him there. After seven rings he answered and I knew at once I had wakened him.

" 'Lo," he said sleepily.

"Aw," I said, "I interrupted your nappy-poo. Sorry about that, chum."

"I'll bet," he said. "What's on your mind—if I may exaggerate?"

"You and I have a date tomorrow," I said.

"Oh goody," he said. "How shall I dress? Long gown?"

"Just shut up," I said. "Al, this is serious."

I told him about the note Mr. Forsythe had found lying on his pillow.

"Son of a bitch," Rogoff said bitterly. "Something screwy is going on in that joint. I hate these family cases; they always turn out to be a mess. Give me a straight, cut-and-dried mugging any day. Who's got the note now?"

I said I did and would deliver it to him when we met at the Forsythes' office at twelve thirty on Wednesday to discuss the situation with Griswold II.

"Why there?" Al asked.

"Because he refused to meet at his home. Perhaps he's afraid the place is bugged. I'm beginning to believe the entire family are paranoids."

"Or maybe just plain wacky. Well, I'm supposed to be off duty tomorrow but I'll be there. Thanks so much for dumping this slumgullion on my plate."

"That's what friends are for," I said and hung up.

I went into the living room and then out onto our little terrace that afforded a good view of the ocean. I saw a lot of whitecaps and decided a swim would be dicey. So I climbed upstairs to my dorm and worked on my journal until it was time for the McNally cocktail hour.

We dined on vichyssoise that night, followed by crab cakes with a salsa that had a zing. Dessert was an almond torte with a white chocolate frosting, which meant that the waistbands of my slacks would continue to shrink.

I huffed and puffed to my lair and continued bringing my professional diary up-to-date. When my phone rang around nine o'clock I was certain it would be Connie Garcia calling to set a time for our dinner date Wednesday night. So I answered with a warm "Hi!"

My caller laughed. "This is Sylvia Forsythe," she said. "Do you customarily answer your phone by shouting, 'Hi!'?"

"Hardly," I said. "But I was expecting a call from my grandfather in Spokane and he's a bit hard-of-hearing."

"What a faker you are!" she marveled. "Archy, I was disappointed you had left when I returned from my ride this morning. I was hoping we might have lunch."

"Sorry about that," I said. "But I didn't know how long you'd be gone. We'll make it another time."

"I'm going to hold you to that," she said. "You and I have a lot to talk about, don't we?"

That was a poser. But it would have been boorish to ask, "About what?" So I said nothing.

There was a pause requiring a pregnancy test; apparently the lady was awaiting a reply. Finally, when there was none, she said, "What did you think of Tim Cussack?"

"Seems like a solid fellow," I answered, lying valiantly. "Very handsome."

"Isn't he?" she said with some enthusiasm. "All the women go gaga over him."

"You too?" I asked boldly.

"Me too," she admitted. "But the competition is fierce."

She talked in riddles and I was lost. I decided to switch to less intimate topics.

"Still playing your harpsichord?"

"Oh yes. I'd go mad without my music."

"And riding."

"And riding," she agreed. "And other things," she added throatily.

The sexual innuendo again.

"As long as you're happy," I said lamely.

"I wouldn't go that far," she said, laughing again. "But I'm working at it. Archy, the next time you're in-residence I insist you give me a few minutes. I may be plinking away at Vivaldi or I may be in my bedroom. In any event, do look me up. Okay?"

"Of course."

"Bye-bye," she cooed and hung up.

I took a deep breath and exhaled noisily. She had just succeeded in putting the kibosh on Geraldine Forsythe's dizzy scenario: Sylvia Forsythe was making nice-nice with Timothy Cussack, her sister-in-law's former lover. But that plot now wilted. If she and the matinee idol were having an affair, why on earth was she coming on to me so blatantly? A puzzlement.

I continued scribbling in my journal and it couldn't have been more than five minutes later when my phone jangled again. This time I was certain it was Connie Garcia. "Hi!" I said ardently.

There was a short silence, and then the caller, a woman, asked, "Is this Archy McNally?"

"It is," I confessed.

"This is Geraldine Forsythe. Do you usually answer the phone by saying 'Hi!'?"

"A slight mistake," I said. "I was expecting a call from my dear old grandmother who's in the hospital with a severe case of shinsplints resulting from her run in the Boston Marathon. How are you, Gerry?"

"Very well, thank you. Archy, I was wondering if you've managed to meet Timothy Cussack."

"As a matter of fact I have, just this morning."

"And what is your take on him?"

"Seems to have a great deal of charm," I said cautiously.

Her laugh was flimsy. "Oh yes," she said, "charm is Tim's stock-in-trade. You're going to follow up on it, aren't you?"

"You're referring to your suspicions?"

"They're more than suspicions, Archy. Believe me, I know I'm right. But I need evidence and I'm depending on you to provide it. You will try, won't you?"

"Of course."

"This is very important to me, Archy. I'm sure you realize that."

"I do."

"Good. I won't be able to pay you with money but I think you'll be happy with your reward. Nighty-night, darling!"

She hung up, leaving me to reflect that Al Rogoff had been correct: the Forsythes were a clan of wackos.

To make a long story short (if it's not too late) when my phone rang fifteen minutes later I was careful to answer formally, "Archibald McNally." And of course it was Connie Garcia. We made a date for the following evening at the Cafe L'Europe at seven thirty. Our conversation was brief because Connie was watching a Bugs Bunny Festival on cable TV.

"Bugs reminds me of you, Archy," she said before she hung up.

After reviewing my three phone calls I didn't feel like Bugs Bunny; I saw myself more like Pepe Le Pew. It made me wonder if since taking on the Forsythe case I had been living in a cartoonish world. I longed for the day I could stutter, "Th-th-that's all, folks!"

Wednesday morning brought reality and I dressed with less than my usual panache, preparing for the meeting with Griswold Forsythe II at twelve thirty. I breakfasted with my parents in the dining room and mother remarked how "spiffy" I looked in my black suit, white shirt, maroon tie.

"Is it graduation day?" father asked with heavy good humor, but I could see he was pleased that for once I wasn't attired like Carmen Miranda.

He drove to work in his black Lexus and I followed in my jauntier surrey. I went directly to my tiny oubliette and began working on my monthly expense account, a fictional masterpiece that might be entitled "Great Expectations." I smoked one cigarette that morning and made one phone call—to the Cafe L'Europe, reserving a table for two that evening.

Shortly after twelve o'clock I left the McNally Building and strolled westward on Royal Palm Way to the structure housing the Forsythes' office. It was a rather grungy three-story edifice of indeterminate age and something of an eyesore. In fact, local newspapers occasionally published indignant Letters to the Editor demanding that the damned thing be demolished in favor of a more attractive building suitable for that prestigious avenue.

It was a warren of small offices, occupied mainly by attorneys and real estate and insurance agents. The Forsythes' cubby, I recalled, was on the top floor, reached by a creaky automatic elevator. I remembered their suite as being a smallish reception room, hardly large enough for the clerk's desk, and a larger office in the rear that held a handsome oak partners' desk, used by father Griswold and son Griswold.

I waited across the street in the shade of a plump bottle palm. At about twelve-twenty I spotted Sgt. Al Rogoff's pickup cruising slowly along while he scanned building numbers. I waved, he saw me, waved back. He turned the corner and apparently parked, for a few minutes later he appeared on foot, trundling along like a fire hydrant on wheels. He was wearing a loose-fitting khaki safari suit and if he was armed, as I assumed he was, it was not noticeable.

"You look like you're going to a funeral," he said, eyeing my duds. "You bring the note?"

I took it from my jacket pocket and handed it over. Al studied it a moment.

"No apostrophe," he commented. "How do you figure that?"

"I figure the writer was not a Rhodes Scholar," I said.

"Brilliant, Mr. Holmes," Al said. "Let's go get this over with. I've got a heavy pinochle game planned for this afternoon."

That elevator was scarcely larger than a coffin and it made alarming thumps and groans as it carried us slowly to the third floor.

"We'd have made better time walking up the stairs," Rogoff groused.

The door to the office had an upper half of frosted glass and bore the inscription GRISWOLD FORSYTHE II and below that GRISWOLD FORSYTHE III, both names in a painted script that had flaked away in spots.

I pushed the door open and we entered the empty reception room.

"Mr. Forsythe," I called. "Archy McNally. We're here." No answer.

The sergeant and I looked at each other.

"Are you sure he said twelve-thirty?" Al asked.

"Yes, I'm sure," I said peevishly and called again, "Mr. Forsythe!"

No answer.

Rogoff tried the knob on the door to the inner office. It turned easily, the portal swung open, we stepped in.

Griswold Forsythe II was lying supine on the worn Persian rug behind the partners' desk. His arms were spread wide and his open eyes stared sightlessly upward.

Al went down quickly on one knee alongside him, leaned close, peered, touched his neck.

"A mackerel," he said.

I took a deep breath. "There goes your pinochle game," I said.

11

Al commanded me to wait outside in the tiled corridor and I obeyed. I paced up and down, smoked two English Ovals, and watched as the investigation got under way. I heard sirens, uniformed and plainclothes officers appeared. Then Tom Bunion, the ME's man, showed up, gave me a cool nod, and disappeared inside. He was followed by a crew of ambulance attendants wearing whites and carrying a body bag and folding stretcher.

Finally, more than a half-hour later, Sgt. Rogoff came out of the Forsythes' office, juicing up one of his fat cigars.

"Heart attack?" I asked him.

"Don't I wish," he said. "Strangled."

"Oh lordy," I said. "Did he have scratches and cuts on his neck similar to the wounds Mrs. Sylvia received?"

"Nope," Al said. "Where's the son?"

"The late Mr. Forsythe told me he had a twelve o'clock appointment with his periodontist."

"And the clerk?"

"Apparently he went out to lunch every day at twelve fifteen."

The sergeant nodded. "Then eventually they'll both show up—I hope. Forsythe told you about the note yesterday?"

"That's correct."

"Why didn't you call me immediately?"

"I tried to persuade him, Al, but he wouldn't have it. He said he wanted to make some inquiries himself last night."

"Maybe he did. And maybe it got him aced."

"You think it was someone from his house or someone he knew?"

Rogoff flipped a palm back and forth. "Could be. But he's got no wallet on him."

"You mean it could have been a stranger, a villain casing the building for a soft touch and stumbling on Forsythe alone in an unlocked office?"

"I doubt it," Al said. "He had a gold pocket watch in his vest with a gold chain heavy enough to moor the QE-Two. It wasn't touched. A grab-and-run scumbag would have lifted that. No, I think all the killer wanted was the wallet—if Forsythe carried one and he probably did. The son or wife will know. Go home, Archy. There's nothing more you can do here."

I nodded. "Keep me up to speed, will you?"

"Sure," he said. "That flock of loonies aren't a laugh anymore, are they?"

"No," I said. "Not funny at all. Just one more thing, Al: when was he killed?"

"Maybe a half-hour ago, give or take."

We stared at each other.

"You mean," I said, almost choking, "the strangler might have been bouncing down the stairs while we were coming up in the elevator?"

"It's possible," the sergeant said grimly. "How does that grab you, sonny boy?"

I started back to the McNally Building, then detoured to the nearest pub for a shot of single-malt Scotch. I was spooked, no doubt about it. As Al had said, the crazy doings at the Forsythe castle were no longer amusing. The wall between comedy and tragedy had come tumbling down.

I found I had no appetite at all (surprised?), returned to my office, and phoned Mrs. Trelawney. She said my father was lunching at his desk and couldn't be disturbed. I knew what that meant: he was having his customary roast beef on whole wheat bread (hold the mayo) and a glass of iced tea. Woe betide anyone who interrupted that sumptuous feast. Mrs. T. promised to call me when he had finished his dessert—a Tums.

I spent the next twenty minutes at my desk, smoking up a storm and recalling those meandering comments Mr. Forsythe had made about death during our first interview. He had claimed he looked forward to dissolution with curiosity and a certain degree of relish.

I didn't believe a word of it. Knowing the man, I was positive he had died outraged that anyone would *dare* usher him so unceremoniously into the hereafter.

My summons finally arrived and I climbed the back stairway to father's office. I found him seated at his rolltop desk, reviewing a stack of blue-bound legal documents.

"Yes, Archy," he said pleasantly enough, "what is it now?"

"Bad news, sir," I said.

I told him of the death of Griswold Forsythe II and how Sgt. Rogoff and I happened on the scene so soon after the murder had been committed. I related the few details Al had revealed and assured father I had done my best to persuade Mr. Forsythe to call the police immediately after I had learned of the threatening note.

The guv listened to my recital in silence. I thought I saw sadness in his eyes but perhaps I was imagining. Then he swung halfway around in his swivel chair so I could not see his face. I wondered if there might be tears aborning.

"I knew that man for forty years," he said, his voice steady. "One of my first clients. I cannot say that I particularly liked him but I respected him. He was an honorable man. Testy occasionally and something of a bore, but honorable. Archy, do you feel his murder has any connection at all with the thefts of his property?"

"It's only a guess, father, but I'd say yes, the two are somehow connected."

"I concur," he said stonily. "I want you to continue your investigation. Is that understood?"

"Yes, sir."

"Has the family been notified?"

"I don't know. I doubt it. It happened only a few hours ago."

He stood up and when he turned to me he was in character again: the conscientious, reliable family solicitor. "I'll call Sergeant Rogoff at once. There is much to be done. I suggest you not visit the Forsythe home for a day or two. Leave them alone with their grief. Unless your presence is requested, of course."

"I'd like to attend the funeral, sir."

"All the McNallys will attend," he said firmly, "if it is not limited to the immediate family."

And on that somber note we parted. I returned to my office, and what I did next may strike you as rather crass and unfeeling. But I considered my actions as deposits (of information) that might possibly earn a profit (of information) in the future. And so I phoned Lolly Spindrift.

"Hi, hon," he said breezily. "What luscious tidbit of gossip are you in need of today?"

"None," I said. "But I have something for you. About

two hours ago Griswold Forsythe the Second was murdered, strangled, in his office on Royal Palm Way."

I heard him gasp. "For real?" he asked.

"Absolutely, Lol. I saw the body—but for God's sake keep me out of it."

"So I shall, sweetie," he said. "I'm going to hang up now and dash over to the news desk. Thanks, luv. I owe you one."

My second call was to Connie Garcia. I told her what had happened. Her reaction was unexpected.

"Shit!" she said furiously. "Is there no end to this madness? Archy, what's happening to our world? When does the killing stop?"

"Never," I said.

"Don't say that!" she cried. "I don't want to hear it."

"I'll call if I learn more," I said. "And if you hear anything about the Forsythe family please let me know. I'll meet you tonight at seven thirty at Cafe L'Europe."

I hung up before she could reply. I didn't feel my two phone calls had been unethical. The murder, I was certain, would be featured on the evening newscasts of local radio and TV stations, so I was revealing no secrets. And by briefing my informants in advance I was convincing them that providing me with inside info was not a one-way street.

People occasionally accuse me of being devious. They may be right.

But now I had an immediate problem. Father had instructed me to continue my investigation but had warned me to stay away from the Forsythe home for a day or two until their mourning had lessened. Unless my presence was requested, he had added. But I thought that an unlikely possibility. How then was I to spend my working hours for two days? The fiddling of my expense account would take only a fraction of that time; I am a rapid fictioneer.

I decided I might profitably use the time to investigate the past and present activities of Timothy Cussack. That dashing lad seemed to be intimately involved with the three Forsythe women—Constance, Geraldine and Sylvia—and I needed to know more about him. If the truth be known (and I would prefer it not be) I was a trifle envious. He was everything I was not—maddeningly slender, catnip to the female gender, and with an aloof self-confidence I could never hope to equal. He seemed a good target for my discreet inquiries—the swine!

I planned the usual credit check with the agencies McNally & Son uses. And there was a new national service to which we had recently subscribed. It had computerized all cases of fraud in insurance and medical claims, including names and addresses of claimants, Social Security numbers, aliases, and disposition of their cases. It really is becoming more difficult to be a successful swindler. Just thought I'd let you know.

But computers, as any street cop will tell you, are no substitute for pounding the pavement and knocking on doors. But before I started traipsing about I looked up the address of T. Cussack in the West Palm telephone directory. I found it. Was I bowled over? A perfect strike! Apparently he lived in the same luxe motel as Rufino Diaz, the Forsythes' gardener.

Remember my telling you the Forsythe ragout resembled one of those kids' puzzles in which numbered dots are connected to form a completed picture? Only in this case, I remarked, all the dots were unnumbered. After discovering where Timothy Cussack lived I realized I had just added another dot.

A less adroit chap might be tempted to phone Timothy Cussack at the Trojan Stables and ask straight out, "I say, old boy, do you and Rufino Diaz occupy the same apartment at that jolly motel?"

To which his reply was likely to be one of the following:

1. "Why do you want to know that?"
2. "Are you investigating me?"
3. "Go dance around the maypole, chum."

Motels are organized more like hotels than condominiums. I mean they usually have a central switchboard through which all phone calls are routed. I tried Cussack's number and was rewarded by a chilly female voice declaring, "The Michelangelo Motel."

I was awfully tempted to say, "The Sistine Chapel, please." But instead I said, "May I speak to Mr. Timothy Cussack, please. I'm afraid I don't know what room he's in."

"We do not have rooms," she stated severely. "All our accommodations are suites. Mr. Cussack occupies Suite 309, but he won't be in until this evening."

"I'll try him then," I said. "Thank you so much for your kind assistance."

That softened her. She replied cheerily, "You're quite welcome, sir."

My next call was to Mrs. Trelawney, pop's ancient private secretary. "How would you like to play detective, Mrs. T.?" I asked.

"Do I get to frisk a suspect?" she asked eagerly.

"Not quite," I said, laughing, "but you'll earn my undying affection. Here's what I'd like you to do . . ."

I gave her the phone number of the Michelangelo Motel and told her to ask for Rufino Diaz. It was almost certain he would not be home but that was fine; all I wanted was the number of the suite he occupied.

Mrs. Trelawney called me back in less than five minutes. "Rufino Diaz has Suite 309," she reported.

"Loverly," I said. "Thanks so much, sweet."

"Archy, what's this all about?"

"I'm setting up a bordello staffed by studs for the convenience of bored and/or lonely ladies."

"You will send me a menu, won't you?"

"For you," I promised, "everything's on the house."

She made a coarse rejoinder to that and I hung up laughing again. Mrs. T. is a glorious antique, wears a wig of wiry gray hair, and may be the raunchiest lady I know. She has served my father for aeons and he still believes her to be the soul of propriety. The governor is tremendously wise, you understand, but in some things he is not too swift. When it comes to street smarts, for instance, he may even be a bit retarded.

You may feel all the foregoing was a roundabout way of determining whether or not Cussack and Diaz shared the same digs. But I did it that way because I did not want either lad to become aware that the famous bloodhound, A. McNally, was sniffing along his spoor. And if I had made a personal visit to the Michelangelo Motel, I might have been remembered and described by the desk clerk. You see how indefatigably sneaky we sherlocks must be?

It was then getting on toward my ocean swim time, and despite the wrenching events of that day I was resolved to maintain my routine. I returned home and, still lunchless, did my two-mile wallow. I then showered and dressed for the family cocktail hour and my dinner with Connie Garcia.

But routine was shattered when mon père did not appear to mix the traditional pitcher of martinis. I did the honors while my saddened mother explained that he was at the Forsythe home, offering what solace he could.

"Mother," I said, "I refuse to have you dining alone. I'll postpone my date with Connie, and you and I shall console each other."

"No, no, Archy," she protested. "Father promised to be home for dinner and you know he always keeps his word. No, you go ahead. Oh dear, I feel so sorry for the Forsythes. I must call tomorrow and ask if there is anything I can do to help."

"Father said we'll all go to the funeral unless it's limited to the immediate family. In any case we must send flowers."

"Of course," she said determinedly. "I'll take care of it."

I moved to her, hugged her shoulder, kissed her velvety cheek. Isn't it odd how death prompts an immediate display of love? I suppose it's realization of human fragility and a desire to hang on to something lasting.

I admit that when I drove to Worth Avenue to meet Connie Garcia I was not in the sprightliest of moods. But I could not allow my megrims to affect our dinner. I decided I would play my usual bubbleheaded self, ready with a silly jape and the sort of surreal nonsense that made Connie laugh uncontrollably. I fancied myself a sufficiently skilled farceur to make the evening a success.

Actually it was Connie who turned the trick. She was at her frisky best, and during that splendid feast she kept our banter light and frivolous. It was not until we had espresso and shared an apple tart that our conversation became weightier and we spoke of the death of Griswold Forsythe the 2nd.

"You know," Connie said, "after you phoned this afternoon I went into the sitting room where Lady Cynthia was

127

playing solitaire. Cheating, of course; she always does. I told her of the murder and she just grunted. Didn't even look up from her cards."

"Typical reaction," I commented.

"Yes, but then when I started to leave the room she said, 'I had a brief fling with that man once. Very brief.' That's what she said, Archy."

I smiled. "I imagine Lady Horowitz has had a brief fling with most of the male population of Palm Beach."

"I suppose. But then she repeated his name, Griswold Forsythe, and said, 'We used to call him Grisly Forsythe. What a lump he was. It was hard to believe the gossip about him.' Well, you asked me to tell you if I heard anything about the Forsythes so naturally I said, 'What gossip was that?' And she said—still laying out the cards—'Oh, it happened years and years ago. Before you were born, Connie.' Then she said, 'Don't you have any work to do?' And I knew it would do no good to question her again and I left."

I was intrigued. "She said it was gossip years and years ago about Griswold Forsythe?"

"That's right."

"Gossip Lady Horowitz found it hard to believe?"

"Uh-huh."

"Flimsy," I said. "Definitely flimsy. But I'll try to pin it down."

"Oh golly," Connie said. "Don't ask Lady Cynthia about it. If she finds out I told you what she said she'll break my face."

"Of course I won't ask her. She'd just tell me to get lost, as you well know."

Connie finished her espresso. She said, "It's funny, isn't it, Archy?"

"What's funny?"

"That years and years ago, before you and I were born, people were misbehaving."

I laughed. "Did you think you and I invented sex?"

She looked at me wide-eyed with mock solemnity. "Didn't we?" she asked.

We left the Cafe L'Europe and reclaimed our cars. I followed Connie home to her condo on the east shore of Lake Worth. I accompanied her upstairs to her trig little apartment. And we invented sex—again.

I departed shortly after midnight and drove home to the darkened McNally manse. I made certain the back door was relocked after I entered, and then I trod as quietly as I could up to my miniature penthouse on the third floor. I undressed and pulled on a robe of black silk—a fitting garment, I mournfully reflected.

I poured myself a very small marc but did not light a cigarette after recalling I had gone through half a pack during that tumultuous day. I sat at my desk, bare feet up, and thought about the curious allusion Lady Cynthia Horowitz had made to long-ago gossip about the murdered man.

I knew it would be hopeless to ask her to tell me more. I liked Lady C. and I think she liked me, but as an aged friend of hers (now deceased) once remarked, "Archy, if you can't be mean, nasty, and cranky, what's the point of growing old?" The lady was a living confirmation of that philosophy. She would refuse to reveal a secret the moment she discovered it might be of value to someone else. She had a net worth of zillions and she didn't amass her wealth by being Lady Bountiful.

And that led me to wonder if every human being is a sanctuary of secrets. We all know things—about ourselves and about others—we will take to the grave—not so? I admit there are several things I know that are better left unwritten and unspoken. You, too.

After a few moments of this dreary pondering I put on earphones and listened to a tape of Ethel Merman singing Cole Porter's "Down in the Depths."

It suited my mood perfectly.

12

Thursday brought so-so weather but I was not discouraged. I awoke molto vivace, ready to challenge fate with a smile on my lips and a song in my heart. And my solitary breakfast—bagel, cream cheese, lox and onion—reinforced my confidence. I was certain that before night crashed I would solve all the Forsythe puzzles that bedeviled me—and possibly discover what happened to Jimmy Hoffa.

I took my second cup of instant black into father's study to search the Yellow Pages for addresses of local pawnbrokers. What a jolt that was! There were almost fifty in the West Palm Beach area, and that made me wonder how our stretch of shore had earned the sobriquet of Gold Coast since so many citizens were apparently in hock.

I am not totally allergic to routine labor, mind you, but it struck me that visiting fifty pawnbrokers scattered over many square miles of South Florida was not the most creative way of spending my time. I compromised by making a list of a dozen hockshops closest to the Town of Palm Beach. Then, carrying my catalog of items purportedly stolen from the late Griswold Forsythe II and his daughter, I sallied forth to play the dogged flic undaunted by the enormity of his task.

It was about three in the afternoon when I stopped at a

pawnshop on Dixie Highway in West Palm. Surprisingly, it seemed to be an upscale joint with an attractive window display of estate jewelry. But what caught my attention was a small, sturdy sculpture, the bust of a young African woman, her neck encircled with yards of necklaces.

I entered the shop, a bell jangled, the proprietor came shuffling from a back room. I estimated his age at 342 but his eyes were clear, sparkling and knowing. He used a cane with the carved head of a fox as a handle. An apt touch.

"Yes, sir," he said brightly, "what can I do for you today?" His voice was firm and vigorous. I hoped that when I was as venerable I would be as fortunate.

"That statue in your window, sir," I said. "Is that a Benin bronze?"

His sly smile was charming. "You have a good eye, sir," he said. "That's exactly what it is—a Benin bronze. Lovely—no? You are a collector?"

"Amateur, sir," I told him. "Is the piece for sale?"

"Not at the moment, sir," he said. "It is still in pawn. But I suspect it may be offered to the public about a week from now."

I knew it would be useless to ask the name of the pawner. He would never reveal that information (except to the police) and the question could destroy our rapport.

"Sir," I said, "if I leave you my business card would you be so kind as to inform me if the bust becomes available?"

"My dear sir," he said, "that would be my very great pleasure."

I gave him my card, he gave me his, we parted with expressions of mutual esteem. A very pleasant encounter.

I sat in the Miata a moment before heading back to the beach. I had no precise description of the statue stolen from Griswold Forsythe II, but how many Benin bronzes could one expect to find in the West Palm Beach area? And a pawnshop seemed the likeliest place for the thief to derive some cash from the loot, even though it would be much less than the actual value.

Driving eastward I reflected it was not the smartest thing for the goniff to do. He or she should have known that pawnshops would be the first places police would check after the theft had been reported. From which I could only conclude I was dealing with an extremely stupid crook or that he or she was confident the disappearance of those pricey items would not be reported to the police. A perplexity, wouldn't you say?

I returned home looking forward to an afternoon swim in a warm, gently rolling sea, but it never happened. As I entered through the back door, Ursi Olson, aproned, came from the pantry to inform me that Griswold Forsythe III had phoned and was quite insistent that I return his call as soon as possible. I used the kitchen phone and eventually got through to the Forsythe heir.

"Archy," he said, "I must see you at once." There was no entreaty in his voice but rather a tone of command—something new for Junior.

"Of course," I said equably. "Where and when?"

"Now," he said, "and not here. You're at home?"

"I am."

"I'll come over. Twenty minutes." And he hung up.

I used the interval to build and drink a vodka-rocks with a splash of aqua. It was my first alcoholic libation of the day and I had an uneasy feeling I would need more before that lucky old sun dipped beyond yon far horizon. So vodka makes me poetic. Sue me.

The Forsythes' Rolls-Royce came purring into our driveway in less than twenty minutes and Griswold III alighted.

I wondered how long it would be before he traded in the family's armored personnel carrier for something a little racier.

We shook hands and I expressed the condolences of the McNallys on the death of his father. He nodded, thanked me in a distracted way, and then asked where we could talk without fear of interruption or being overheard.

"We might take a stroll on the beach," I said giddily. I confess it was a somewhat derisive suggestion, for he was dressed in a three-piece suit of heavy wool and wearing black wingtip brogues.

He missed the irony completely. "Good idea," he said. "Let's go."

So we crossed Ocean Boulevard and descended the rickety wooden stairway. It was a cloudy afternoon and sultry. I figured the temperature hovered around 80° and I had a wild vision of him swooning of heat exhaustion in his cumbrous costume. Then I'd be forced to hoist him aloft in a fireman's carry and lug him back to air conditioning.

But he seemed oblivious to the heat. We went down close to the water where the sand was firmer and began to plod northward.

"Have funeral arrangements been completed, Griswold?" I asked.

"What?" he said, his thoughts obviously elsewhere. "Oh. No, the police haven't yet released the body. In any event it will be a private interment. Just the family and staff."

"I can understand that," I told him. "But it seems a shame that friends and neighbors won't have an opportunity to pay their respects."

"You think so?" he said, and I think he was genuinely

surprised by my comment. "Well, I suppose we can always have a memorial service later, can't we?"

I didn't reply but glanced sideways at him. I could see he was beginning to perspire as we trudged along and it did my heart good.

"So much to do," he said fretfully. "I'm having lunch with your father tomorrow. The will and all that. Settling the estate. I'm not certain I understand it."

"I'm sure my father will explain."

"I guess we'll be coming into a bundle. Mother, Geraldine, and me, I mean. With a trust fund for Lucy and something for the servants. Dad handled all those things." He turned his head to give me a toothy grin. "Making money is the most fun you can have without taking your clothes off."

Ordinarily I might have considered that a mildly amusing remark. But under the circumstances I thought it crude. This twit seemed positively gleeful a day after his father had expired and I found it offensive. But possibly the death of his papa had lifted his spirits by freeing him from the domination of an imperious paterfamilias. Meanwhile I was happy to note the Forsythe scion was sweating bullets.

"But that's not what I wanted to discuss with you," he went on. "I mean talking about money is vulgar, don't you think?"

"Only if you have plenty," I said, and he had the grace to laugh. One short, feeble laugh.

"What happened was this . . ." he continued. "On Tuesday night, after dinner, father went prowling around asking questions of the family and staff."

"Did he? What sort of questions?"

"All I know is what he asked me. Very personal questions. Was I happy with my wife? Was she happy with me? How much money did we have in our bank accounts? Very odd. And apparently he was asking everyone in the house similar things about their private lives. Got the staff quite upset, I can tell you that."

"I can imagine."

"Well, after he finished making all those inquiries I went into the library, where he was sitting behind his desk, just staring into space. To tell you the truth, Archy, he looked like someone had sandbagged him. I asked him what was going on. Then he told me."

"Griswold," I said, "I think we've walked far enough. Shall we go back now?"

He was beginning to look a bit puffy about the gills and I feared my wild vision of him collapsing might well become a reality. I was happy when he acquiesced and we turned around to retrace our steps.

"Your father told you what?" I asked him.

"That several valuable things had disappeared from the house and he was sure someone in the family or on the staff was stealing them. What a shock it was to hear that! But that was why father had been asking all those questions— to try to discover if anyone was desperately in need of money."

"I see."

"Also," Griswold said, almost panting as he spoke, "he told me he had employed you to investigate and try to identify the thief. Is that right?"

I thought half a mo and decided the truth wouldn't hurt—a dreadful mistake. "Yes," I said, "that's correct."

"Well, father said he had determined to his satisfaction who was doing the stealing and he had made certain it would not continue. He was very firm about that. In fact, he said he intended to tell you to end your investigation. That's what I wanted to relay to you, Archy: you can stop snooping around because there won't be any more stuff disappearing. Dad said so."

"Uh-huh," I said. "And did your father tell you who the thief was?"

He turned his head to look out over the ocean. "No," he said, "he wouldn't reveal it."

He was a very unskilled liar. If he had stopped there I might have been inclined to believe him, but he continued to embellish his yarn.

"I begged him to tell me who it was," he went on, "but he refused. He just kept repeating the robberies would end and you could stop your search. Of course I expect McNally and Son to bill us for the time you've put in."

"Of course," I said.

By the time we climbed that stairway to Ocean Boulevard, Griswold III was tottering. He finally made it to the Rolls in the McNally driveway and grabbed a door handle for support. Oh, how I enjoyed his discomfort!

"So you'll wind up your investigation, Archy?" he asked anxiously.

I nodded and didn't even murmur, "When shrimp fly."

"Good," he said, whipping out a handkerchief to swab his dripping face. "But I do want you to continue cataloging the library. After the estate is settled I plan to sell off all those moldy books. Maybe turn the library into a billiard room. That would be jolly, don't you think?"

"Oh yes," I said. "Jolly."

He gave me a damp hand to shake and then he drove away. I stood there a few moments considering what he had told me.

I did not believe it was wholly a falsehood. I thought

Griswold II had actually made those inquiries the night before he was murdered (he had told me he intended to), and I reckoned his son had talked to him later as he had claimed. How else could Griswold III learn I had been employed to investigate the thefts?

But I definitely did not trust him when he said his father refused to identify the thief. Why did he lie about that? The natural assumption would be that he lied because he himself was the crook. But I found that difficult to accept. I thought him a twit but not a larcenist. Which left only one other possibility: he was lying to protect someone else. But whom?

That puzzle continued to excite the McNally neurons during the cocktail hour, dinner, and after I ascended to my belfry to bring my journal up-to-date. My labors were interrupted by a phone call. Sgt. Al Rogoff was abrupt.

"You got anything?" he demanded.

"*Nada*," I said. "You?"

"Zilch. The alibis of the son and clerk hold up. Griswold Three was at his dentist and the clerk was eating a tuna salad at Ta-boo. No one in the building saw the proverbial stranger lurking about. I figure it was family, servants, or friends who did the dirty deed."

"I agree. Or their accomplices. What about the missing wallet?"

"Oh yeah, he had one. Black calfskin with gold corners. He usually carried a couple of hundred cash and his credit cards."

"Where do you go from here, Al?"

"Out to the Forsythe place tomorrow for a day of talking to the screwballs. I'm looking forward to that. I also look forward to root canal work. I wish you'd come up with a lead, old buddy."

"So do I," I said. "But do not fear; McNally is here."

"Stuff it," he said and hung up.

I sat at my desk in a broody mood. But I was not thinking of the skimpy information Al Rogoff had just revealed; I was reviewing my afternoon meeting with Griswold the Third and wondering why I had an antsy feeling that I was missing something.

It took a small marc to identify the reason for my unease. The son apparently had an intimate conversation with his father on Tuesday night. But he made no mention that daddy had said anything about the threatening note he had received. Which meant the senior hadn't told the junior, or he had and Griswold III was deliberately concealing his knowledge.

I was in the midst of these gloomy musings when I received my second phone call. Sylvia Forsythe. I repeated the McNallys' condolences on the death of her father-in-law.

"Thanks, Archy," she said. "I really liked the old fart."

I did not feel that expressed sincere grief but I said nothing.

"Listen, boy," she said, "you promised me a feed. Hubby dearest is lunching with your father tomorrow, so how about it?"

I was more dismayed than shocked. "Surely the family is in mourning," I said.

"The family may be," she said, "but I'm not. Where can we meet?"

Ticklish. Definitely ticklish. I didn't wish to offend hubby dearest but neither did I want to reject overtures from one of the personae of this drama—comedy—farce—tragedy—soap opera—whatever.

"The Pelican Club," I suggested, and gave her instructions on how to find it. "Twelve thirty? How does that suit you?"

"It suits, it suits!" she cried merrily. "See you there, darling!"

I hung up somewhat shaken. It is not that I object to or am frightened by forthright women—Connie Garcia is a paradigm of unambiguity—but let's face it: this eager and apparently randy lady was the wife of a client of McNally & Son and possibly a suspect in an investigation of both robbery and homicide. A man would be a fool to become involved with a woman like that.

I'm a fool.

13

On Friday morning I yawned my way to work fashionably late (about ten thirty), having overslept and then pigged out on a breakfast of eggs scrambled with shallots and more buttered scones than I care to mention. I collapsed at my desk and decided to complete my larcenous expense account if only to delay wrestling with the puzzle of connecting all those unnumbered dots.

Shortly before noon I dropped my magnum opus on the desk of Ray Gelding, treasurer of McNally & Son. He inspected the total.

"You jest," he said.

"You are fortunate," I said loftily, "that I did not bill the company for job-related mental and emotional stress."

"Mental I can believe," he said. "You are obviously suffering."

I withered him with a glance and went on my merry way.

I arrived at the Pelican Club in time to order refreshment at the bar before the arrival of Mrs. Sylvia Forsythe.

"Tonic with a twist, please, Mr. Pettibone," I said.

He stared at me in astonishment. "Have you changed your religion, Mr. McNally?"

"*Mens sana in corpore sano,*" I told him. "Which freely

translated means I do not wish to get tanked before the lady shows up.''

''Very wise,'' he nodded approvingly, and served that noxious concoction.

Sylvia was only twenty minutes late and well worth the wait. She came floating into the club clad in a filmy jacket and Bermuda shorts of honey-colored silk. She had a presence. She had an attitude. And sixty years ago observers would have said she had *It*.

I introduced her to Mr. Pettibone and she asked for a grasshopper, a drink I thought suited her nature famously. I drained my tonic and ordered a vodka-rocks which I suppose suited my nature as well.

''Have any trouble finding the place?'' I asked her.

''Oh no,'' she said. ''I've been here before. A year ago, or perhaps it was more than that, Griswold and I had dinner with Geraldine and Tim Cussack, and we stopped here for a nightcap.''

''Tim Cussack?'' I said, feigning surprise. (I'm a topnotch feigner.) ''He and Geraldine were dating?''

''For a while,'' she said. ''Hot and heavy. Then he dumped her or she dumped him; I never did get it straight. I thought you knew.''

I was saved from replying when our drinks were set before us and we both sipped.

''Yummy,'' Sylvia said. ''Fattening, I expect, but who cares?''

''Surely you don't have a weight problem.''

''Not me,'' she said. ''I can eat anything.''

It was the kind of comment that invited a ribald response but I resisted. ''Tell me,'' I said, ''how is your daughter reacting to her grandfather's death?''

"All right, I guess. Lucy lives in a world all her own. Sometime it's hard to know what she's thinking or what she's feeling."

"A deep child," I observed. "Charming and deep."

"I suppose," she said and took another gulp of her syrup. "She was an unplanned child, you know, and perhaps she senses it."

That was not a revelation I cared to hear. "Why don't we go into the dining room," I suggested. "In another half-hour it may be mobbed."

It was already crowded, but Priscilla found us a table for two. Not the one, I was gratified to note, that was favored by Connie Garcia. Sylvia and I decided on a salad of Florida lobster, which unfortunately have no claws, the poor dears. We also ordered a basket of garlic bread and a bottle of sauvignon blanc.

"On a diet?" Priscilla inquired.

"You know me, Pris," I said, "lean and mean."

She giggled. "Honey," she said to Sylvia, "keep your eye on this cat. When he's in his cups he'll proposition the Goodyear blimp."

She bopped away laughing and my companion said, "I gather you two are pals."

"Long-standing," I assured her.

"Keep it that way," she advised. "Standing."

I thought that a thigh-slapper and told her so.

"I do have a brain, you know," she said. "But I don't get much chance to use it."

"Oh?" I said idly. "Why is that?"

"I'm sure you know what my husband is like," she said. Then she paused and apparently decided not to detail his failings. "I just feel stifled," she concluded.

"Where are you from, Sylvia? Not Florida, I presume."

"You presume correctly. Milwaukee. I left because I wanted to see what the sun looked like."

"And how did you meet Griswold?"

She smiled. "He picked me up. In the bar at an airline terminal. And they lived happily ever after. Only they didn't."

I was spared further disclosures by the serving of our salads and wine.

"I've got to get out," she said, stabbing at her clawless lobster as if it were her own malignant fate.

"Out of where?" I asked her. "And into what?"

"Out of the Forsythe crypt," she said. "And into some-place open and airy and free."

"Divorce?" I asked, not looking at her.

"Whatever it takes," she said determinedly, exhibiting a steel spine in a velvet back. "Life is short, isn't it?"

"Someone once said we must strive to die young at a very old age."

She brightened. "That's exactly right," she said. "That's how I feel and what I intend to do. This salad is scrumptious and I'd like another glass of wine, please."

I poured. "Your husband is now a very wealthy man," I mentioned casually.

"Yes," she agreed, "and it does change things, doesn't it? Before the old man died we were on a mingy allowance. But now hubby dearest is loaded in his own name, and I've got to plan."

"What about Lucy?"

"She'll have her own trust fund."

"You'd be willing to give her up?"

"Yes, I would," she said defiantly, staring at me. "It's my life and I want to live it."

"It may not prove to be more satisfying than what you have now."

"I'm willing to risk it," she said boldly. "Risk doesn't scare me. Never has, never will."

I had thought her an airhead but now I was getting a glimpse at the demons that drove her. It was True Confessions time and I wanted to hear more, but she put an end to it.

"Enough of this whining," she said, pushing back her naked salad bowl. "Never complain and never explain—isn't that the First Commandment?"

"For the haut monde."

"That's me. Now let's talk about what we're going to do this afternoon."

I looked at her. "I assumed you'd want to return home. The funeral arrangements and all that."

"Is that what you assumed?" she said. "Wrong!"

It wasn't difficult to infer what she meant. And because mama didn't raise her son to be an idiot, I could guess where we were heading. That prospect didn't spook me. What I found worrisome was that Ms. Garcia would indubitably learn of my lunch with this attractive lady (Connie's snitches were everywhere) and I didn't wish to imagine her reaction. Violent, I had no doubt.

I signed l'addition, we left the Pelican Club and, as expected, Sylvia Forsythe said, "Why don't you follow me?"

"To Timbuktu?" I asked.

"Not quite that far. To a fun place. You like fun places, don't you?"

I'm sure my grin was glassy. "Be lost without them," I assured her.

It was the Michelangelo Motel, as anticipated. I had

already decided the Cussack-Diaz suite in that elegant bagnio served as a trysting place for most of the Forsythe family and staff. A sort of home away from home. I could now understand how the mustachioed gardener could afford such costly digs. He was paying a monthly rental and in turn was collecting a daily rental—or at least a generous pourboire. A win-win arrangement.

There was absolutely no problem when we arrived. We sailed past the desk with scarcely a glance from the clerk on duty. Sylvia had a key to Suite 309, and I had a mad vision of that key hanging from a hook in the Forsythe pantry, available to any member of family or staff who suddenly fell victim to his or her carnal appetites and needed a cozy auditorium for an afternoon of giggles.

The two-bedroom apartment wasn't quite as garish as I had imagined, but I would hardly call the decoration in subdued good taste. There were several colored prints of Florida beach scenes complete with palm trees and bikinied sun-freaks.

I spotted evidence of Timothy Cussack's occupancy: polo mallets and boots tossed into a corner. But I saw no signs of Rufino Diaz's presence; apparently he was more discreet. The suite boasted an enormous TV set equipped with a VCR. I suspected a library of porn videos might be available on request. I did not request.

"Who owns this place?" I asked Sylvia.

"A friend," she said evenly, and then, "A glass of vino?" she inquired pleasantly as if she were welcoming a guest to her own home.

"That will do me fine," I said.

She looked at me thoughtfully. "No," she said, "I think brandy would be better."

She marched into the kitchen, obviously familiar with

the layout, and returned a few moments later with small snifters. She handed me one and I took a cautious sip.

"Calvados," I pronounced.

"Close," she said. "It's an American applejack."

"Vintage of last Tuesday?"

"Probably," she said, shrugging. "But who cares?"

"That's the second or third time you've said that," I observed. "You keep repeating, 'Who cares?' Don't you really care?"

"Nope," she said, "I really don't. And if you're trying to lay a guilt trip on me, forget it. I'm immune."

"Not me," I protested. "It's your life."

"You bet your sweet patootie it is. Now can we stop this chatter and get down to business?"

She took me by the hand and led me into one of the bedrooms. Perhaps boudoir would be a better word. Lace, chintz, and ruffles everywhere. No mirrors on the ceiling but definitely an intimate chamber designed for lovemaking. The coverlet on the king-sized bed had been turned down and I could see the fresh sheets were peach-colored satin.

"I guess I better take off my shoes," I said.

She laughed, punched my arm, and began to undress.

"Matinees turn me on," she said.

How can I describe that charged afternoon and stay within the bounds of decorousness? I'll try.

She was a sprite, a mindless sprite, and absolutely delightful. Her long hair was the color of butterscotch, her skin ivory and untouched by Ol' Sol. There was a wispiness in all her gestures. In all her caresses. More fey than feh! I feared I might break her but she was too pliant for that. And compliant.

I was convinced it wasn't the two glasses of wine and sip

of applejack, but she seemed inebriated on—what? On her passions, I reckoned, and her dreams. She was dwelling on her own planet, wherever that was, and I was merely a visiting astronaut.

"More," she kept breathing. "More."

I must admit that for one brief moment during our vigorous session I had the most awful feeling that I was abusing a child.

I was freed from that notion when, depleted and apart, she sighed, smiled at me, and said, "That was a smasheroo!" Then I definitely knew I was dealing with a willful and experienced woman. I wondered how many sets of horns Griswold III was wearing.

Our parting was totally without the awkwardness that usually attends first affairs. We finished our applejack, dressed, exchanged a chaste kiss and parted, all in great good humor with no vows, promises, or entreaties. Two civilized people sharing their jollies. Quite bloodless.

I suppose I should have been in a triumphant mood when I drove home, or at least plumped with peace and satisfaction. Instead I found myself in a melancholic mood. Sylvia Forsythe's unhappiness had been palpable that afternoon. And although she had seduced me, I had the nags that rather than help alleviate her miseries I had contributed to them. It bothered me. I make no claim to nobility, you understand, but neither do I delight in jostling the blind. All actions involve moral choice, do they not?

When I arrived at the McNally spread I sought out my mother and found her in our little greenhouse, chatting up her begonias. She lifted her cheek for my kiss.

"Mrs. McN.," I said, "you are a very wise woman."

"Oh Archy," she said, "are you broke again? I can't lend you very much."

148

"No, no," I said hastily. "Nothing like that. I just need a word of advice. When a wife cheats on her husband, what might her motive be?"

"Unhappiness," she said promptly.

"I know that, dear. I'm asking the reason for the woman's unhappiness. Lack of affection from her spouse? Silly dreams that can never be realized? Or finding another, more attractive mate?"

Momsy went on watering her plants for a moment before she replied.

"It could be any of those things, Archy," she said finally. "A wife can become unhappy for so many reasons. Those you mentioned and more. But do you know what I think it is in many cases?"

I waited.

"Boredom," she said firmly. "They can't find enough to keep them occupied. Oh, they may have clubs and charities and hobbies and sports, but those are just surface things. In their personal lives, their deep emotional lives, they are just bored. 'Is this all there is?' they keep asking."

I thought about that awhile. "Yes, mother," I said, "I believe you are right. As usual. Thank you for your help."

"That's what mothers are for," she said brightly.

It was a reflective swimmer who braved the ocean's wimpy ripples that afternoon. As I plowed along I thought of what mother had said of wives who stray from the fold. She was right, you know. Sylvia's flapdoodle about seeking someplace open and airy and free was simply a cloak for her basic motive: the woman was bored out of her skull.

During the cocktail hour and dinner my parents and I were unable to avoid discussing the brutal murder of Griswold Forsythe II, for it had become a cause célèbre in the Town of Palm Beach and was featured in all our local newspapers and TV newscasts. Many theories as to the identity of the killer had been suggested, but scanty information had been released. "Several promising leads are being investigated" usually means the police are stymied.

I retired to my cupola to record in my journal the events of that day. As I scribbled a brief (and discreet) account of my tumble with Sylvia Forsythe I fell to wondering how many other men she had granted a "smasheroo" and who they might be. Timothy Cussack? Anthony Bledsoe? Rufino Diaz? Zeke Grenough? Groucho Marx? Ben Turpin? I stopped, fearing I was verging on madness.

I welcomed the interruption of a phone call, hoping it would bring me back to reality. It did—with a jolt.

"Who was she?" Consuela Garcia demanded.

"Who was who?" I asked. "Or who was whom—whichever is grammatically correct."

"Screw grammar," she said wrathfully. "That dolly you had lunch with today at the Pelican Club. Who was she?"

"The lady happened to be Mrs. Griswold Forsythe the Third," I replied stiffly. "I was merely attempting to console her on the death of her father-in-law."

"I'll bet you consoled her right into bed."

"Connie, I am aghast, utterly aghast. What a frightful accusation."

"Keep talking, buster; you're just making it worse."

"Would I lie to you?"

"Constantly," she said bitterly. "And sometimes when you don't have to—just to keep in practice."

"It's the absolute truth. If you don't believe me, ask Simon Pettibone. I introduced Mrs. Forsythe to him."

"Why did you have lunch with her?"

"Because the Forsythes are valued clients of McNally

and Son, and it was the first opportunity I had to express our sympathy."

"And what did you do after lunch?"

"Why, we each returned to our respective homes. She had her car."

"I can just see your nose getting longer and longer."

"Connie," I said earnestly, "do you really think me the sort of bloke who would take advantage of a young woman devastated by the murder of her beloved father-in-law and consumed by sorrow?"

"Yes," she said and hung up.

It hadn't been as bad as I had feared. I was confident I could eventually smooth things over, nurture that shrunken belief she had in my devotion. I *want* to be faithful to Connie, really I do, but fate conspires against me; I am constantly offered opportunities to betray her trust and I did not have a resolve strong enough to resist.

It is positively amazing that Connie has endured my infidelities as long as she has. What is even more amazing is that her forbearance increases my affection for her.

Diversity makes the heart grow fonder—ask any philanderer.

14

During that weekend I played the blade-about-town. Tennis. Golf. A poker game with a quartet of felonious cronies. And a riotous bachelor party for one pal who had decided to desert his wild, dissolute life and seek marital somnolence. I must admit I felt a wee twinge of envy.

The only happening during those two days that concerned the Forsythe case occurred on Saturday afternoon when I met with Sgt. Al Rogoff, at his request. He came to our home in his pickup and we sat in the cab while he smoked a cigar and, in self-defense, I inhaled more cigarettes than I should have.

"Anything new?" he asked.

"Nothing of any consequence," I said. "You?"

"I've practically been living at the Forsythe place," he complained, "and it gets nuttier by the hour. You know Rufino Diaz?"

"The gardener? The chap with the jungly mustache?"

"That's the guy."

"Yes, I've met him."

"I checked him out. He used to be a cop in Havana. That's interesting, isn't it?"

"I guess," I said. "But what does it mean?"

"Not much," Al admitted. "But he lives in a swanky

153

motel in West Palm. And meanwhile he's mowing lawns. I can't figure that, can you?"

"Nope," I said.

He turned to look at me. "Why do I have this itchy feeling that you're holding out on me?"

"Al, would I do that?"

"Sure you would."

"Nothing that would impede a homicide investigation and you know it."

"Maybe," he said grudgingly. "I'm going to keep digging at Rufino. And also on Fern Bancroft."

"The maid? The one who found Mrs. Sylvia half-strangled?"

"Yep. She's got a ticket. An old sheet with no convictions. But she was racked up twice for committing a public nuisance."

"Such as?"

"Archy, you're not going to believe this."

"Try me."

"For taking her clothes off in public places. Once in a supermarket, once in a movie theater."

"You were right," I said. "I don't believe it. You think the Forsythes were aware of her record when they hired her?"

"That I doubt."

"Al, did it ever occur to you that craziness is engulfing the world?"

"Occasionally I have that thought at three in the morning when I can't sleep."

"Tell me something," I said. "Did you check the whereabouts of the Forsythe clan at the time Griswold the Two shuffled off this mortal coil?"

"I love the way you talk," Rogoff said. "You mean when

154

the old guy got iced? Of course I checked their alibis. What do you think I am—a potted palm? They all claim they were at home, with two exceptions. Sylvia Forsythe says she was out at the family's horse farm in Wellington. Anthony Bledsoe—the butler or houseman or whatever—says he had driven the Rolls into town to fill the tank and get the car washed. I'm still trying to pin down their statements."

We were silent awhile. The sergeant relighted his cold cigar and I started another English Oval. The atmosphere in that truck cab was so noisome I suspected both of us might soon require CPR.

"Al," I said, "I know your investigation has hardly started, but if you had to choose the villain right now who would you select?"

"John Dillinger," he said.

I laughed. "He died sixty years ago."

"I know," Al said gloomily. "But maybe he came back from the grave. That makes as much sense as everything else in this mishmash. Have you talked to the kid?"

"Lucy? Yes, we've spoken."

"I can't get a thing out of her," he fretted. "She just clams up. I have a feeling she knows something but just won't spill. And I can't lean on her because she's practically an infant."

"Not quite," I said.

"Well, see what you can do with her, will you, Archy? Maybe she saw something or heard something."

"I'll try," I promised. "You still figure it was someone in the family or one of the servants?"

"What the hell else can I figure?" he demanded. "It wasn't a coked-up intruder who throttled the old man. I'm practically certain of that. You agree?"

"Yes, I think that's a reasonable assumption."

"Thanks a bunch," he said bitterly. "And a Happy New Year to you."

We were both grumpy when we parted. Neither of us enjoyed insoluble puzzles. They were an affront to our talent and intelligence. Which implies we shared a healthy dose of chutzpah: as if all the problems of the world can be solved by talent and intelligence. Rubbish, of course. Still, we were being challenged—by the killer—and no one likes to be snookered.

I wasn't in the greatest good humor when I arose Monday morning. To tell the truth (a rarity) I felt totally unraveled. I simply could not concentrate and feared I might be a victim of premature senescence. But then I realized my befuddlement was caused by the Forsythe investigation: all those unconnected and unnumbered dots.

The weather didn't help: unseasonably warm, humid, overcast. Definitely not the sort of day to inspire one to shout a hosanna or dance a flamenco. But with gritted bicuspids I pulled myself together, showered, shaved, dressed, breakfasted, and drove to the Forsythe abode.

Mrs. Nora Bledsoe opened the door for me. I was startled; the woman looked destroyed: drawn features, soiled bags under the orbs, slumped shoulder, a general air of hopelessness and despair. I had an immediate and probably base impression that her grief was excessive. I mean she had served the deceased for many years, and sorrow for her employer's death was understandable. But she seemed totally overwhelmed.

"A sad time, Mrs. Bledsoe," I said.

"It is that, Mr. McNally," she said in a choked voice, and I feared she might begin weeping.

"Mr. Forsythe," I began and then added hastily, "—the younger—has asked that I continue cataloging the books."

She nodded and led the way down that crepuscular corridor to the library. I noted that all the strength had disappeared from her formerly stalwart figure; she seemed shrunken and defeated.

"Mrs. Bledsoe," I said, "is Lucy at school?"

"Not today," she said dully. "Because of what's happened—the funeral and all—her parents thought it best to keep her home for a few days. I think she's out back somewhere."

That library was even gloomier than before. I suppose it's a fanciful notion but the death of the owner made all the leather-bound volumes seem equally defunct, fit for no place but an auction house. A nutty feeling, I admit, but I thought the books had died when the owner expired and could only regain a second life from the love and respect of a new owner.

I shuffled listlessly through my cataloging notes and then tossed them aside. When I thought Mrs. Bledsoe and the others might be safely out of sight I went looking for Lucy. I knew where to find her—in the Secret Place, and I now capitalize it because I was certain she did in her own mind.

Sure enough, I found her seated on the greensward in her minuscule amphitheater. She was not reading a book, there was no pad or pencil in evidence. Clad in a wrinkled romper, she was simply staring into space with a wooden expression that alarmed me. Her eyes were reddened and puffy. But when she became aware of my presence she looked up with a timid smile that warmed the old cockles.

"Hi, darling," I said. "How's by you?"

Her smile grew. "Hello, Archy," she said. "Gee, I'm glad to see you. Did you hear what happened to granddad? He's dead."

"I know," I said, flopping down beside her. "It's awful and I feel very bad about it. Don't you?"

"Oh yes," she said sadly. "He was very nice to me. Sort of like very cool, you know, but nice."

"Sure he was," I said. "A nice man. You know what I think you should do, Lucy?"

"What?"

"Write a poem about him."

She brightened. "Hey," she said, "that's a good idea. What kind of a poem?"

"That's up to you," I told her. "How you felt about him and how sorry you are that he's gone."

She nodded. "I'll do it," she said determinedly. "I'll write it tomorrow or maybe even tonight before I go to bed. Archy, do you know more keen poems?"

"Of course I do," I said. "How about this one?"

I recited the verse beginning "As I was going up the stair / I met a man who wasn't there."

When I finished she hugged her ribs and rocked with merriment. "That's neat," she said. "I love it."

"So do we all," I said and took her little hand in my paw. "Lucy, about your grandpop, try not to cry too much or too long."

"I didn't," she said, lying bravely. "I don't cry anymore. I told you that."

"You did but I'm not sure it's right *never* to cry. Sometimes it's best. Then you feel better afterward."

She looked at me dubiously. "Are you sure?"

"Absolutely."

"Do you ever cry?"

"Not often," I said, "but occasionally. It does help."

She considered that a moment. Then: "I guess," she said, sighing. "I know grown-ups cry. I saw Nora and she couldn't stop. But it wasn't about my grandfather dying. She was having a fight with Tony. They're always fighting."

I was dreadfully tempted to ask her about what but I refrained. I must emphasize again that never did I attempt to pump this child. I have, now and then, acted ignobly in my life but I draw the line at interrogating an innocent as young as Lucy.

"I don't know what it's about," she said, answering my unspoken question. "They're always fighting. I hate it when people fight, don't you?"

"I certainly do."

"Everyone in our house is always fighting," she went on. "Like Fern and Sheila. And my mother and my aunt. Fighting all the time. I wish they'd stop. It scares me."

"Lucy, you and I will never fight, will we?"

"Well, I should hope not," she burst out indignantly. "Because we're friends and friends never fight, do they?"

"Never," I assured her. "They may argue but they don't fight."

"Of course not," she said. "That would be silly because then they wouldn't be friends anymore."

What a wise child she was! I released her hand and rose to my feet. Is it a sign of aging when rising becomes much more of an effort than sitting? I reckon gravity is the final victor.

"Lucy," I said, "I've enjoyed talking to you, and when you finish your poem about your grandfather I hope you'll let me read it."

"Okay," she said cheerfully. "I love you, Archy."

So artless it made the old ticker skip a beat.

"And I love you, sweetheart," I vowed and meant it.

I wandered back to the main house, doing some heavy

cogitating on what Lucy had said. All those fights. Mrs. Nora Bledsoe and son Anthony. Fern and Sheila: maid versus maid. And Sylvia against Geraldine. Of course it was possible that what Lucy, in youthful trepidation, described as "fights" were merely noisy and brief disagreements, soon forgotten. But I didn't think so. I was beginning to believe the Forsythe household was riven and the fault lines ran deep.

I used the phone in the library to call Sgt. Rogoff. He was as grouchy as he had been the last time we conversed.

"Will you do me a favor, Al?" I asked.

"Why the hell should I?" he demanded. "No one does me any—including you."

"I'm doing you one now," I said. "Run a trace on a lad named Timothy Cussack. Two s's in the last name. He works on a horse farm owned by the Forsythes out in Wellington. He used to be a polo player and now he trains jumpers."

"Interesting—but not very. Why should I check up on this guy?"

"Because he lives in the same apartment Rufino Diaz occupies at the Michelangelo Motel."

I waited patiently until Al's silence came to an end. "Now that *is* interesting," he said finally. "All right, I'll sniff him out. Local, national, or worldwide?"

"Local," I said. "For starters. You'll let me know?"

"Don't I always?"

"No," I said, and he was laughing when we hung up. That was a plus.

I was feeling better too and I didn't know why; I hadn't really learned anything meaningful that morning except that cornflakes with milk and sliced bananas followed by a filet of pickled herring with onions does not constitute the most felicitous breakfast combo. But I seemed to be recovering and went out to my car whistling, the McNally juices once again at tsunami strength.

I found Anthony Bledsoe wiping the hood of my Miata with a shammy.

"Hey," I said, "you don't have to do that. I appreciate the attention but the baby just had a bath."

"I can see," he said. "But while you were inside a gull hit the target."

"In that case," I said, "keep swabbing. Do you mind if I call you Tony?"

"Why should I mind?" he said, that note of surliness creeping back into his voice. "Everyone else does."

"Just to make us even," I told him, "everyone calls me Archy. Is it a deal?"

"I guess," he said.

I was trying to charm the fellow and obviously making little progress. He seemed in a constant state of resentment and I hadn't a clue to the reason. Envy, I supposed, or jealousy—or both. Whatever was gnawing at him appeared perpetual; I had never seen him lighthearted or flashing a "What, me worry?" grin. Condemned to the doldrums, this chap.

I thought him reasonably handsome. Not a young Clark Gable, you understand, but with a brooding intensity I imagined would be attractive to women. The odd thing was that his rather heavy, squarish features reminded me of someone and I could not think of whom. Not a movie star, not a public figure, but someone with whom I was familiar. I gave up trying to identify the resemblance.

"A bad week, Tony?" I suggested.

He finished polishing and stood back to examine his handiwork. "Bad enough," he said. "The old man was king around here, and now with the prince taking over no one knows what's going to happen. Like today is supposed to be my day off but the new boss said No. Everything is all screwed up."

His words were innocent enough but there was venom in his voice.

"Surely your job is secure," I said.

"Maybe," he said. "Maybe not. I don't give a damn. Believe me, I'm not going to be a gofer all my life."

"Tony," I said gently, "I think you're more than a gofer for the Forsythe family."

His laugh was sarcastic: a contemptuous laugh. But whether the contempt was for me, his employers, or himself, I could not tell.

"If you leave the Forsythes," I said, "what will you do?"

He stared at me. "I'll live," he said, and trudged back to the house.

"Thank you for the cleaning job," I called after him, and he gave me a casual wave of his hand without turning around.

A very troubled young man, I reckoned, beginning to believe everyone in that wealthy and idiosyncratic household was troubled.

I was granted added evidence of that a moment later. I started to pull out of the driveway and then stopped to allow entrance of a new Ford Taurus Wagon, pearly blue. It halted and Mrs. Constance Forsythe emerged. She slammed the door and the Taurus backed onto Ocean Boulevard, but not before I recognized the driver—Timothy Cussack.

Mrs. Forsythe came over to my Miata and I climbed out. We shook hands.

"I'd like to express the sympathy of—" I started, but she waved my sympathy aside.

"Understood," she said, "and appreciated. It's a downer, I admit, but I'm not about to do the sackcloth-and-ashes bit. No one will do it for me when I croak."

I tried not to be but I was amused by her sangfroid.

"What the hell," she continued, "life goes on. At least mine does, thank God. Hey, want to come back in the house for an early pick-thee-up?"

"Thank you," I said, "but I'll take a raincheck. I have a heavy lunch date awaiting."

She looked at me speculatively, head to toe and back again. "Yes," she said with a roguish smile, "I can imagine. Like the girlies, do you, Archy?"

"I enjoy feminine companionship," I admitted.

"And I'll bet they enjoy yours," she said. "And why not? What other pleasures does life have to offer—except horses, of course."

This feisty woman never ceased to amaze and I wondered how she had ever brought herself to marry such a hidebound man as Griswold Forsythe II. But maybe she had developed her forthright persona *after* marriage—perhaps as a reaction to finding herself wedded to a stick. There will be no extra charge for that Jungian analysis.

She was wearing jodhpurs and the badly stained bush jacket. Her face was free of makeup and she seemed to flaunt her wrinkles. Her hair was a mess and I guessed she had her last manicure shortly after the Korean War.

"Was that Tim Cussack driving the Taurus?" I asked.

"Sure it was," she said. "My right-hand man. I don't know what I'd do without him. Timmy makes me feel young again. He's such a scamp I've just got to love him."

I thought her praise somewhat effusive and, coming from a new widow, in questionable taste. But I knew better than to expect tender feelings from this bumptious lady. I don't know why, but every time I saw her I thought of Teddy Roosevelt waving a saber and shouting, "Charge!"

I was about to make my farewell when she stepped closer to me and clamped a heavy hand on my arm.

"My son tells me you're to continue cataloging the library."

"Those were my instructions."

"It makes sense," she said. "We'll probably sell off all those old books. Did Griswold tell you anything else?"

She spoke very intently, her uninhibited brashness suddenly gone. I found the abrupt change startling. And her question posed a kind of Hobson's choice. Griswold III had told me to scratch my investigation into the thefts, but I didn't know if he had revealed that to his mother. I wanted to respect his confidence, but if Mrs. Forsythe *was* aware of it, I didn't wish to appear a barefaced liar. And so, as usual, I temporized.

"Griswold said merely that I was to confine my activities to cataloging the library."

There was no mistaking her relief. Her grip on my arm fell away, her smile was huge, and her hearty manner was reborn.

"And so you shall!" she cried, clapping me on the shoulder. "Why, you've practically become a member of the family."

Mother of pearl! I prayed. Save me from that!

She gave me a final blow on the clavicle and strode to the house. I watched her go, convinced now that she knew I had been assigned to investigate the disappearance of Forsythe valuables and was delighted to learn my inquiry had come to an end.

I believe it was at that precise moment that I began to get a glimmer of what was going on in the Forsythe booby hatch. And Connie Garcia had called these people dull! Au contraire, dear Connie. They made the Jukes Family look like saints.

It was all ludicrous, of course, except that a woman had been half-strangled and a man totally. I found it difficult to snicker.

15

Did you ever see one of those old movie melodramas about life on a daily newspaper? The star reporter was usually played by Lee Tracy, and he'd come rushing into the newsroom, press pass tucked into the band of his fedora, and scream, "Stop the presses! I've got a yarn that's going to tear this town wide open!"

I now have a similarly dramatic announcement to make: On that particular Monday I skipped lunch. Yes, I did. The continued shrinkage of the waistbands of my slacks alarmed me and I was determined to regain the Apollo-like physique that had formerly been the envy of my compadres and had elicited whistles from female construction workers.

So upon arriving home I marched resolutely past the kitchen and went directly to my quarters, manfully ignoring the excruciating pangs of hunger. It was my intention to work on my journal for as long as it took to bring my record of the Forsythe case up-to-the-minute.

Instead, I found myself seated behind my desk, feet up, staring blankly into space while I pondered an oddity that puzzled me. I had already established the fact that Anthony Bledsoe and Timothy Cussack were pals. And I had noted—as I am sure you did too—that both lads took Mon-

167

day as their day off. I had decided to look into that coincidence to determine if the two spent the day together and, if so, what their activities might include.

But on that Monday Tony Bledsoe was working, apparently at the command of Griswold III. That was understandable; the new lord of the manor wished to assert his authority immediately. But Tim Cussack was also working on that Monday. At least he was chauffeuring Mrs. Constance, and she had been dressed as if she had just come from the Trojan Stables.

It was a minor mystery, I admit, but I found it perplexing. I could think of a dozen innocent explanations for Cussack being busy on a Monday, driving his employer hither and yon. But I could devise a dozen other scenarios not quite as innocent.

Obviously I had insufficient information at the moment to come to any reasonable conclusion, so I put that riddle aside for the nonce and ruminated on another enigma that had been stirring in that bowl of tapioca I call my brain. It concerned what Connie Garcia had told me was related to her by Lady Cynthia Horowitz; to wit, years and years ago Griswold Forsythe II had been the subject of Palm Beach gossip that Lady C. found difficult to believe.

It was a very small nugget indeed, and even if I was able to assay it I had no insane hope it would prove to be the "smoking gun" that would solve all the Forsythe mysteries in one swell foop. But it would certainly do no harm to attempt to learn more, and so I phoned Lady Horowitz.

Her housekeeper, Mrs. Agnes Marsden, answered and I identified myself.

"Mr. McNally!" she said. "How nice to hear from you again."

We chatted a few moments about this and that, for we

were old friends, and then I asked if I might speak to Lady Horowitz.

"I don't know," she said doubtfully. "She's out at the pool having a pedicure and hates to be disturbed when she's having her tootsies treated."

"It's really not necessary that I speak to her," I said hastily. "Would you be kind enough to act on my behalf and ask if I may visit? At her convenience of course. It's a matter of some importance."

"I'll try," she said. "You hang on now and don't get impatient. This might take some time."

"I'll wait," I promised.

It was almost six minutes by my Mickey Mouse watch (an original, not a reproduction) before Mrs. Marsden came back on the line.

"Mr. McNally?"

"I'm still here."

"Lady Horowitz says that if you come over at one o'clock she'll be glad to see you."

"Splendid."

"But she wants you to bring a bottle of gin. We're running low and won't get a delivery until tomorrow."

I laughed. Lady Quid Pro Quo was at it again.

"I'll be happy to," I said. "Will Beefeater gin be okay?"

Mrs. Marsden humphed. "I think bathtub gin would be okay," she said.

I had about twenty minutes to get to the Horowitz estate. But that was no problem; it was a short drive up the coast and I knew we had a case of Beefeater in our utility room, a sufficient supply for many family cocktail hours to come. So I freshened up, bopped downstairs, and filched a liter, slipping it into a blue Tiffany shopping bag.

The Horowitz spread is only slightly smaller than the

State of Delaware and is surrounded by a high wall of coral blocks topped with razor wire. Within is a Tara-like mansion that lacks only Spanish moss dripping from cypress trees. The large patio area is at the rear and has been the scene of many a memorable bash, usually ending with guests leaping fully clothed into the enormous swimming pool.

Loyal readers need no introduction to Lady Cynthia Horowitz, but for the benefit of newcomers I should explain that Lady C. is one of the wealthiest matrons of Palm Beach, as well she should be since she's had six moneyed ex-husbands. She is about seventy years old, give or take, and in her youth had been a famous nude model for painters and photographers. Happily, age has not withered her physical beauty from the neck down. It would be ungentlemanly to comment on the neck up.

I found her at poolside, lounging on a chaise in the shade of an umbrella table. As usual she was protected from the semitropical sun by a wide-brimmed panama hat, a long flannel robe, white socks, and long white gloves. And, as usual, she was sipping her customary gin-and-bitters.

"Hallo, lad," she sang out. "You've been neglecting me."

"Shamefully, m'lady," I agreed and proffered the Tiffany shopping bag. "Perhaps this will make amends."

She peered at the contents. "God bless," she said. "Would you care for a belt?"

"Not at the moment, thank you, but could we chat for a few moments?"

"First you must tell me what mischief you've been up to."

"Regrettably little," I said, pulling a webbed patio chair close so I could share the umbrella's shade. "I've been involved in investigating the death of Griswold Forsythe."

"Have you?" she said indifferently. "What's your interest?"

"Ma'am, he was a valued client of McNally and Son."

"That's nonsense," she said. "Leave it to the cops, lad. It's their migraine."

"Well, yes," I admitted. "But we would like to provide as much cooperation as we can."

She stared at me over the rim of her glass. "Who's handling the case?" she asked.

"Sergeant Al Rogoff."

"That animal!" she said wrathfully. "Why, he smokes cigars."

"I know, but he's a very capable detective."

"Cowpats! If he's in charge the murder will never be solved."

"I'm not so sure of that," I said. "He came across something he wants me to ask you about."

My reason for lying, of course, was to protect Connie Garcia, my source.

"Why doesn't Rogoff ask me himself?" she demanded.

"Perhaps he knows how you feel about him."

She laughed. "And he's right, lad; I wouldn't give him the time of day. What does he want to know?"

"He heard a rumor that years ago the victim was the subject of some hot gossip, but Rogoff can't pin it down. Because you've lived in Palm Beach such a long time he hoped you might remember what it was all about."

She opened the bottle of Beefeater I had brought and poured a generous dollop into her crystal tumbler. She drank without a grimace. I am not a devotee of warm gin. Are you?

"No," she said finally, "I think not."

171

"Ma'am, don't you want to help investigate a heinous murder?"

She shrugged. "It makes no nevermind to me."

"I find that hard to believe," I said boldly. "Forsythe was a man of your generation. Palm Beach is a small town; surely you must have known him."

"Of course I knew him. What a stiff he was—even before he died. And when you speak of my generation you make me sound like an antique."

"That was not my intention, I assure you."

She looked at me thoughtfully. "Your father is also of my generation," she said. "And he knew Griswold better than I did. Why don't you ask him about the gossip?"

I sighed. "Because my father is a self-righteous fuddy-duddy, as you well know, and would never even consider repeating an unsubstantiated rumor."

"You've got that right, lad," she said, laughing. "But I hate to talk about the past. Nostalgia can be addictive, you know. Once you start down that path your life becomes a constant 'Remember when . . .' and your brain turns to mush. Retreat into the past and you're lost. You've got to keep facing up to the present and the future."

"Is that what keeps you so young?" I asked.

She laughed again. "What a clever, devious lad you are! Have you ever considered the understanding companionship of an older woman?"

"Frequently."

"Put me first on your list," she urged. "We could play fun games. Like the prince and the shepherdess."

It was my turn to laugh. "More like Catherine the Great and a serf," I said. "I thank you for your kind offer but I must respectfully decline. After all, you are a client of McNally and Son, and we do have ethical standards."

172

"Since when?" she said.

It was apparent to me that this conversation had strayed from the main track and wandered into byways I had little wish to explore. I was wondering how I might get back to the purpose of my visit when the mercurial Lady Horowitz solved the problem.

"So what you want from me," she said, "is a tidbit of foolish gossip that must be almost thirty years old."

"Yes," I said eagerly, "that's exactly what I want."

"It's important to you?"

"It is," I said. "Very."

She stretched inside her voluminous robe and gave me a tantalizing glance. "You may be a clever, devious lad," she said, "but you have a lot to learn about negotiation. To be specific, what's in it for me?"

"The satisfaction of knowing you have assisted in solving a homicide."

The tantalizing look turned to mockery. "Not a very solid reward. Try again."

I thought a moment. "A case of Bols?" I suggested.

She came alive. "Genever!" she cried. "Oh lordy, I haven't had a sip of that stuff since my third husband kicked the bucket. Flavored with caraway, isn't it?"

I nodded. "Not for cocktails," I admonished. "Cold and neat."

"You've got a deal," she said. "But if you tell anyone I told you I'll cut out your heart."

"My job is discreet inquiries, m'lady," I reminded her. "With emphasis on the discreet."

"Well, it's an impossible story and I really didn't believe it when I heard it. We used to call him Grisly, you know. Anyway, there was talk that Griswold Forsythe the Second was having a mad, passionate love affair with a married woman who worked in a West Palm bakery. Grisly mad? Grisly passionate? It was not to be imagined! But the rumors persisted and after a while it became common knowledge, so to speak."

"Forsythe was married at the time, of course."

"Of course."

"I'm disappointed," I said. "I'm as surprised as you must have been to learn that such an unadventurous man could have an extramarital liaison. But it's the territorial disease of Palm Beach. I can't see how it might affect the investigation of his murder."

"Wait a minute," she said, and took another sip of her warm gin. "There's more to the story. Apparently they were careless and the woman got preggy."

"Uh-oh," I said.

"About the same time the woman's husband disappeared. Just vamoosed. I guess he knew what had been going on and figured it wasn't his kid. He took off for parts unknown, deserting his pregnant wife. Grisly did the honorable thing and took care of her and their infant son."

That was the moment I decided I had been a fool for rejecting my hostess's invitation to share her gin.

"Are you going to tell me," I said hoarsely, "that the woman in question is now the Forsythes' housekeeper, Mrs. Nora Bledsoe, and her son Anthony is the illegitimate offspring of Griswold Forsythe the Two?"

"You've got it," Lady Horowitz said cheerfully. "The boy is Grisly's bastard. Or so the gossip has it. Satisfied?"

"Stunned," I said, and I was.

"I told you I don't believe a word of it," she went on. "But where there's smoke there's fire."

"Yes," I agreed. "One never knows, do one?"

I arose, somewhat shakily, and made a farewell oration:

"I thank you, ma'am, for your kind cooperation. And I promise that what you have told me shall remain entre nous."

"And don't forget the Bols," she called gaily as I departed.

I drove directly to the McNally Building. I was not looking forward to bearding daddy-o in his den but I consoled myself with the thought that it was the only way I could verify what Lady Horowitz had just told me—providing father would relax his cast-iron rectitude sufficiently to breach a client's confidentiality.

I phoned Mrs. Trelawney the moment I arrived in my office. "Listen, dear," I said, "I must see hizzoner at once for about ten minutes or so."

"No can do," she said firmly. "He's reviewing briefs and doesn't want to be disturbed."

"Try," I urged. "Tell him it concerns the murder of Griswold Forsythe. That should persuade him to put aside his briefs—even if they're his own."

She giggled. "I'll give it a go," she promised.

She came back on the line a few moments later to say I had been granted a ten-minute audience. I galloped up the backstairs and found the don seated at his desk. He swung around in his walnut swivel chair when I entered.

"Yes, Archy," he said irritably, "what is it now?"

"Sir," I said, "in my investigation of the thefts at the Forsythe home I've come across a story that needs verification. I hope you may be able and willing to provide it."

I repeated what Lady Horowitz had told me of Griswold Forsythe's dalliance years ago with the married lady from the West Palm bakery and how she was now ensconced as the Forsythes' housekeeper while Griswold's illegitimate son served as butler-houseman.

Father was silent when I finished and I could see he had slipped into his mulling mode. I had expected it and waited patiently. You cannot hurry a man capable of pondering three minutes whether or not to put piccalilli on his cold roast beef. Finally the oracle spoke.

"I don't know from whom you heard that story," he said in rather testy tones, "and I don't wish to know. Essentially the story is correct."

"Father, if you had told me from the start it might have aided my investigation."

"I could not tell you," he said sharply. "The client was alive when this thing began and I had to respect his confidence. But now that he is deceased I believe I may ethically reveal details of the matter. I said the story is true and it is, with one glaring inaccuracy. Mrs. Nora Bledsoe's husband had deserted her *before* Mr. Forsythe and she began their affair. Her child was his responsibility—there was no doubt of that in his mind—and he was willing to provide for her future and for her son's. I told you he was an honorable man."

"Perhaps," I said. "Honor is an elastic word, is it not?"

"Just what are you getting at, Archy?"

"For instance," I said, "do you think his relationship with Mrs. Bledsoe continued after she entered his employ and his home?"

He looked at me stonily. "I have no way of knowing that," he said. "Forsythe never volunteered the information and naturally I never asked."

"Would you care to hazard a guess, sir?"

"No, I would not."

I went at him from another angle. "Father, when you spoke to me of the disposition of Mr. Forsythe's estate you mentioned nothing of a specific legacy to Mrs. Nora

Bledsoe or to Anthony Bledsoe. Had he made such provisions in his will?"

He drew a deep breath. "He had. Amply, I might add."

"Do you think the Bledsoes were aware of his bequests?"

"I have no idea. In any event the matter is now moot."

"No, sir," I said. "I beg to disagree."

He stared at me a long moment in silence. Then: "Are you implying Mrs. Nora Bledsoe and/or her son Anthony may be implicated in the murder of Griswold Forsythe?"

"It is certainly a possibility, is it not?"

He shook his head sadly. "Perhaps," he said. "Archy, are you continuing your investigation of the thefts?"

"Yes, sir."

"And working with Sergeant Rogoff on the homicide?"

I nodded.

"Good," he said. "I want you to keep at it until this nasty business is cleared up. I hope to see both the thief and the killer brought to justice."

"Father," I said softly, "it may be the same person."

"So it may," he agreed. "Now I suggest you return to your job and allow me to return to mine."

But I felt I had toiled in the vineyards sufficiently for one day. I stopped at a local liquor emporium and, paying with plastic, had a case of Bols sent to Lady Horowitz. I then returned home, donned my fuchsia Speedo trunks and Daffy Duck cover-up, and went down to the ocean for a two-mile swim. The family cocktail hour and dinner followed in due course and during all that time I resolutely restrained myself from brooding about the Forsythe tangle.

But when I went upstairs to resume scribbling in my journal I was faced once again with the puzzle of those unconnected dots. I did not despair of eventually finding the solution, mind you, but at the moment I felt I was sans paddle and up the famous creek.

But the travails of that confusing day had not ended. I received a phone call around nine thirty.

"This is Geraldine Forsythe," she said crisply. "I must see you at once."

16

She came for me in an oldish Buick sedan I presumed was her personal car. It was, in fact, so old that it had a bench seat up front with an armrest that could be lowered from the middle of the back to form two quasi bucket seats. When I climbed into the passenger side Geraldine flipped up the armrest so there was no divider between us. It was, well, um, uh, cozy.

We exchanged brief greetings and without another word she headed out of the McNally driveway and turned south on Ocean Boulevard. She made no mention of our destination.

"Miami?" I inquired pleasantly.

"Anywhere," she said. "I have to talk to you privately and this seemed the best way. Have you done anything about my missing jewelry?"

"No significant progress," I reported. "Your father's death has complicated things. I am sure you and everyone else in your household has been questioned by the police."

"Endlessly," she said gloomily.

"Of course. Which temporarily puts your personal problem on the back burner."

"But you're not forgetting about it, are you, Archy?" She sounded desperate.

"No way," I assured her. "I promised you I'd do what I can and so I shall."

"Good," she said. "Because another of my lovely things has been stolen. A necklace of gold rose petals. I wanted to wear it last night and it was gone."

"Expensive?" I asked.

"About five thousand. But it meant a great deal more than that to me. It was a birthday gift from my father years and years ago, and now it's gone."

"What a shame," I said. "Where was it kept?"

"In its original velvet case hidden under lingerie in the top drawer of my dresser. The case was still there but it was empty."

"Not a very secure place to keep a five-thousand-dollar necklace," I remarked.

"What do you expect me to do?" she said angrily. "Put all my jewelry in a safe deposit box?"

I swung sideways to look at her. She was wearing a black silk jumpsuit, zippered to the chin, and she appeared to be under considerable tension. She was gripping the wheel tightly, leaning forward, her formidable jaw clenched. If she was gritting her teeth I wouldn't have been a bit surprised.

We drove in silence until we were south of Manalapan. Traffic was light, the night cloudy. A hard onshore wind was kicking up whitecaps on the sea, and far out I could see the twinkling lights of fishing boats and the blaze of a cruise ship. Nothing seriously amiss with that scene but I would have much preferred being home, enjoying a small marc and listing to Sarah Vaughan singing "Lost in the Stars."

Gerry abruptly made a wild and totally unexpected U-turn, pulled into a parking space on the corniche, and braked so violently that I was thrown forward against my seat belt.

"Hey," I said in mild protest.

She killed the engine and snapped off the lights. Then she grabbed my arm. "It's my sister-in-law," she said fiercely. "I know it is. You believe me, don't you, Archy? She's giving that bum all my lovely jewelry."

"Timothy Cussack?"

She nodded.

"Gerry," I said as gently as I could, "you may be correct but you have no real evidence, do you?"

"But I know how to get it," she said eagerly. "I'll bet if you search his apartment you'll find my things. Maybe not all of them because he's probably sold some by now. But I'm sure you'll find enough to prove what I'm saying is true."

"And how do you suggest I search his apartment? Break into the place? I don't even know where he lives."

"Suite 309 at the Michelangelo Motel in West Palm," she said rapidly. "And you won't have to break in because I have the key."

She dug in the pocket of her jumpsuit and handed me a key slipped onto a large paper clip.

"How do you happen to have this?" I asked.

"From when Tim and I were going together. Then we broke up but I never gave back the key. Will you do it for me, Archy? You'll find my things, I know you will."

"And if I do? What will you do then?"

"Go to the police," she said promptly. "Report what's been happening and have them arrest Sylvia and Tim for stealing."

It was, I reflected mournfully, Looney Tunes time and I had a starring role.

"You will do it for me, won't you, Archy?" she repeated in a breathy voice and pressed closer, lifting her face.

I don't know what it's termed in these hyperkinetic days but it used to be called smooching or necking, and I hadn't indulged in such amorous and ultimately frustrating behavior since I was a lustful and frantic teenager. And limped home simultaneously exhilarated and disappointed. Ah, the joys and pains of youth!

Our juvenile grappling became so de trop that I had to interrupt a soulful kiss long enough to giggle.

"Why are you laughing?" Gerry demanded.

"Because I'm so happy," I lied valiantly, and she accepted that.

Eventually she apparently felt she had bestowed a sufficient reward for suborning a criminal act (breaking and entering) and pulled away from me, raising her zipper to its original position.

"Wasn't that nice?" she whispered.

"Sublime," I said, thinking my granddaddy, Ready Freddy McNally, a famous second banana on the old Minsky burlesque circuit, would have been proud of me.

Having accomplished what she had set out to do, she drove me home and dumped me—just like that. I felt like Passion's Plaything.

"I expect you to do what you promised," she said firmly before departing.

"Of course," I said and watched her drive away, more convinced than ever that the entire world had gone bonkers—including, I am sure you will not be shocked to learn, me. Because I had every intention of doing exactly what Geraldine Forsythe had requested: entering Timothy Cussack's apartment and searching for items Gerry had told me were stolen.

It would be illegal and I am ordinarily a law-abiding cuss, except when circumstances dictate otherwise. But later that night, snug in my chambers, a tot of marc in my fist and a tape of the Divine Sarah playing softly, I stared at the key to the Cussack-Diaz motel apartment lying on my desk blotter and realized a surreptitious break-in represented a risk I need not take.

There was a way of gaining entry to Suite 309 at the Michelangelo that held little danger of my being nabbed for committing a felony. I must tell you from the start that the caper I planned was not honorable, chivalrous, or estimable in any way, shape, or form. But my motive, I assure you, was irreproachable: I wanted justice to triumph. And if, in the process, I profited personally—well, that was just honey on the croissant, was it not?

I retired to my trundle trying to recall who it was who said morality is merely a matter of time and geography. I swear it wasn't me.

I might still be sleeping to this day, a mod Rip Van Winkle, if I hadn't been awakened by a phone call on Tuesday morning. I glanced bleary-eyed at my bedside clock and saw it was close to nine thirty.

"What's *with* you?" Sgt. Al Rogoff groused. "Don't you ever get up?"

"Actually," I said, yawning, "I've been awake for hours, just lying in the sack quietly contemplating."

"Uh-huh," Al said. "And I've been sitting in my squad car doing macramé. Are you conscious now?"

"Of course I'm conscious," I said indignantly. "What's up?"

"Not you," he said. "That's for sure. About that guy you wanted me to trace—Timothy Cussack . . ."

"He has a record?" I asked eagerly.

"A sheet as long as a piano roll. The thing that grabs me is that it starts out with penny-ante things like shoplifting and committing a public nuisance."

"Such as?"

"Peeing in the middle of Worth Avenue. Then he graduates to slightly heavier stuff like writing bad checks and attempted fraud. And finally to robbery and felonious assault."

"Has he ever done time?"

"Not a day. Made restitution, paid fines, or drew short-term probation. Two things that get me: One, his cons show a steady progression from minor to major. And two, he's got a lot of pals in high places who wrote letters to the court saying he's just a naughty, high-spirited lad and please go easy on him. That's understandable if he was a good polo player running with the richniks."

"Al, did you find anything that ties him to the Forsythes?"

"Nope. Except that, like you said, he shares a motel apartment with the Forsythes' gardener."

"*As* you said," I admonished him. "Not 'like you said.' "

"Thank you, professor. It's a treat having my grammar corrected so early in the morning. Have you got more on Cussack?"

"Nothing conclusive," I said, "but I'm working on it."

"I'll just bet you are. And if you dig up something juicy I'll be the first to know—right?"

"You can count on it," I told him.

His reply is unprintable.

I rose and moved somnambulistically through my morning routine. Cussack's record of illegal activities seemed to confirm Geraldine Forsythe's accusations—but then things are not always what they seem, are they? All of which lent added importance to the caper I had devised.

After a lone and Spartan breakfast (OJ, toast, black coffee) I pointed the Miata northward to the Forsythe manse, beginning to have a few quivers of doubt if the action I planned would be as easy and rewarding as anticipated. But then I remembered Admiral Farragut's famed command and the McNally chutzpah revived.

Sheila Hayworth opened the door for me and she looked uncommonly attractive. I thought she was wearing a trifle too much makeup for a servant in a house of mourning but, on occasion, I can be as blimpish as mein papa.

"Hi!" she said brightly. "Back on the job again?"

"You betcha," I said. "Life goes on."

"I hope so," she said, looking at me with a smile I can only describe as inviting. "I could use a little life."

"I'm sure you could, after the events of the past week. Sheila, you haven't borrowed any books from the library, have you?"

"Not me," she said. "I don't read much except the tabs. Mostly I watch TV. But that can be a drag too."

Again she smiled and now it was positively lubricious. At another time I would have been tempted to continue this suggestive chatter and discover where it might lead. But at the moment I had other devilry in mind.

"Must get to work," I said briskly. "By the way, is Mrs. Sylvia at home? I must ask her about borrowed books."

"Yeah, she's here, playing her harpischord."

"Harpsichord," I corrected, thinking I was rapidly becoming a fusspot—and at such a tender age.

"Whatever," Sheila said indifferently. "You know where her studio is?"

185

"I can find it. Thank you for your help. I hope to see more of you."

"That's up to you," she said saucily, and I was glad to escape. I recalled those nude photos Griswold III had snapped, and I also recalled hearing that he once had eyes for Sheila until his father lowered the boom. I was beginning to believe that all the rumors about the Forsythes weren't gossip, they were incontrovertible facts. It was just your average all-American, Norman Rockwell family. And I am Ethelred the Unready.

But I was ready enough when I paused outside the door of Sylvia's studio. I could hear her plinking away on the harpsichord. It sounded like bored noodling to me and I hoped it was. I knocked and won a shouted, "Come in!"

I entered and received a sizzling welcome.

"Archy!" she yelped, leaped from the bench, and rushed forward to embrace me. "Where have you been? I thought you had forgotten all about me."

"Not a chance," I said, beginning to recite the playscript I had, in my own mind, entitled "Seductio Ad Absurdum." "But because of Mr. Forsythe's death I thought it better to stay out of the way for a while."

"Oh pooh," she said. "That's ancient history."

And so it was; the poor man had been deceased for almost a week.

"Sylvia, I stopped by hoping you might be able to join me for lunch."

"Frabjous!" she cried. "And I want to eat in a diner. You know, one of those places made of shiny aluminum that looks like a railroad car."

"I know exactly what you mean. I practically lived in diners during my undergraduate days."

"Well, this morning when I woke up," she rattled on,

"the first thing I thought was that I simply *must* have meat loaf with mashed potatoes and gravy."

"And peas."

"Or pale string beans. And you got two slices of white Wonder bread with one small pat of soft butter."

"Memories, memories," I said. "And if you didn't want the meat loaf there was always fried liver with bacon and onions, or corned beef and cabbage."

"And a choice of desserts. Vanilla or chocolate ice cream, or lemon Jell-O."

"Formica-topped tables," I reminded her.

"With a paper lace doily under your plate."

"And cutlery stamped U.S. Army," I added, and we both burst out laughing. "Sylvia, every diner from New York to L.A. must have had the same menu. But where can we get food like that today?"

"A new diner opened up on Dixie Highway about a month ago. Lolly Spindrift wrote that it's the new *in* place, a perfect replica of a vintage diner. Archy, can we have meat loaf for lunch?"

"Only if they have a crusty bottle of ketchup on every table."

"You wait right here," she said breathlessly. "I'll go change and be right back."

She hurried away leaving me to question why she would want to change; she had looked fetching in a linen shift in a yummy molasses shade. I wondered if she intended to dress in true diner fashion: a felt dirndl skirt decorated with a large appliqued poodle (complete with chain) and a pink cardigan sweater set.

Sylvia came scampering back still wearing the molasses shift and I could only fantasize about the "changes" she had made. She asked that we drive in my Miata and I readily agreed. We left by the front door and found Anthony Bledsoe and Rufino Diaz standing in the driveway engaged in what appeared to be a very intent conversation.

They stopped speaking as we approached. Diaz tipped his baseball cap respectfully to Sylvia but I earned a dark glower from Tony, as if my presence offended him. After what I had learned about his antecedents I could sympathize with his perpetual ill-will. It must be awful to be in a constant state of biliousness that no antacid can cure.

The joint on Dixie Highway turned out to be a paradigm of diners, and the owner's efforts to duplicate the glories of yore even included an antique Wurlitzer jukebox with those glorious neon tubes. It was loaded with music of the Diner Dynasty: e.g., "The Yellow Rose of Texas" and "Sam's Song." Surely you're not too young to recall those monumental melodies.

The meat loaf turned out to be just as I remembered it: wonderful and completely tasteless. The gluey gravy was ladled on abundantly and, sure enough, we both received two slices of spongy white bread with one small square of melting butter. That lunch was a time warp and I must admit I enjoyed every morsel of it.

"Dessert?" I asked.

"Of course," Sylvia said, giving me a tender glance. "But not here."

"If not here," I said, "then where?"

"You know," she said, and so I did, much encouraged that the scenario I had planned was progressing so smoothly.

Of course we ended up in Suite 309 of the Michelangelo Motel. I refuse to apologize further for my actions.

Our second sexual rapprochement exceeded the pleasure of the first. She was, as she had claimed, a free spirit seeking only to satisfy her whims. I would never claim she found me impossible to resist. Let's just say I was handy, and I wondered how many other men had played the same role of temporary consort.

We concluded our barbaric coupling and lay depleted, panting like greyhounds that had caught the rabbit. It was time, I reflected muzzily, to engineer the second part of my caper: I had to separate myself from my companion long enough to search the second bedroom, used by the apartment's residents.

I hadn't envisioned how it might easily be accomplished but had consoled myself with the thought that if I failed on the first attempt, a second or even third try might be necessary. I assure you it was not a prospect that daunted me.

But fate sometimes favors the undeserving, as it did in this case.

"I've got to go to the john," Sylvia said.

"I also," I said immediately.

"Use the one in the other bedroom," she advised, the darling, and whisked out of bed.

And as soon as she was out of sight I whisked into the adjoining bedroom. Twin beds in there with matching chests of drawers, two lamps on two bedside tables. There was enough careless masculine disarray to convince me it was the sleeping chamber of Timothy Cussack and Rufino Diaz.

The first dresser I opened obviously belonged to the latter, for the top drawer contained a baseball cap, several copies of Spanish language newspapers, and three folded denim coveralls. I switched to the second chest and found a jumbled collection of memorabilia of the former polo player: programs of games, reviews, photos, invitations to parties of years past. I searched as swiftly as I could, anxious to finish before Sylvia began to wonder at my absence.

The bottom three drawers of the bureau were jammed with a tangle of shirts, socks, bikini briefs, and the oddments of a horseman. I delved into this disorder frantically but found none of the jewelry Geraldine Forsythe claimed had been stolen from her. But in the bottom drawer, far in the back, I discovered a tissue-wrapped package. I drew it out carefully.

It was a worn and stained first edition of Edgar Allan Poe's "Tamerlane." Staring at it, stunned, I realized it was one of the items the murdered Griswold Forsythe II had listed as having been looted from his home.

Zounds!

17

We drove slowly back to the beach sorry that our meat loaf matinee had ended. At least *I* was and, glancing sideways at Sylvia, I hoped she felt as radiant as she appeared. Her cornsilk hair flickered in the breeze and I had never seen her look so vibrant, so zestful. I knew she was a woman who lived for excess, who welcomed it, and I admired her foolish courage.

"Thank you for a marvelous afternoon," I said politely.

"And will you love me always?" she asked with mischievous solemnity.

I smiled, not so much at her mockery as at the recollection of what my buddy Binkie Watrous had once said. He insisted the Irving Berlin lyric should be sung, "I'll be loving you all ways." Good, but not as good as George S. Kaufman's comment that it should be "I'll be loving you Thursdays."

"Sylvia," I said, "I've never asked you who inhabits that motel suite we use. It's none of my business but I *am* curious."

"I thought you knew," she said. "Timmy Cussack and Rufino Diaz, our gardener, live there. They're very good about letting friends use it. For an occasional tenner or a bottle of booze, of course."

"And you have a key?"

"I borrowed it from Rufino this morning when I left you alone in the music room."

Then I understood why Tony Bledsoe had shot me such a venomous glance on the Forsythe driveway before we departed. He knew very well we were planning fun and games in Suite 309. But why should that infuriate him? Unless . . .

"Tell me something else, Sylvia: does Cussack have a steady?"

She laughed immoderately. "Half a hundred steadies. Our Timmy is quite a playboy."

"I can imagine; he has the charm. Where does he hang out—do you know? I'd like to look him up and slip him something for the use of his digs."

"You don't have to do that, Archy. Tim is very well taken care of, I assure you."

"It wouldn't do any harm to buy him a drink or two."

She laughed again. "He'd like that. Tim is not an alcoholic, mind you, but he's never learned how to say 'When!' Connie told me he favors the Sea Turtle off Worth Avenue. Do you know the place?"

I had a brief instant of cardiac arrest because I thought she was referring to Consuela Garcia, my one-and-almost-only.

"Connie?" I said hoarsely.

"Constance," Sylvia said, puzzled by the terror in my voice. "My mother-in-law."

"Oh," I said, much relieved. "Yes, I know the Sea Turtle. Not exactly my cup of oolong. In fact, I consider it somewhat unsavory."

"It is," she agreed. "Hopeful young chicks and old men

with fat wallets and skinny buns. But Timothy seems to like it."

"I'll look him up one of these days," I said casually and let it go at that.

I delivered her to the portal of the Forsythe fortress and we exchanged a firm handclasp and a complicit grin. Sylvia ran inside and I drove home through the waning afternoon sunlight thinking I should be ecstatic because my caper had succeeded beyond expectations. But I was definitely not gruntled. My guileful plot had resulted in more questions than answers.

I had returned the first edition Poe to its original place in the bottom drawer of Timothy Cussack's bureau. But his possession of that valuable volume was a puzzlement. How on earth had he managed to filch it? There was one obvious explanation, of course. Geraldine Forsythe had been correct and Cussack was having a lunatic affair with Sylvia. To keep him supplied with walking-around money she was swiping her sister-in-law's jewelry. But in addition she was also stealing those items the late Griswold Forsythe II had said were disappearing.

It was a neat solution to all the thefts but I could not buy it. Too simple. Sgt. Al Rogoff is continually complaining that I have a taste for complexity and he may be right. But in this case I thought my doubts were justified. Geraldine's accusations, if verified, could account for the thefts. But they provided no solution to the cruel murder of the senior Forsythe.

We had a splendid skirt steak for dinner that evening. Father was in an uncharacteristically jolly mood and contributed an excellent bottle of a vintage merlot from his sequestered stock. The reason for his good humor became apparent when he remarked that McNally & Son had just signed on a new client: a chain of prestigious funeral homes in the South Florida area. I drank to that.

I retired to my upstairs sweatshop in a mellow mood. I made entries in my journal, pondered the events of the day and what significance they might have, if any, and then exchanged my duds for a costume more suitable for a foray to the Sea Turtle, Timothy Cussack's hangout. I wore a shrieking plaid sport jacket, mauve Izod, and slacks that looked as if they had been dipped in Welch's grape juice.

I must tell you now that the name "Sea Turtle" is fraudulent. If I used the actual name of the nightclub I might find myself a defendant in a libel action. The place has been the scene of several mini and a few gross Palm Beach scandals. It is a popular pickup joint for the in-season crowd but most year-round residents shun it. It really is awfully infra dig. I mean how can you, with a clear conscience, patronize a bar willing to serve drinks topped with little paper parasols?

It was late September but the snowbirds had already started to flutter down and the Sea Turtle was cranking when I arrived. The scene was as expected: women in tight leather miniskirts; men with gold medallions; the air swirling with smoke smelling of pot; and laughter too loud and too harsh.

Most of the roisterers were seated at tables or squirming on the dance floor and I had no trouble finding a place at the bar. I was waited upon by a lissome maid wearing black net hose, short shorts, and a Spandex halter top refuting the notion that Less is More. The young lady was living proof that More is More.

"What's your pleasure, sir?" she asked.

"If I told you," I said, "you'd be shocked. But right now I'd like a Sterling on the rocks."

"Fruit?" she said, and for a half sec I feared it was an accusation.

"No, no," I said hastily. "Just the vodka with a splash of water."

She built my drink swiftly and expertly, placed it before me and, leaning elbows on the bar, cupped her face in her palms.

"I'll bet you're visiting from up north," she said.

"Not me," I protested. "I live here."

"In Palm Beach?" she said, astonished.

I nodded.

"Then how come I've never seen you before?" she demanded. "Everyone in Palm Beach comes here."

"I dropped by—oh, it must have been a year ago. You weren't here then."

"I started about six months ago. I love it. It's a real fun place. My name is Gladdie. For Gladys, you know. What's yours?"

"Archy. For Archy, you know." We both laughed and shook hands.

"Looking for someone special, Archy?" she asked, giving me a knowing grin.

"Right," I said. "But not the girl of my dreams. I'm looking for Timothy Cussack so I can buy him a drink. You know him?"

Her expression changed. "Sure," she said. "Everyone knows Timmy."

"And likes him?"

"Mostly," she said cautiously. "He's sure to come in

tonight. He practically lives here. You just hang around and he'll show up."

She moved away to serve another customer. I sipped my drink slowly, observing the frenzy on the dance floor. Few of the gyrating couples had any talent. They were trying but it was all ersatz boogie. I rarely attempt to dance to rock, but if you ever saw me glide about to "Ole Buttermilk Sky" you'd swoon with delight.

I beckoned Gladdie, pointing at my empty glass. She brought me a refill.

"Thank you, nurse," I said.

She laughed. "You're cute," she said.

"Not as cute as you," I told her.

"I get off at two," she said in a low voice.

"I'll be unconscious by then. Another time. If you get a chance, slip me your phone number."

"No problem," she said happily. "Oh—hey! There's Tim Cussack. He just came in."

I turned to look. He was standing in the doorway surveying the action. He was clad totally in black: leather jacket, turtleneck pullover, denim jeans, mocs. I think he meant his half-smile to be sardonic; I thought it smarmy. But I could not deny he was lean, self-assured, and mucho macho—three things I am not. And so, naturally, I detested him.

I left the bar and approached him before he found other companions.

"Hello, Cussack," I said genially. "Buy you a drink?"

It took him a mo to recognize me. "McNally," he said finally. "The lawyer fella."

"You've got it," I said. "How about that belt?"

"Sure," he said. "First of the night. And if you believe that, I've got a rhinestone mine I'd like to sell you."

We moved back to the bar. He was drinking Jack Daniel's Black Label, a potent potable. He took it straight with a water chaser he never touched. If I tried that I'd have to change my address to Intensive Care.

"What's the occasion?" he asked idly. Very bored, very affected.

"I just wanted to thank you for the use of your dorm."

"Yeah," he said indifferently, "Rufino told me we had guests this afternoon. Had a few laughs, did you?"

"A few," I acknowledged.

"That's the name of the game, isn't it?" he said. But even as he spoke his head was on a swivel, gaze floating everywhere. It was obvious he was casing the joint looking for—what? Opportunities, I supposed. Female opportunities.

It had been my intention to ask him about his work at the Trojan Stables and gradually, ever so subtly, inquire about his relations with the Forsythe women: Constance, Geraldine, and Sylvia. But it was not to be; this stud simply wasn't much interested in my company. I wasn't wearing a skirt.

He slugged his sour mash, slid off the barstool, and squared his shoulders. "Thanks for the refreshment," he said. "I see someone I want to—"

At that moment a bulky chap stalked up and confronted him. The guy was in his middle forties, I guessed, but well put-together: barrel chest, no paunch, aggressive thrust of head. There was no doubt he was steaming.

"I told you to keep away from her," he said to Cussack in a gritty voice. "Don't you listen to me?"

Timmy looked at him coldly. "No, I don't listen to you," he said. "I listen to the lady. Why don't you?"

Their voices had become louder during this taut exchange and I stood and prudently moved out of the range of a flying fist. There was a sudden quiet at our end of the bar. Gladdie started toward us but a beefy bartender shouldered her aside and leaned toward the two antagonists.

"Take it easy, gents," he said softly. "We don't want no trouble here."

"Stuff it," Cussack advised him.

"You need a lesson," the interloper said to Tim. "Let's go outside."

"Suits me," Cussack said. "Come on, schmuck."

By this time their altercation had attracted fascinated attention from bar patrons and a few couples at nearby tables. When the two moved outside, a small crowd of perhaps a dozen would-be spectators followed, including me. I had no desire to get involved in this fracas but I wanted to witness how Timothy Cussack handled it.

We all marched out to the small parking area, the accuser leading the way. His back was toward Cussack, which proved to be a mistake. Before he had a chance to turn around and face his foe, Cussack swooped, grabbed one of the man's ankles, and pulled sharply backward and upward. Naturally the hapless fellow went thudding facedown on the blacktop.

Cussack straddled his fallen opponent, clutched his hair to raise his head and then smashed it down. There was a sickening crunch that brought a gasp from all of us, and I had no doubt that a nose had just been splintered.

The former polo player released his grip on his adversary's hair and turned to the spectators with an ugly grin.

"The show's over, folks," he said. "Keep those cards and letters coming. Now let's go have a drink."

He reentered the Sea Turtle. I followed him, leaving a few kind souls to minister to the injured man. He was still lying prone and groaning. There was blood. I was shaken by the speed and viciousness of Cussack's attack. He had struck swiftly, callously, with no mercy whatsoever.

I saw him move casually to a table of two middle-aged ladies and begin to chat them up. I went to the bar and asked Gladdie for my bill.

"What did Tim do to him?" she asked anxiously.

"Not nice," I said. "Did anyone call the police?"

She nodded.

"Then I must be on my way," I said, leaving her a generous tip. "The only enjoyable thing about this evening was meeting you."

"Likewise," she said and handed me a slip of paper. "My phone number. If a man answers it'll be my father. You may have to shout because he's hard-of-hearing."

"I'll shout," I promised and got out of there before the guardians of the law arrived. The victim was sitting up on the parking lot, holding his face. One woman, a matron, was bending over him, rubbing his neck and speaking to him solicitously. I boarded my Miata and departed, hearing the sound of an approaching siren.

That night I made sure every door to the McNally sanctuary was securely locked and bolted. That is my father's task and I was certain he had not neglected his duty. But I needed to check. Witnessing senseless violence was the reason for my irrational behavior of course.

I climbed the stairs to my personal refuge and then ran up the last flight when I realized my phone was ringing. I grabbed it thinking it might be Timothy Cussack asking if I could provide bail.

"Hello?" I said breathlessly.

"What were you doing at the Sea Turtle?" Connie Garcia demanded.

"How do you know?" I cried despairingly. "How *do* you know?"

"My spies are everywhere, laddie," she said. "And don't you ever forget it. Well? I'm waiting. What were you doing there?"

"Having one drink with an old pal—a classmate at Yale. He's passing through Palm Beach on his way to Key West and wanted to renew acquaintance."

"And you didn't make a play for any of the available tootsies?"

"Connie, I swear the only woman I spoke to was the barmaid, and she's eighty-three and has a glass eye."

"And you're going to have a black one if I find out you've been doing what I think you've been doing. When are you going to buy me a feast?"

"As soon as humanly possible," I vowed.

"Liar, liar, pants on fire," she said and hung up.

What a bodacious woman!

I emptied my pockets before putting my duds away. I found Gladdie's phone number and tucked it into my wallet hoping she might be able to provide eyewitness accounts of Cussack's previous shenanigans. Then I poured myself a marc to put lead in the McNally Faber #2.

I am not a stranger to violence, you understand, but it always troubles me. I keep hoping for a mannerly world and instead of civility I find only throttled clients and former polo players gallivanting about mashing noses on parking lots. It's very discouraging. Perhaps my sensibility is too fragile for a career as an investigator. I might be happier teaching the tango at nursing homes.

I mean people like Tim Cussack (and Sylvia Forsythe) scare me. They never seem to consider the consequences of their actions but simply plunge ahead, whistling, as they follow their fancies. I imagine Alexander the Great was like that—and so was Charles Manson.

In my opinion their temerity springs from a dark, abiding hopelessness. They feel they have nothing to lose and so they are doubly dangerous.

This analysis comes to you through the generosity of Dr. Sigmund McNally at no additional cost.

18

Wednesday began auspiciously. A client of McNally & Son, vacationing in Oregon, had sent us a package of smoked steelhead trout. I had a goodly portion with a few rings of red onion for breakfast and almost howled with bliss. That's what I want to be when I grow up: a smoked steelhead trout.

I had the day's activities planned but, as usual, fate dealt me a cruel blow as it always does when I attempt to organize my untidy life. But "There's a divinity that shapes our ends . . ." I think Gypsy Rose Lee said that but I may be wrong.

I stopped at the McNally Building on the off chance I might have received an answer from the credit agency I had asked to investigate the financial condition of Timothy Cussack. Mirabile dictu, their reply was on my desk and revealed the poor chap was suffering from a bad case of plastic dehydration. In other words, loss of liquidity; his credit card debts were enormous and the interest charges positively enfeebling. If I had been in his position I might ponder escape via Chapter 7. Not of this tome but Chapter 7 of the Bankruptcy Code.

Even more intriguing than the report on Cussack's lack of lucre was a message asking me to return a phone call from a person named Simeon Gravlax. I had a short-term memory loss and then recalled he was the superannuated pawnbroker who had taken in hock the Benin bronze stolen from Griswold Forsythe. I dug out his business card, called instanter, and identified myself.

"Good morning, my dear sir," he said cheerily. "I trust you are in good health."

"Tip-top," I said. "And you, sir?"

"I am in working order," he said. "Which, for a man of my age, may be the ninth wonder of the world."

"Oh?" I said. "And what is the eighth?"

"That I am still alive," he said with a throaty chuckle. "Mr. McNally, you asked me to inform you when the Benin bronze you admired had not been reclaimed and was available for sale. That has happened. Are you still interested?"

I didn't give him a direct answer—another of my nasty habits. "May I visit you this morning, Mr. Gravlax?" I inquired.

"I shall be overjoyed to see you, sir," he said and disconnected.

I had intended my first order of business that day would be a drive to the Trojan Stables to determine if Tim Cussack had been arrested by the cops for his nose-bashing spree. But a stop at the pawnshop would not require much of a detour and so I set out in the Miata on a blindingly brilliant morning with a dazzling sun and pure sky.

I found Simeon Gravlax in a chipper mood, leaning heavily on his cane and regarding the world with some bemusement. The Benin bronze was still on display in his window and after an exchange of pleasantries I asked the price.

"Twenty-five thousand," he said softly. Then, apparently noting my shock, he added, "It is a museum piece, my dear sir."

"I have no doubt of that whatsoever, sir," I said. "But it's a little rich for my blood. Actually, I am more interested in the person who pawned this work of art. I realize you cannot legally or ethically reveal that information."

"That is true," he said, nodding.

"And I would never attempt to bribe you, sir," I told him.

It was his turn to be startled. "You are not familiar with the ancient wisdom?" he asked. "Never trust a man you cannot bribe."

I thought a moment. "In that case, sir," I said, "I am prepared to make you an offer. I shall describe the person I believe pawned the bronze. I ask only that you tell me if I am correct or wrong. I shall not ask you to name the pawner."

"In that case," he said somewhat ironically, "I am prepared to accept your offer."

I handed over fifty dollars and then, smugly, I described Timothy Cussack to a T: a tall, well-built young man, willowy, probably in his early or mid-thirties, deep suntan, very white teeth, with a sardonic smile.

Mr. Gravlax slowly folded my fifty-dollar bill and tucked it into a waistcoat pocket. "My dear sir," he said sorrowfully, "I must inform you that you are totally and completely incorrect. The pawner had absolutely no resemblance to the person you describe."

I gulped. "Thank you for your kind cooperation, sir," I said, giving him a glassy smile, and departed with as much aplomb as I could muster, which wasn't much.

I drove away, heading for the Trojan Stables, so piqued

I could have kneed myself in the groin if that were humanly possible. I believe Mr. Gravlax had told me the truth; he had no reason to lie. It meant my theory that Tim Cussack was the thief was seriously if not fatally flawed. But if not him, then whom?

I was in a splenetic temper when I drove into the grounds of the Forsythes' horse farm. I enjoy a challenging riddle as much as any tot but when it turns out to be as difficult as the *London Times* crossword one can only feel frustration and fury at being such a lamebrain.

No one greeted me but I spotted Mrs. Constance Forsythe, foot up on the lowest rung of a rail fence, watching a helmeted young lady—12? 14?—taking a bay mare over low hurdles. I strolled toward her and was almost at her side before she became aware of my presence and turned.

"Hullo, Archy," she said with a broad grin. "Slumming, are you?"

"Hardly," I said. "It's such a splendid day I wanted a taste of the Great Outdoors. What better place than here?"

That plucked a chord. "Yes," she said, gazing out over the green acres, "it *is* nice, isn't it? I think of it as my home rather than that pile of stones on the beach."

"The Forsythe mansion is impressive," I offered.

"It's a dungeon," she said flatly. "From cellar to roof. A prison. Out here I can breathe. I love this place. It was part of Griswold's estate, you know, and now it's mine. My son and daughter can have the castle. I'll build a home out here, a small ranch house." She laughed. "No one around but me and the horses. Who needs people?"

She was trying to keep it light but I could guess the intensity of her dream. I am not an outdoorsy person myself but I could understand how she felt about this open spread. It was sweet freedom: sleek horses, eager riders, a rolling turf, and the glory of hot sun and limitless sky. I happen to prefer the smoky bar at the Pelican Club on a rainy night. But different strokes for different folks.

"I really stopped by to see Timothy Cussack," I told her. "Is he about?"

"Not today," she said shortly, turning back to the practicing horse and rider. "One of our customers is thinking of buying a jumper at auction and asked our advice. Tim went over to take a look."

"I'll catch him another time," I said. "Have a great day."

"How can I miss?" she said.

I paused at my chariot and looked back. She was still at the fence, one foot up, and looked planted there. I wondered a lot of things: Did she know Tony Bledsoe had been fathered by her husband, now deceased? Was she aware of all the thefts from the Forsythe household? And why on earth was she employing a harum-scarum chap who had treated her daughter so shabbily?

I seemed to be drowning in questions and, hoping to find water wings, I headed for what Mrs. Constance had called that pile of stones on the beach. I was convinced that if answers were to be found they lurked in the murky corridors of the Forsythe home, which could well be pictured on the cover of a Gothic paperback novel (with one window alight high in a turret). And within, bodices were probably being ripped.

I was admitted by Fern Bancroft. To refresh your muzzy memory she was the twitchy maid who had discovered the half-strangled Sylvia Forsythe and was convinced she was being blamed for the assault. She had also posed for Griswold the Third's eager Polaroid. Do try to pay attention; I hope no more reminders will be necessary.

But Fern was hardly in an agitated state that day. Instead she was all beams and softness, said she was delighted to see me again, and inquired as to the condition of my health. A transformation had taken place and I could only hope it would not prove temporary.

"You're looking very well, Fern," I told her and it was the truth; she had a glow.

"Thank you, sir," she said, coming dangerously close to simpering. "I'm as happy as a pig in the mud."

I laughed. "Where did you learn that expression?"

She thought a moment. "From Tony, I guess," she said finally. "Why? Is it gross?"

"Not at all," I assured her. "Very picturesque."

I went along to the library thinking that if, for the want of a nail, a kingdom was lost, then it followed that with the addition of a nail a kingdom might be won. And I had the curious feeling that my brief and casual exchange with Fern had provided such a nail. But at the moment I was incapable of hammering it home. I will readily admit to cool competence but prescient I am not.

I wandered about that gloomy chamber looking dolefully at the stuffed shelves and questioning if Griswold III actually thought I would ever complete my assigned task. I mean how eager can you get by contemplating a leather-bound set of Trollope that seemed to stretch for miles.

I was just beginning to take up my cataloging chores once again when the clown prince himself came barging in. I was not so much surprised by his entrance as by his appearance. The pupa had emerged from the cocoon and the imago was now complete. And what a butterfly it was!

Heliotrope slacks. A rugby shirt with mauve stripes. A jacket of inflammatory madras. Pink mocs with vermilion socks. A sight? You wouldn't believe! I favor jazzy colors in my dress but this dolt was a rainbow on amphetamines.

"Hallo, hallo, hallo!" he caroled with a disgusting excess of good-fellowship. "Poking about my books, are you?"

"Something like that," I said dourly. I mean the man was a walking toothache. Now they were "*my* books." This heir was more than apparent.

He stalked up and down, a preening fop inspecting his domain. I really can't explain why I held him in such contempt. I guess it was a case of hate at first sight; he was *such* a yuck. And then, of course, there was his hobby of snapping nude photos of his sister and female employees. Even granting their willing cooperation it was not the avocation of a gentleman.

"Listen, Archy," he said, and I detected a note of anxiety, "that business we talked about—your investigating the thefts. There's been no further action—right?"

"Right," I agreed, soothing him with a half-truth. "No further action."

"Good-oh," he said, obviously relieved. "As I told you, the matter's been cleared up. No more thefts, I promise you that."

"Glad to hear it."

"Oh yes," he said, "one more thing . . ." And he snapped his fingers as if it were a matter of little importance he had suddenly recalled. It was the phoniest display of casualness I've ever witnessed. "Gerry tells me you're a member of the Pelican Club."

"That's correct."

His short cough of laughter was pure sham. "How do I go about joining?" he asked. "Naturally I belong to my father's club. And your father's too."

I nodded.

"Nice club," he said. "But a bit stodgy, wouldn't you say?"

"I'd say so."

"So I've been thinking about joining a younger club. Something jazzier, if you catch my meaning. Not so frumpy."

"Well, yes," I admitted. "The Pelican *is* looser. But you realize it has no golf course, pool, or tennis courts. It's really just an eating and drinking establishment. Emphasis on the latter."

"Just what I'm looking for!" he cried enthusiastically. "A place to let down one's hair, so to speak. How do I get a card?"

"I'd be happy to propose your name to the membership committee," I told him. I refrained from adding that I chaired that committee, there was a long list of would-be Pelicanites ahead of him, and I'd do my damndest to keep his name at the bottom.

"Good man!" he almost shouted. "I knew I could depend on you. I'm looking forward to spending a lot of time there. Let me know when I'm elected."

He gave me a hand flap and sauntered out, leaving me to reflect on how the death of the papa had wrought such a radical change in the son. But we all know, do we not, that where there's a will there's a way. I am, of course, referring to the will of the deceased Griswold Forsythe II.

Feeling I had done enough cataloging for one morning (zilch) and beginning to feel the stirrings of lunchtime hunger, I decided to return home and explore the McNally larder. I was almost at the front door when my escape was interrupted by the bouncy appearance of Sheila Hayworth. She seemed in an even more exuberant mood than Fern Bancroft, and I wondered if the Forsythes' chef was sprinkling hashish in the squid stew.

"Hi!" she said brightly. "I was hoping to see you so I could say goodbye before I leave."

"Leave?" I said. "You're going to Disney World? Say hello to Mickey for me."

"No, no," she said laughing. "I'm leaving the Forsythes."

"Are you indeed? I'm sorry to hear that, Sheila."

"I'm not sorry," she said forthrightly. "I wasn't cut out to be a maid. I'm just too independent. I don't like waiting on other people."

"That's understandable," I told her and meant it. What a surly (and oafish) butler I'd make! "What do you plan to do?"

"Well, I'm taking a small condo in West Palm for starters. It's just a little studio apartment but it'll be all mine. And I've saved up some money, and if I can get a bank loan I want to open a boutique that sells lingerie. Like Victoria's Secret, you know. Do you think that's a good idea?"

"An excellent idea," I assured her, forbearing to mention that her chances of getting a bank loan to open a shop that sold thong bikinis ranged from anorexic to impossible.

"Well, that's what I want to do," she said determinedly. "Anyway I just wanted to say so long, wish you the best, and hope I see you again sometime."

She held out her hand. I took it to shake and noticed she was wearing a tennis bracelet. The diamonds weren't large—quarter- or half-carat I estimated—but it was an attractive trinket.

"That's a lovely hunk of jewelry," I said. "New?"

"Brand-new," she said joyously, holding up her wrist and turning it this way and that, admiring the glitter of the stones.

"A gift from an admirer, no doubt."

"Yep," she said and grinned. "Me! I'm so happy about leaving this draggy place I had to buy myself a going-away present."

"Good for you," I said, not believing a word she said.

She gave me an air kiss before we parted and I had twinges of regret at never having accepted her earlier come-ons. Whittier wrote: "For all sad words of tongue or pen/The saddest are these: 'It might have been'!" I don't think so. To me the saddest words of tongue or pen are these: "Who ate all the turkey bologna?"

On the drive home I had my first epiphanic moment of the day. After reviewing the conversations of that morning with Constance Forsythe, Fern Bancroft, Griswold III, and Sheila Hayworth, I realized the slaying of the senior Griswold had popped the cork from a jeroboam of champagne and everyone in the Forsythe ménage seemed in a giggly mood. It was cruel to impute their good spirits to the old man's demise but so it appeared.

Which suggested they all had a motive for doing him in. Which also meant yrs. truly was still out in left field, gloved and ready, vainly searching the sky for a ball that might come his way.

My luncheon was delayed and that was a shame because Ursi Olson had prepared a cold seafood salad with endive and watercress bedding chunks of shrimp, crabmeat, and Florida lobster. Ursi likes to add a tablespoonful of Dijon mustard to the dressing.

But there was a message from Sgt. Al Rogoff asking me to call him. So I postponed my noontime banquet, went into my father's study, and used his phone.

"I'm eating an anchovy pizza," Al said. "What are you having?"

"A liverwurst sandwich," I said, not wishing to upstage him.

"Rather you than me," he said. "You got anything?"

I thought it a propitious time to give him a tidbit. Al and I are competitors, in a sense, but our investigations are also cooperative ventures. If we don't share *all* the information uncovered by each of us it's understood we trade salient discoveries.

So I told Rogoff about my recent chat with Sheila Hayworth: she was leaving the Forsythe household to take her own place in West Palm and hoped to open a lingerie boutique if she could secure a bank loan.

"And I am Queen Marie of Romania," the sergeant said. "How do you figure?"

"Well, she was wearing a diamond-studded tennis bracelet she claims she bought for herself."

"Ho-ho-ho," Al said. "Who do you guess was the donor?"

"Griswold the Third," I said. "He had a thing going with Sheila until his father broke it up. But now that daddy's gone I think he's yielding to his baser instincts. I reckon he bought her the bracelet, is picking up the tab on her new apartment, and will probably finance her boutique. It's all glands, Al."

"What else?" he said. "Sex and money. If it wasn't for that cops wouldn't have a thing to do."

"What have you got for me?" I asked him.

"Not much," he admitted. "We found the calfskin wallet that had been lifted from the victim. It was in the bushes behind the building. The cash was gone but everything else was there, including credit cards. So it wasn't your ordinary, run-of-the-mill creep who offed Forsythe. He'd have taken the plastic."

"Did you dust the wallet?"

"What do you think?" he said indignantly. "We're not mutts, you know. The wonks picked up a fuzzy partial that didn't belong to the owner. It's not something you can take to court but it's a teaser."

"Any ID?"

"No, but they're working on it. By the way, your pal Timothy Cussack was involved in a barroom brawl last night. The other guy got his nose smashed and wants to bring charges of assault. He hasn't got a chance; witnesses say he was the one who started it. Anyway, just for the fun of it, I went out to the Forsythe horse farm this morning, picked up Cussack, and brought him in for questioning. Son, that lad is one cool customer. He knew we couldn't hold him and we didn't. He waltzed out in a couple of hours. That bum goes bad-assing his way through life and never draws more than a wrist slap."

I thought about what he had just told me. "Al, when you went out to the stables to pick up Cussack, what time was it?"

"Time? Early. Around nine thirty I'd say. Why?"

"Was Mrs. Constance Forsythe there when you took him in?"

"Sure she was."

"And she knew why you were taking him—for questioning about the barroom brawl?"

"Of course she knew. And gave us a lot of mouth about it. That's one tough cookie. But what's your point?"

"Al, I went out there about an hour or so later, looking for Cussack, and she told me he had left to inspect a horse a client was thinking of buying. I was just wondering why she thought it necessary to lie to me."

We were both silent a long time. I was the first to speak.

"Toto," I said, "I have a feeling we're not in Kansas anymore."

"Yeah, Dorothy," Rogoff said. "I think you're right."

19

I returned to the Forsythe manor after lunch. I assure you I did not anticipate proving or disproving a grand theory that explained all the goings-on in that household. I had no such theory. I was not yet certain of *anything* concerning the Forsythes but I was curious—nay, obsessed!—about the passions that were riving the family. I have mentioned in previous narratives my unquenchable nosiness, and now I found myself plunged into the middle of a living, breathing soap opera. It was heaven!

But perhaps, regarding my lack of a theory, I am being too modest—a fault of which I am rarely accused. I did have some vague notions of what had happened and was happening—and I am certain you do too. Human behavior is endlessly fascinating, is it not? I began this magnum opus with a few well-chosen remarks on the craziness of human primates, and my involvement with the Forsythes had only reinforced that opinion. They were loons! And if you mutter it takes one to know one, you may be correct.

I had no specific program planned for the afternoon. After Ursi Olson's seafood salad (with a glass of chilled pinot grigio) I was in a benevolent mood and willing to accept whatever fate shoveled my way. I did hope I'd have a chance to exchange a few giggles with Lucy, that lorn child. It seemed to me she was the only true victim in this tragicomedy. The others were riddles.

Mrs. Nora Bledsoe opened the door for me. Unlike the other residents I had met that morning, she seemed subdued. There were two little vertical lines of worry between her heavy brows.

"I trust you are in good health, Mrs. Bledsoe," I said. "I'm sure it's been a troublesome week."

"I'm surviving, sir," she said with a sad smile. "I'm good at that."

"Of course. I presume you and the rest of the staff will continue as before."

"I don't know what's going to happen," she said fretfully. "Things are so mixed up since Mr. Forsythe passed. Sheila Hayworth is leaving and Zeke Grenough threatens to quit because the younger Mr. Forsythe told him the short ribs we had last night weren't spicy enough. And Miss Gerry is moping and has hardly come out of her room since her father died. I just wish things would settle down and get back to normal."

"I'm sure they will," I comforted her.

"I don't know," she said gloomily. "Everything seems to be breaking up." She was silent a moment as if debating a decision. Then: "And I have a personal problem that's bothering me. I wonder if I might speak to you about it, Mr. McNally, and ask your advice. I trust your judgment, sir."

That was flattering and completely mistaken. I mean I'm the guy who said rock would never replace bebop and who voted for the loser in every Presidential election since I came of age.

"Of course, Mrs. Bledsoe," I said. "I'll be happy to offer what help I can. Why don't we move into the library."

We did, and the housekeeper sat in the armchair along-side the desk while I occupied the giant swivel, tapped fingertips together, and prepared to listen with solemn mien. Meanwhile I reflected that asking me for advice in a personal problem was akin to requesting Godzilla's aid on protecting the environment.

"It's Tony," Mrs. Bledsoe started. "My son. He'll be coming into some money soon. Mr. Forsythe's will, you know. He was very generous. I was hoping Tony would go to college and get a good education, but he wants to open a bar in Palm Beach."

"A bar?" I said, thinking that was just what we needed: another bar.

"A sort of nightclub," she said. "Dancing and all. He has a friend named Timothy Cussack. Do you know him?"

"We've met," I said cautiously. "I can't say I really know him."

"Well, I think he's a lowlife. I've told my son not to associate with him but Tony won't listen to me."

Oh-ho. I wondered if that was the cause of the slap, son to mother, I overheard during my first visit to the Forsythe home.

"Anyway," she continued, "he's convinced Tony they could make a lot of money if they opened this—this *saloon* for rich young people. I guess Cussack knows a lot of them. And that's how my son wants to use the money he'll get from Mr. Forsythe's estate. I've tried to talk him out of it but he won't listen to me and it's keeping me awake nights. I just don't know what to do."

"Mrs. Bledsoe," I said gently, "there are some things we can't change no matter how strongly we feel or how right we might be. Tony is an adult and can do whatever he pleases with money that is legally his. If you can't persuade him to invest it wisely, I don't believe you have any choice but to let him live his own life, make his own decisions, wish him well, and hope for the best."

"I don't trust that Timothy Cussack," she said angrily. "I think he's a conniver and he's going to cheat Tony."

"You may be correct, Mrs. Bledsoe, but I doubt if your telling Tony so will change his mind. There's a point you haven't considered: it will take months, perhaps a year, before Mr. Forsythe's estate is settled and your son receives his bequest. What I'm suggesting is that this is not an immediate problem. A lot can happen during the next year. Perhaps Tony and Cussack will have a falling out. Perhaps your son will find a more attractive opportunity to invest his legacy. I don't have to tell you the future is unpredictable. That's why I think you are worrying unnecessarily about something that may never come to pass."

I was gratified to see her brighten after listening to my Solomonic discourse.

"Of course," she said. "You're right, Mr. McNally. Things can change, can't they?"

"They always do," I assured her, refraining from quoting *"Plus ça change,* etc."

"Yes," she said, "and I must think positively. That's very important."

"It is indeed."

She rose and reached across the desk to shake my hand. "Thank you so much for your help," she said earnestly. "Since Griswold died I've had no one I can talk to."

Then, realizing she had used her former employer's given name and implied an intimacy she had kept hidden for so many years, she blushed and fled. She left me feeling proud of the way I handled a rather delicate situation and at the same time realizing I now had another motive for the murder of Griswold II. The only person I could confidently absolve from complicity in that violence was little Lucy, and I went looking for her.

But I was told by Anthony Bledsoe—in a definitely surly manner, I might add—that Lucy would be late returning that day since she was rehearsing a school play in which she was acting the part of a tangelo. I thought it a fitting role for such a sweet child.

But what I could not comprehend was Tony's enmity toward me. It went beyond his quite understandable rancor at not having been legally fathered: a sullen railing against fate. He obviously had an antipathy toward me personally. I was not aware of ever having offended him yet he treated me with a mixture of dislike, envy, and scorn. It was off-putting and another part of the Forsythe puzzle.

Searching about wildly for any activity to delay my cataloging chores, I traipsed up to the music room and put my ear to the door. I heard no jingling of the harpsichord. Just to make certain Sylvia was not present I knocked but received no answer. She was apparently busy elsewhere. Possibly Suite 309 of the Michelangelo Motel, I acknowledged.

I then sought Mrs. Bledsoe and asked directions for finding the private chambers of Geraldine Forsythe. Finally, after a few wrong turnings in those labyrinthine hallways, I found the correct door and rapped softly.

"Who is it?" she called.

"Archy McNally."

After a moment I heard the sounds of a bolt being withdrawn and a chain unlatched. Superfluous security for the daughter of the house, I thought, but perhaps the attack on her sister-in-law had spooked her.

She opened the door and stood blocking the entrance. "Yes?" she said.

It was not what one might call a warm, enthusiastic welcome.

"Just wanted to say hello, Gerry," I said as breezily as I could. "And give you a progress report on the investigation—or lack of progress I should say."

"Oh," she said, thawing, "that. I want to talk to you about it. Do come in."

I entered and she bolted and chained the door behind me. She had a small suite: sitting room, bedroom, bath. But the ceilings seemed at least twelve feet high and there were enormous windows facing northward. It was heavily furnished with velvet drapes and overstuffed furniture, everything in maroons and lifeless blues. There was a depressing dinginess about her quarters and I looked in vain for some evidence of lightheartedness. Zip. A fun place it was not.

She led the way into the bedroom. It was in disarray, with two large suitcases and one small, all on the floor, opened and half-filled.

"I'm packing," she said unnecessarily.

"So I see. Where are you off to, Gerry?"

"First to London. I have friends there and I'll stay with them a few days while I make up my mind where I want to go next. Vienna perhaps. I love strudel. I'm glad you stopped by, Archy. I was going to give you a call before I left. I want you to end your investigation of my missing jewelry."

"Oh?" I said. "Why is that?"

"I changed my mind."

I stared at her. "You have every right to do that of course, but I'm curious as to why."

"I just decided it wasn't important."

When some people lie they first lick their lips to lubricate their falsehood.

"You seemed to think so when you asked me to undertake the inquiry."

"That was then," she said. "This is now. I want you to drop the whole thing. Okay? They were just things. I can always buy more things."

"I thought they had considerable sentimental value."

She shrugged. "I can live with their loss. You'll stop looking into it?"

"If you say so."

"I do. Let's just forget about the whole thing. I really don't care if my sister-in-law is having a fling with Timothy Cussack. It's all a bloody bore."

I was silent, trying to evaluate this switcheroo and link it to the recent orders I had received from Griswold Forsythe III to cease investigating the theft of his late father's property. I was certain there was a link but what it might be I could not at the moment conceive.

Those north windows filled the room with a dullish afternoon light that had the hue of sullied brass. A desultory breeze billowed lace curtains. I was struck by the dead quiet of stodgy rooms enclosed in thick stone. I wondered if that was the reason for the Forsythes' behavior: everyone was trying to break out—dig tunnels, smash walls, fly, whatever it took.

"Listen, Archy," she said, "I don't know if I'll have a chance to see you again before I leave. I keep a bottle of Jack Daniel's Black up here to help when I can't sleep. Could we have a goodbye drink?"

"I'd like that."

"I don't have any ice."

"No problem," I said.

She went back into the sitting room while I reflected that Jack Daniel's Black was Timothy Cussack's choice and wondered what significance that had—if any.

She returned with two reasonably clean tumblers, each holding what I estimated to be about two ounces of 90-proof plasma.

I raised my glass. "Bon voyage," I said.

I sipped, she gulped. It seemed to have no effect on her but I was aware of a sudden jolt to the red corpuscles and looked at her with altered and slightly concupiscent interest.

She was wearing cutoff denim shorts with frazzled cuffs and a white T-shirt that bore no printed legend or image. A blank white T-shirt makes a statement, does it not? In her case it did; I mentioned before she was a robust woman. I imagined her capable of lofting me into the bleachers or perhaps out of the park. I jest, of course, but I was willing to accept the challenge.

She must have seen libidinous thoughts reflected in my expression because she smiled and said, "I always keep my promises, Archy."

"I wasn't aware you had made any."

"Oh yes," she insisted. "I asked you to do a job for me and promised a reward. The fact that I've ended the job doesn't relieve me of my obligation. It's payday, Archy."

I refuse to apologize for my conduct. I was less seducer than seducee—and if there isn't such a word there should be. Suffice to say that I allowed myself, heartily, to join in her desire to pay what she apparently felt was a debt. I considered her complaisance more than adequate compensation for my labors on her behalf and would gladly accept more employment at a similar salary.

What a stalwart woman! And what a vigorous lover. All firm muscle and glossy skin. My one objection to her behavior during our frantic joust was that she was so vocal—yelps, bleats, and yowls. Thank God for thick walls!

In all honesty I must confess I might have been guilty of a yodel or two.

Away we flew and a pleasant time was had by all. So pleasant, in fact, that after we had completed our escape and returned, perforce, to harsh reality, Gerry turned to me and said, "If you ask me to, Archy, I'll unpack."

"No," I said promptly, "don't do that."

She accepted it calmly as if she had long ago recognized that rejection by men was her destiny. I could have given her a lot of blather about my own personal obligations and how a closer relationship would prove awkward if not catastrophic. But I thought it best to make our parting short and sweet. Cowardice of course. Another go-around with Gerry and I reckoned I'd be using a walker.

Our farewell turned out to be happily casual with no recriminations and, I hope, no regrets.

"Send me a postcard from Vienna," I said lightly.

"I may even send you a strudel," she said.

We both laughed, kissed, and parted.

I had accumulated enough experiences that day to keep me scribbling in my journal for hours. I returned home and decided to forsake my two-mile ocean swim. I was in such a frail condition that even wading up to my ankles might have caused collapse. But collapse I did, in my bed, for an hour's nap that was more resuscitation than sleep.

The family cocktail hour and a splendid dinner of broiled wahoo helped restore my vigor and confidence. But before I set to work that evening recording the day's events in my

professional journal I phoned Connie Garcia. I always do
that after I have been unfaithful. Guilt, naturally.

"Hi, hon," I said. "How are you?"

"You're alive?" she said. "Good heavens, I was sure you
had passed away ages ago."

I snickered, a mite falsely I must admit. "I've been chasing my tail," I told her. "Busy, busy, busy."

"As long as you're not chasing someone else's tail. What
are you up to?"

"All sorts of things, most of them gruesome. Dinner tomorrow night?"

"Can't make it. Lady C. is having a sit-down for a passel
of politicos. Black tie. It's about local taxes."

"Which she thinks are too high."

"You've got it," Connie said. "But I can grab a quick
lunch."

"Sounds dandy to me," I said. "Tomorrow at the Pelican
Club. Let's make it at noon. I haven't seen you in years."

"And whose fault is that?" she demanded before she
hung up.

I wish I could understand my attachment to that lady. I
want her and I need her. I think she wants me and needs
me. But we can never make a final commitment. It's not a
love-hate relationship; it's more like a yep-nope. Nothing
endures but the struggle—which ain't bad.

I settled down to my bookkeeping entries. And as I jotted
rapidly in my scrawly script I came across something I
found intriguing. Both Griswold III and Gerry Forsythe
had instructed me to end my investigations into the thefts.
Their orders had come after the murder of their father. But
I could not see how his death could possibly influence their
decisions.

Then, flipping back through my journal, I found something interesting and possibly meaningful. On the afternoon before the day he was slain Mr. Forsythe had told me about the pernicious note he had received: YOUR NEXT. He had forbidden me to report the matter to the police because, he said, he intended to make inquiries himself that evening in an attempt to discover the author of the threat.

It occurred to me that perhaps, as his son claimed, he had succeeded and in the process had learned the identity of the person or persons responsible for the disappearance of his artworks and his daughter's jewelry. If so, he had paid dearly for his success.

And what the king of the hill had uncovered had led to his son and daughter commanding me to cease and desist from any further inquiry into the thefts. It all made a crazy kind of sense. I began to draw tentative lines between those unnumbered dots. It might result in a recognizable picture but it was not a pretty one.

I yearned to spend the remainder of that evening ruminating on the complexities of the Forsythe affair while tasting a marc and listening to a tape of Leadbelly singing "Goodnight, Irene." But my peace was disturbed by a phone call from—guess whom? Timothy Cussack himself.

"I hear you were looking for me this morning," he said bluntly.

"Well, yes," I admitted. "I wanted to ask how you made out after your imbroglio at the Sea Turtle last night."

"Imbroglio?"

"The fight."

"Shit," he said, "that was no fight. The guy asked for it. The cops pulled me in but they had no case and they knew it. I walked out. Listen, I'm calling from the Sea Turtle right now and—"

"How did you get my personal phone number?" I interrupted.

"It's in the book."

"No, it isn't."

"You gave me your card."

"No, I didn't."

"Hey," he said, "don't make a federal case out of it. I got your number from someone—okay? Like I was saying, I'm calling from the Sea Turtle and I want to talk to you. How about joining me and we'll hoist a few."

"Sure," I said. "Give me twenty minutes or so."

It was not a prospect I welcomed, but when duty calls, A. McNally stands to attention and salutes.

20

Cussack was clad in his ninja costume of black jeans, black turtleneck, black leather jacket. What's even worse was that he was wearing a musky cologne I loathed; it called to mind an ox that had neglected to shower for several days.

We sat at a corner of the bar and were served by Gladdie, who gave me a nervous smile and, when Cussack wasn't looking, rolled her eyes to express—what? Nervousness or perhaps fear, I reckoned. But Timothy seemed in an equable mood, sipping his sour mash peaceably and paying no attention to the frenetic action on the dance floor behind us.

"Nice of you to join me," he said. "How's it going?"

I had no idea what he meant. Just a casual inquiry about life in general I supposed.

"The madness rolls on," I answered.

"Yeah," he said, "doesn't it. Listen, the reason I wanted to talk to you may be nothing but it may be something."

I turned sideways to look at him. The man had a profile as grim as an Easter Island statue. I took a sip of my vodka gimlet. Gladdie had missed on that one: too puckery by far.

Since Tim was silent and seemed to be awaiting a reply to his inexplicable opener, I said, "What's it all about?"

He may have been a lowlife as Mrs. Nora Bledsoe had

claimed but he was a dynamite salesman: manner serious and intent, eyes steady, voice lowered to give the impression he was revealing a valuable confidence. "You know Tony Bledsoe?" he asked.

I nodded.

"Tony and I are close," he said earnestly. "We party around together. He's a lively one, Tony is, when he gets out of that Forsythe zoo. He's an okay pal but he's got one fault: he's a bad drunk. Gets mean and wants to take on the whole world. Confidential?"

"Of course," I said.

"Well, the reason I'm telling you this," Cussack went on, "is that Tony's got a grudge against you."

"He does?" I said. "I can't think why. I've never offended him."

He signaled Gladdie for a refill—for himself, not for both of us. It was just as well; I wanted to keep the McNally brain (both halves) clear and undulled by strong drink. I had the distinct impression that I was being manipulated but for what purpose I could not guess.

Cussack took a gulp of his fresh jolt. "It's Sylvia Forsythe," he said, leaning toward me and lowering his voice even more. "Tony has eyes for her but she won't give him a tumble. I told him why: Sylvia can't stand men who try to put the make on her. She doesn't want to be hustled. But treat her like you couldn't care less and she's a pushover." He paused to laugh shortly. It was not a pleasant sound. "Ask me," he added. "I know."

I said nothing. I detest men who brag about their conquests. Definitely not pukka.

"That's why Tony hates your guts," Cussack continued. "He knows you're making it with Sylvia and it's driving him right up the wall. I've tried to calm him down, tell him she's just a chippy."

"I don't think she's a chippy," I said.

"No?" he said. "Well, whatever. Here's the problem: Tony is dead serious. I mean the poor guy is truly, madly in love with her and told her so. That turned her off. Some women are like that, you know."

"I suppose," I said. I thought he might possibly be correct in his analysis of Sylvia Forsythe. He was a man eager to exploit the weaknesses in women but utterly incapable of recognizing their strengths.

"Sure," he said. "I mean what does Tony have to offer? He's a fucking servant—right? Good for a roll in the sack if she feels like it. But now he's driving her nuts and talking about them taking off together. And all the time she's married to a rich cat so why should she even listen to this idiot? That's the way things were when you appeared on the scene. You've been spending a lot of time at the Forsythes' lately—am I correct?"

"Yes, I've been given the job of cataloging the books in their library."

"Uh-huh," Cussack said. "But all Bledsoe can see is that you and Sylvia are having fun and games. And like I said, he's stewing. The reason I'm telling you all this is to warn you how he feels. As much as I like the guy I know he has a ferocious temper and I really think he might go off the deep end. I've seen him completely unwired after a night of boozing. What you do about it is your problem; I'm not going to make any suggestions. But you've always treated me fair and square, and I just thought you should know about the situation."

"Thank you for your concern," I said, trying hard to keep

any trace of irony out of my voice. "I'll certainly think about my best course of action."

"You do that," Cussack said. "The guy can be a killer if you push him too far. And I do mean *killer*." He swung about and began casing the crowded nightclub, sizing up the possibilities (unescorted women) no doubt. "There's someone I've got to see," he said abruptly and drained his glass. "Thanks for the shots."

I wasn't aware I had offered to pay for his drinks; he had invited me. But there wasn't much I could do about it, was there?

Gladdie took my money with a sympathetic smile. "He's a card, isn't he?" she said.

I agreed. But whether Timothy Cussack was a joker or a knave I did not yet know.

I drove home in a legal fashion utterly flummoxed by Cussack's reasons for requesting that brief meeting. He may have been completely honest and sincere, of course, wanting only to warn me of Tony Bledsoe's enmity toward me and his potential for violence. But I suspected Cussack had more cunning motives. I thought him a deep man— deep in the sense that while his actions might seem logical to him, they were obscure to others.

Mrs. Nora Bledsoe had also called him a conniver. I was beginning to respect the wisdom of that lady.

I had the small marc I had promised myself, listened to "Goodnight, Irene" through earphones, and lapsed into a Scarlett O'Hara mode: "I'll think about it tomorrow."

I was true to my resolve, for when I awoke on Thursday morning I sat on the edge of my bed a few moments, still dopey with sleep, and thought again about that weird conversation with Timothy Cussack. He had casually mentioned he had enjoyed the favors of Sylvia Forsythe. If that was mere braggadocio, and I suspected it was, it helped solve part of the puzzle that had been bedeviling me. Now, if I did not see a blinding light at the end of the tunnel, I did glimpse a flickering candle flame.

Cussack had spoken of the "Forsythe zoo." A more apt metaphor, I decided, was that all the denizens of that cobwebby manse were playing the kids' game of Snap the Whip. Griswold Forsythe II had been on the tag end—and he had been spun off.

I went through my usual morning routine and, remembering my noontime lunch with Connie Garcia, I dug out my puce beret, which always puts her in a felicitous mood—after her hysterical laughter has calmed. Then I clattered downstairs to a late breakfast with Jamie Olson, who was kind enough to scramble me a brace of eggs with sliced shallots sautéed in butter. O cholesterol, where is thy sting?

It was over our coffee refills that I asked if he was aware Sheila Hayworth was leaving the Forsythes' employ.

"Yep," he said. "I heard."

That didn't surprise me. In the Palm Beach milieu the servants know what is going to happen before it does.

"Taking a condo in West Palm," I said. "Thinking of opening a lingerie shop." Frequently, while conversing with Jamie, I found myself mimicking his elliptical speech pattern.

"Uh-huh," he said.

"Costs money to open a shop," I observed.

He looked at me. "The boy," he said. "They took up again after the old man passed."

It was gratifying but a mite depressing to have my suspicion confirmed. "What about the other maid?" I asked. "She seems happy enough to stay."

LAWRENCE SANDERS

"Loopy, that one," he remarked. "Ursi says her brassiere size is larger than her IQ."

I laughed. "That's cruel," I said.

"Yep," he agreed. "Since she's flat-chested."

"Why do you suppose she's staying on with the Forsythes? Needs the job?"

"Thought you knew," he said, chewing on his pipe stem. "Talk is she's in heat over that young butler."

"Tony Bledsoe?"

He nodded.

"Thank you," I said and slipped him a sawbuck.

I returned to my barrack and began scribbling furiously in my journal. There was much to be recorded for I had been neglecting my journalistic chores. As I jotted down all the tidbits I had recently collected, the pattern of what had happened and was happening in the Forsythe menagerie began to take shape. When I clapped on the puce beret and set out for my luncheon date I had a theory that put numbers on most of those dots. And what a nasty picture they formed.

I was seated at the bar of the Pelican Club, enjoying a vodka gimlet and chatting idly with Mr. Simon Pettibone when Connie came sailing in. Her glossy black hair swung free and she was wearing a slip dress of some shimmery stuff in a soft butterscotch color. Be still, my heart!

She waltzed over, gave me a peck, and looked accusingly at my empty glass.

"You started without me," she protested.

"My dear," I said loftily, "I assumed you were aware that the universe is composed of five elements: earth, air, fire, water, and vodka."

"I thought vodka *was* firewater," she said.

234

"Not a bad joke as jokes go," I told her. "And as jokes go, it went. What'll you have?"

"Food," she said. "And lots of it. I'm famished."

"Mr. Pettibone," I said, "I regret I must leave you now. I am faced with the problem of a famished lady."

"Such is the way of the world," he said philosophically.

Priscilla seated us at our favorite corner table in the dining area. She seemed in a churlish mood.

"Pris," Connie said, "is anything wrong?"

"My guy-of-the-month," Ms. Pettibone said grumpily. "He's turning out to be a first-class louse."

"Welcome to the club," Connie said, looking at me. "I know exactly how you feel."

"Food!" I cried heartily. "Pris, we're in dire need of nourishment. Starving, in fact. What's Leroy pushing today?"

"Humongous club sandwiches on whole wheat buns. With grilled chicken breast, Swiss, bacon, lettuce, tomato, and mayo."

"That's for me," Connie said happily. "With a glass of chardonnay."

"I'll go along," I said to her, "but only if you promise not to look at me while I'm eating. It's going to be messy."

"Try not to dribble," she urged.

The sandwiches were as good as described and I didn't dribble too much. It's a bit twee to eat a club sandwich with fork and knife—don't you think? We were halfway through our lunch, gossiping of this and that, when I said, "Listen, dear, there's something I'd like you to do for me."

She stopped nibbling on a curl of bacon to stare at me. "Oh?" she said. "And what is that?"

"Well, you know I'm involved in the investigation of the

LAWRENCE SANDERS

murder of Griswold Forsythe. Not officially of course; just
trying to lend what assistance I can to Sergeant Al Rogoff,
who's a good cop but a little lost when it comes to Palm
Beach anthropology. I mean he's just not plugged in. Anyway, when this whole foofaraw started you mentioned that
the daughter, Geraldine Forsythe, had been taken over the
jumps by a former polo player."

Connie said nothing.

"You were right," I went on. "His name is Timothy
Cussack and your tip may prove to be significant. Now
what I need to know is exactly why they split up. Do you
think you could find out?"

"Why are you so interested in Geraldine Forsythe?" she
asked suspiciously. "Is there hanky-panky going on between you two?"

I laughed merrily. "Perhaps a soupçon of hanky," I said,
"but definitely no panky. How about it? Will you try to find
out?"

"Maybe," my dearest one said. "What's in it for me?"

I sighed. "Connie, I do believe you've contracted the
quid pro quo syndrome from Lady Horowitz. Very well,
what do you want in return—assuming you can obtain the
information I seek?"

"A weekend in Freeport," she said.

"Done," I said promptly. "Get me what I need and we'll
be off for two days of unbridled delight. Plus bowls of that
marvelous conch chowder."

"Okay," she said happily. "I'll try."

We finished our lunch, I signed the tab, and we moved
outside to the sunbaked parking lot. I donned my puce
beret and, as expected, Connie collapsed with guffaws.

"It's *you!*" she screamed. "Oh lordy, is that hat ever
you!"

We exchanged a smeary kiss and, still giggling, she drove away in her new green Camry. That woman changes cars more frequently than I change my unmentionables. I stood there a moment after she departed, pondering my next move. I had a grand theory about the Forsythe affair and sooner or later I'd have to put it to the test. But that scared me; if I flunked I'd be up sc without a p.

But buoyed by my vodka gimlet, chardonnay, and calorie-stuffed lunch I decided to go for broke. So I headed for the pawnshop of the urbane Mr. Simeon Gravlax. I found him in good health, his sly smile intact—the soul of amused curiosity as if the world had been created for his enjoyment.

"Sir," I said, "several days ago we had a small transaction during which I paid to ask you to approve or reject my description of the person who pawned the Benin bronze. I lost."

"I remember, sir," he said, nodding vigorously. "A most interesting negotiation. And profitable, I might add."

I withdrew a fifty-dollar bill from my wallet. "May I try again?" I asked.

A claw reached out and snatched the half-yard from my grasp. "Delighted," he said.

I then delineated in great detail the person I now believed had pawned the work of art stolen from Griswold Forsythe II. Mr. Gravlax listened to my recital closely.

When I had finished he smiled and reached up to pat my shoulder. "My dear sir," he said, "you are absolutely correct."

What a rush that was! I wanted to do a small entrechat but controlled myself. "Thank you, sir," I said huskily. "You have made me a very happy man."

"As you have me," he said. "It was a dull day until you

arrived. Dealing with poverty as I do is not the most exhila-rating of professions. Even if your business with me is concluded I hope you may stop by occasionally if only to schmooze for a few moments."

"An honor, sir," I said.

"A pleasure, sir," he said.

I drove back to the beach singing another of my favorite songs—"It's Only a Paper Moon." They don't write songs like that anymore. I wonder why?

It was almost four o'clock when I arrived at the Forsythe mansion which, in my own mind, I now labeled the Hôtel des Kooks. I drove around to the back and parked close to their mammoth garage. Then I headed into the greenery, hoping to find Lucy Forsythe in her Secret Place.

The young miss was there, seated on the lawn with a notebook open on her lap and pencil stub in hand. Her head was lowered, wings of silky hair hiding her face.

She looked up as I approached. "Hi, Archy," she said. "Gee, I'm glad to see you. I thought you had forgotten all about me."

"Nah," I said, plumping down beside her, "not a chance. How are you, darling?"

"Okay," she said. "Sort of. I'm writing that poem about my granddad but I'm not going to show it to you until it's finished."

"That's best," I assured her. "I know it's going to be fine because you're very creative."

"Creative? What does that mean?"

"You're very good at making things up."

"I guess," she said and stared at the thick shrubbery surrounding her miniature amphitheater. It occurred to me that she hadn't yet smiled. "Archy, may I ask you some-thing?"

238

"Of course."

"Can I come and live with you?"

How do you handle something like that?

"Lucy," I said, "this is your home, right here with your family."

"I know," she said, "but I don't like living here. Besides, I don't think I'm going to have a family. I heard my mother and father yelling at each other and what I think is that they're going to get a divorce. I know what that is. A lot of the kids at school, their parents got a divorce."

"It happens," I said. "But the kids are still living with their mother or father, aren't they?"

"Most of them. Except for Emma Bradbury; she's living with her grandmother. But what if neither my mother or father wants me?"

I swallowed. "I don't think that's possible, honey."

She turned to look at me, eyes brimming. "But what if it *is?* It worries me. That's why I'd like to come and live with you. Do you have a house?"

"Yes, I live with my parents."

"Well, couldn't I come and stay? I'd just need a little room and I promise I wouldn't cry or get sick or anything like that."

I had been right: she was the main victim. The adults went their selfish, screwball ways and this child was hurting.

"Tell you what, Lucy," I said. "If no one wants you, I promise you can come and stay at my home. I don't think that's going to happen because even if your parents get a divorce, one of them will want you and the other will want to visit and take you on trips and things like that. Please try not to worry about it. You're never going to be left alone."

That seemed to brighten her a bit. She finally gave me a smile, a small, frail thing. Hope is hard to kill in kids.

"You promise, Archy?" she said.

"Positively," I said with more confidence than I felt. I climbed to my feet. "Now you finish your poem. And don't forget that you and I are going to have a picnic right here. But you must let me bring the lunch."

That quickened her; the shy smile turned to a grin. "You know what I'd like?" she said, excited now.

"What?"

"A pizza."

"Good choice," I said. "With lots of cheese."

"And maybe those funny little pieces of meat that look like coins. I like those."

"Pepperoni," I said. "You're so right; they're good. That's what we'll have."

"Thank you," she said gratefully. "I love you, Archy."

It came close to being a mawkish moment but her innocence saved it.

"And I love you, Lucy," I mumbled and stumbled out of there.

21

I had time for my ocean swim, a melancholy wallow I must admit because I could not sluice away my memory of Lucy's misery. Adults are supposed to be able to cope with troubles but we want kids' lives to be a constant joy—and they so rarely are.

No family cocktail hour that evening because my parents were leaving early to have drinks and dinner at the home of septuagenarian friends. It would be followed by a ferocious contest of high-stakes bridge. The victorious couple might win as much as forty cents.

And so I dressed casually, planning to dine in the kitchen with the Olsons. To my delight, Ursi had prepared a rabbit stew made Italian-style with, amongst other goodies, salt pork, garlic, and red wine. Served with small roast potatoes. Also a round of pepper focaccio. Luscious.

I was in the pantry uncorking a bottle of the Chianti Classico we keep on hand in case of an impending nuclear catastrophe when the phone rang and I picked it up in the kitchen. Sgt. Al Rogoff was calling.

"Interrupting your dinner?" he said gruffly.

"Not yet. What's happening?"

He didn't answer that. "Can you and I get together tonight?" he asked.

"Easiest thing in the world," I told him. "My parents are out this evening and I'm going to scarf with Ursi and Jamie in the kitchen. Come join us."

"Oh, I couldn't do that," he said. "We'll meet later."

"It's rabbit stew and roast potatoes."

"Be right there," he said and hung up.

"Ursi," I said, "Sergeant Rogoff will be joining us for dinner. Is that all right?"

"Of course," she said. "There is plenty."

Al showed up bearing our dessert: a chocolate cake layered with raspberry mousse, and my diet immediately became a dim remembrance. What a merry feast we had! Good food, good wine, good talk. Like all cops Al had an inexhaustible store of amazing and amusing true tales to relate. My favorite was of a well-known investment banker of Palm Beach who was arrested pedaling his ten-speed bicycle along Worth Avenue at midnight while wearing his wife's lingerie. How many times must I tell you that madness is engulfing the world?

Rogoff and I retired to my father's study after dinner. I broke out a bottle of the pater's Rémy Martin and poured us ponies of cognac. We sat in facing club chairs and simultaneously sighed with content.

"Great dinner," Al said.

"Great dessert," I said. "No-cal, of course."

"Of course. Would your old man object if I smoked a cigar? He'll smell it."

"Go ahead," I urged. "I'll tell him we had a conference on the Forsythe investigation."

"That's the truth." He lighted up one of his Louisville Sluggers and I had an English Oval, wondering how many I had had that day. Two, three, four or more—I couldn't recall. And I was in such a replete mood I didn't much care.

"How are you coming along on the Forsythe homicide?" I asked lazily, for to tell you the truth I really didn't want to think about it. That raspberry mousse cake was stupendous! And guess who had two slices.

"I'm not coming along," the sergeant said grumpily. "No hits, no runs, just errors. I can't get this thing off the ground. That's why I'm here. You got anything? Anything at all?"

I hesitated half a mo. I had a lot I could tell him but it was all suspicions, conjectures, presumptions. Still, I reckoned it was time to reveal *some* of it. At least I could give him a few bones to gnaw, and he had the resources and official heft to find answers to the questions troubling me.

"As I recall," I said, "you told me Sylvia Forsythe and Anthony Bledsoe were not at home when the murder occurred. Did you check out their alibis?"

He nodded. "She's clean. She was having a pedicure and a massage at the time Forsythe was offed, just like she claimed. Bledsoe is a little more iffy. He drove the Forsythes' Rolls in for a wash and wax, as he said, but he didn't hang around while the work was being done. Says he just wandered around window-shopping and then had a hamburger. Maybe. We haven't pinned it down."

I took a deep breath. "Al," I said, "Tony Bledsoe is the illegitimate son of the recently deceased Griswold Forsythe the Second."

He looked at me, blasted. Suddenly he chomped down on his cigar and bit off the tip. He made a grimace of disgust and deposited the severed smoke in a nearby ashtray.

"Is that for real?" he demanded.

"It is," I said. "Reported to me as gossip and then confirmed by an unimpeachable source."

"Why didn't you tell me before this?" he said harshly.

"Because I only learned of it a few days ago and I thought it of little significance. A footnote, so to speak. But then I heard that Bledsoe has a propensity for violence, especially after he's had a few drinks."

"Propensity for violence," the sergeant repeated. "Love the way you talk. Couldn't you just say the guy's a hot-head?"

"All right," I said. "Anthony Bledsoe is reputed to be a hothead."

"And you have a propensity for prolixity," said Al who, as you may have guessed, is no fool. He looks as if he was hacked from a side of beef by a careless butcher but he is an extremely astute and conscientious detective. He also happens to be a closet balletomane—but that's neither here nor there.

"Okay," he said, "so Tony is the dead man's bastard. What does that get us?"

"Motive?" I suggested. "Resentment and anger. He was a servant in his father's home. That couldn't have been easy to endure."

"Who's his mother?"

"Mrs. Nora Bledsoe, the Forsythes' housekeeper."

Rogoff shook his meaty head in wonderment. "That place is a zoo," he said.

"You're the second person who's said that."

"Who was the first?"

"Timothy Cussack."

"Oh-ho. And have you any secrets about that bum you'd care to reveal?"

"I'm leery about him," I admitted, not answering his question directly. "But I can't imagine what his motive might be for strangling Mr. Forsythe. Surely not for the few hundred dollars in his wallet."

The sergeant hunched forward. "But you figure he's a possible?"

I nodded.

"And Bledsoe is another?"

"Or the two of them in cahoots. Al, they're close friends, drinking buddies. They may have cooked up the whole thing together. Bledsoe gets a nice bequest after his father dies. The two of them, Bledsoe and Cussack, want to open a saloon or nightclub or whatever. Maybe they got impatient and decided the old man was worth more dead than alive."

That wasn't *quite* the way I saw it, but I knew the suggestion would be sufficient to start Al digging deeper into the whereabouts of the two suspects at the time of the murder.

The sergeant sat back, finished his brandy, and began to juice up a fresh cigar. "You know," he remarked, "the only reason I put up with you is that you're one of the beach people. They'll talk to you and tell you things they'd never tell me because I'm just a lousy cop."

"You know," I said, "the only reason I put up with you is that you can flash your potsy and get the street people to tell you things they'd never tell me because I'm just a lousy civilian."

We glowered at each other, then burst out laughing.

"Not a bad team," Rogoff said.

"Not bad at all," I agreed.

He rose to depart without lighting up his new cigar, for which I was thankful. I walked him out to his pickup truck. It was a splendid night, cool and clear.

"Thanks for the feed," Al said. "And for the leads. I'll take a closer look at Bledsoe."

"And Cussack," I said. "Don't forget him."

"I won't," he promised. "And if you learn anything new don't be bashful. Support your local police."

"Don't I always?"

"Sometimes," he said. "After a delay. But better late than never."

"What a brilliant expression," I told him. "I wish I'd said that."

"Go to hell," he said cheerfully and drove away.

I went back inside and cleaned up father's study, taking brandy snifters and ashtray into the kitchen to rinse. I asked Ursi to give me a wakeup call on Friday morning. Eight o'clock, no later.

"Make sure I'm out of the hay," I urged.

"I'll make sure, Mr. Archy," she said, smiling. "If necessary I'll have Jamie play his concertina in your bedroom."

"That'll do it," I acknowledged and climbed the stairs to *my* Secret Place. I undressed and pulled on a Japanese kimono imprinted with a scene of a samurai battling dragons. Fitting?

I worked on my journal awhile and then surrendered. I treated myself to a marc, lighted a cigarette, and put on a tape of Tony Bennett singing cabaret songs. What a balladeer he is! Did you ever catch his "Night and Day"? Magic.

While I sipped, smoked, and listened I reflected on my conversation with Sgt. Al Rogoff. I was satisfied with the way it had gone, confident I had spurred him to do the donkeywork needed to add flesh to the bones of my theory of what had happened. I was not absolutely sure of it, you understand, but there is little I am totally certain of—

except that a stock will rise in price the day after I sell it.

I finished my drink, cigarette, and Tony Bennett's tape. His last song was "I'll Be Seeing You." It was beautifully done but had no relation to the discreet inquiry that concerned me. A more apt selection might have been "The Lady is a Tramp."

Ursi was true to her word and pounded on my door at eight A.M. Friday morning and continued pounding until she heard my strangled shout, "I'm up, I'm up!" I cannot claim I bounced out of bed at that ungodly hour full of p & v. But I did manage to drag myself through the morning's ablutions, shaving, dressing, and arriving downstairs in time to breakfast with my parents in the dining room.

It was not a festive repast. As usual, father kept his nose buried in *The Wall Street Journal*, checking the current status of his Treasury bonds, and I was in no mood for brilliant chatter, aching for at least another hour of slumber. Poor mother had to provide what conversation there was, relating a droll tale of a woman in her garden club whose springer spaniel apparently had an insatiable appetite for her impatiens.

After breakfast we all separated. Father drove his Lexus to the office, mother retired to the greenhouse to wake her begonias, and I set out in the Miata on my morning program, planning to visit the Trojan Stables. Horse people, whether engaged in the activities of farm or racetrack, are notoriously early risers, sometimes (ugh!) before dawn. So I expected Mrs. Constance Forsythe would be present when I arrived.

And so she was, supervising a morning exercise of all the horses entrusted to her keeping. The riders were mostly her stable boys, plus a few owners, plus Timothy Cussack atop a handsome chestnut mare. I was glad to see him so occupied; I had no desire to have an immediate encounter with that scalawag.

Mrs. Constance was all beams. "Hiya, Archy," she said genially. "You awake so early?"

"Barely," I said.

She was looking a bit puffy about the gills that morning, as if on the previous night she had enjoyed a pajama party with a regiment of dragoons. I had noted her ruddy and ravaged face on our first meeting, and wondered if she might be a heavy drinker. Now I was convinced of it. The outdoor life was not the cause; hers was an 80-proof complexion.

"Ma'am," I said, "I don't know whether or not you are aware of it but I have been working with the authorities in the investigation of your husband's murder."

She looked at me sharply. "Are you now?" she said. "And why on earth would you be doing that?"

"Griswold Forsythe was an old and valued client of McNally and Son. Naturally we want to provide the police with whatever assistance we can."

"Uh-huh," she said, turning to look at the cantering horses. "I hope that doesn't include revealing any confidential information."

"Of course not," I said stiffly. "As I'm sure you know, my father is a very principled man."

She wheeled around to stare at me again. "I believe he is," she said. "I'm not so sure about you."

"You can trust my discretion," I assured her.

"I don't have much choice, do I?" she said with a hard laugh.

"Mrs. Forsythe, I would think you'd be eager to aid in solving this brutal crime."

"Of course I am," she said peevishly. "But the cops ask such stupid questions. I don't think that clunky sergeant—what's his name?"

"Al Rogoff."

"Yes, well, I don't think he's got a clue."

"Don't underestimate him," I advised her. "He may move slowly but he's very determined."

"So what?" she said sardonically. "I've seen thoroughbreds who move slowly but are very determined. They finish twelve lengths back."

I didn't feel like smiling but I did. "Actually," I said, "I'm here more or less on Sergeant Rogoff's behalf. He is so occupied analyzing the physical evidence he has had little opportunity to interrogate the people who may or may not be personally involved. That is why he has deputized me—not officially of course—to ask questions and try to provide him with profiles of relatives, employees, friends, and acquaintances of the victim."

It was a long, rambling speech, pure fudge, and I wasn't sure she'd buy it. But she did.

"All right," she said, tightening the belt on that scrofulous riding jacket she wore, "what do you want to know?"

"Anthony Bledsoe," I said. "What can you tell me about him?"

"A barrel of laughs he ain't," she said with that whinny of hers. "A sullen kid. Oh, he does his job; no complaints there. But he's got a grudge against the world."

"Any evidence of violence?"

"Occasionally."

"Against whom?"

"His mother, for one. There seems to be a constant squabble going on between those two. I've never asked about it. None of my business. If they do their jobs that's all I ask."

"Does Tony drink?"

"Don't we all?" That whinny again.

"Do you think he'd be capable of assaults against others while under the influence?"

She considered that a brief moment. "I think probably he would. He's got a ferocious temper. To tell you the truth, Archy, I'm not sure he's got both oars in the water."

"Is he having an affair with Fern Bancroft?" This was a supposition on my part but evidence pointed to it and I reckoned it was time for verification.

Constance Forsythe gave me a crooked grin. "You do get around, don't you?" she said. "Well, she's as nutty as he is and it wouldn't surprise me a bit if they had a thing going. Listen, why are you asking all these questions about Tony Bledsoe? Is he a suspect in my husband's murder?"

"There are several," I replied. "He's one of them."

She nodded. "I can understand that. I'd hate to believe it but he's hyper and strong enough to have done it, especially if he was in one of his wicked moods."

"What would be his motive?" I asked her.

"Money," she said promptly. "What else? Tony has dreams he'd never realize on what Griswold was paying him. Maybe he went to the office that day, asked for a raise, got turned down and blew his stack."

"That's possible," I said. "Thank you for your help, Mrs. Forsythe. I'm sure it will aid the investigation."

"You'll report to Sergeant Rogoff what I've just told you?"

"Unless you have any objections."

"No," she said. "No objections."

She walked away from me abruptly to meet the returning riders. I headed for the Miata but stopped when I saw Sylvia Forsythe's silver-gray Saturn come gliding into the parking area. It stopped and she hopped out, wearing white jeans and an aqua tank top. No matter what her costume, it had a dégagé look, as if she had grabbed the first things in her closet that came to hand. The result was elegant insouciance.

She came bopping over to me with a sassy smile. "And a jolly good morning to you, Archy," she said. "Sorry, luv, but I can't have lunch with you today."

I laughed. "I don't recall inviting you."

"However," she said, drawling the word and looking at me speculatively, "I should be free by three o'clock. The Michelangelo Motel. Okay?"

"Why not?" I said hoarsely, hating myself for the weak-kneed craven I am.

"That's what I like in a man," she said saucily. "Uncontrollable passion." She tossed me an air kiss and scampered over to Mrs. Constance and the sweated horses.

Stay tuned.

22

I pointed the Miata toward West Palm, singing mightily and revising the lyrics of that old spiritual to "Swing high, sweet chariot." For I was in a frolicsome mood. That verbal fencing with Constance Forsythe had added confirmation to my ramshackle theory. I began to glimpse the end of the Forsythe affair and could imagine the whole story being condensed in *Soap Opera Digest*.

It was then about eleven o'clock or so. I stopped at the first public telephone kiosk I could find and dug into my wallet for Gladdie's number. Surely you remember Gladdie—the barmaid at the Sea Turtle. I reasoned that because of the hours she worked it was possible she was now astir and ready for breakfast.

"Yeah?" a man answered in a croaky voice.

"May I speak to Gladdie, please."

"Who?" he said. "What?"

Then I remembered her warning about a hard-of-hearing father. "Gladdie!" I shouted. "Your daughter!"

He grumbled but in a few moments she came on the line, sleep in her voice.

" 'Lo," she said. "Who's this?"

"Archy," I said, then added modestly, "I don't suppose you remember me."

253

"Archy!" she said. "Of course I remember you. You're that cute redheaded boy with the funny little goatee."

Somewhat discomfiting. "Not quite," I said. "I'm the cute boy who was drinking with Timothy Cussack."

"Of course," she said. "Now I remember. You're a vodka gimlet."

"You've got it," I said gratefully. "That's exactly what I am. Gladdie, I realize I probably woke you up and I apologize. But I was hoping I might treat you to breakfast."

"Hey," she said, "that sounds utter. I usually go to our local IHOP. I love their pancakes—don't you?"

"Divine," I said.

Which explains why, thirty minutes later, I was seated across the table from her, watching with fascination while she attacked plates of pancakes, a T-bone, eggs, potatoes, toast, a pint of OJ, and enough heavily creamed coffee to float the *USS Wisconsin*. I had already enjoyed an abstemious breakfast of a single English muffin (admittedly slathered with Rose's lime marmalade) and I could not believe this young miss was gobbling a meal that would have staggered Lucullus.

"Archy," she said, "you don't think all this is fattening, do you?" Oh yes, she was quite serious.

"I'm not a doctor," I told her, "but I play one on TV. In my judgment your breakfast is not fattening providing you get sufficient physical exercise."

She gave me a bright smile. "I try," she said.

She really was a *nice* woman, destined, I was sure, to marry a handsome rake who would starve her shamefully, not recognizing what a treasure he had won.

I took a sip of my black coffee. "Gladdie," I said, "I must be honest with you. I need some information from you for which I am willing to pay."

She stopped gorging long enough to ask, "Information? About what?"

"You have a drop of maple syrup on your chin," I mentioned. "It's about Timothy Cussack. Two questions, and if you don't wish to answer them, that's your prerogative and I'll understand completely."

"What are they, the questions?"

"What kind of a car does he drive, and do you know of any particular woman with whom he has been closely associated. Recently, that is."

She wiped her chin. "This won't get me in any trouble, will it? Timmy is a meanie when he's riled. You saw that."

"Our conversation is confidential, Gladdie. I promise you he'll never hear about it."

"Okay. How much?"

"Fifty."

"Works for me," she said blithely, starting on her dessert: a bowl of chocolate ice cream. "Tim used to drive an old beatup Pontiac, a real clunker. Then, a couple of months ago, he showed up in a new Taurus wagon, pearl blue. A real beauty. Okay?"

"Fine," I said. "And his favorite woman—if he has one."

"There I can't help much," she said. "The guy's a real Don Juan." (She pronounced it Don Joo-ann.) "But I've noticed he's got a thing for older women. Not ancient, you know, but older than him. Does that help?"

"Immeasurably," I said and watched, disbelieving, as she stole the salt and pepper shakers and glass ashtray, slipping her loot unconcernedly into her shoulderbag. The only thing I've ever lifted was a stein from McSorley's Old Ale House in Manhattan.

I paid for our breakfast and in the parking area outside the IHOP I passed a fifty to Gladdie.

"Thank you, sir," she said pertly.

"My pleasure," I said.

"When will I see you again?" she asked eagerly.

"Soon," I promised. But I didn't think so.

It was nudging one o'clock when I finished that bacchanalia with Gladdie but I was in no mood for lunch. Watching her gourmandize had somehow robbed me of an appetite. I mean, who puts catsup on scrambled eggs? That qualifies for the icky category, wouldn't you say?

So I had two hours to slay before my rendezvous with Sylvia at the Michelangelo Motel and, despite the travel involved, I resolved to make a quick trip back to the beach and do a spot of discreet inquiry. My flaccid theory was beginning to sit up and bay at the moon. I was convinced a few more bits of info would prove me the most brilliant detective since Nancy Drew.

Arriving at the Forsythe Bedlam, I drove around to the back, intending to enter through the rear door. But the man I sought was standing outside, smoking a twisted cigar that looked like two entwined pieces of rope that had been soaked in tar. Zeke Grenough was wearing chef's whites, his wire-rimmed pince-nez clamped to the bridge of his nose.

His greeting was affable enough and we exchanged news about the most recent of the season's hurricanes, which was now apparently weakening and would exhaust its remaining fury in the North Atlantic.

"Mr. Grenough," I said, "I heard a distressing rumor that you may be leaving the Forsythes' employ. Surely that can't be true."

"Oh no," the little man said calmly. "No, no. I admit there was a minor disagreement right after Mr. Forsythe was killed. But things were so upset, you know. Now we've all calmed down. No, I'm staying and young Mr. Griswold has promised me a new microwave."

"Glad to hear it," I said. "I know how much the family depends on you." (McNally's Law: If you wish to seduce by flattery, pile it on.)

"I try," he said modestly. "When I arrived they were strictly beef and potatoes people. Gradually I have been introducing them to more subtle dishes. For instance, this evening we are having veal medallions and scallops sautéed with sundried tomatoes and fresh basil."

"With a good white wine," I gurgled, my appetite suddenly returning in full force.

"Of course. Perhaps a chablis or sauvignon blanc."

"The Forsythes have a good wine cellar?"

"I am gradually creating it," he said complacently. "When I started I was horrified to find most of their bottles had screw tops and handles."

"Incredible," I said, shaking my head. "So in addition to increasing their fondness for haute cuisine you are also teaching them the glories of good vintages."

"Oh yes," he said, apparently happy to discuss what was not only his job but his passion. "As they say, life is too short for cheap wine. Mrs. Constance has been especially supportive of my efforts."

"And what about Anthony Bledsoe?" I asked lightly. "I hear he enjoys a glass or two."

He stared at me through those crazy specs. "Tony?" he said. "Oh no, you have been misinformed. Tony has no interest in wine—or any other spirits as far as I know. He drinks Diet Pepsi with my *chef d'oeuvre:* poached salmon with pears. That offends me."

"I should think it would," I said.

We chatted a few moments on vital topics, such as which

is the best sauce for tournedos, béarnaise or bourgui-
gnonne. We came to no agreement but parted firm friends,
each recognizing in the other a fervor for tasty vittles. I
hopped back into the Miata having determined, in my
opinion, exactly what I had hoped.

I sped back to the Michelangelo Motel in a mood more
depressive than manic. It was gratifying, of course, to have
added confirmation that my analysis was correct but it gave
me no joy. Instead I was saddened by human perfidy. I am
no saint, mind you, but my sins were small spuds compared
to the evils committed by the miscreants who had con-
spired to murder Griswold Forsythe II.

My visit to the doldrums was mercifully short. By the
time I arrived at the Michelangelo the McNally spirits
were once again bubbling like an uncorked magnum of
Bollinger. I espied Sylvia's silver Saturn in the parking area
and found her already in Suite 309, nibbling on a small
beaker of applejack. She was wearing a grin of luxurious
content. And nothing else.

I realized we had enjoyed only two passionate scrums
but sometimes brief encounters are more meaningful than
a lifetime of intimacy, are they not? In any event this flighty
woman still had the magic to entice me. It was, I decided,
a clear case of déjà voodoo.

She was in no mood to waste time, nor was I. In the blink
of a gnat's eye we were jousting on sea-foam-colored satin
sheets and howling (pianissimo) with delight. What a mad-
cap she was! She gave new meaning to the phrase "fancy-
free." But I was not so insensible with passion that I did not
recall Ms. Browning's words: "How do I love thee? Let me
count the ways." Before that afternoon ended I was up to
fourteen.

Finally, dizzy with rapture and exhaustion, we lay panting as if we had just set a record in the high hurdles, which I believe we had. I staggered from the track and stumbled to the kitchen where, with trembling hands, I prepared transfusions of applejack on ice. Lots and lots of ice.

"Bless you, my child," Sylvia murmured when I delivered her glass. "That was quite a go, was it not?"

"The only trouble," I said, "was that it went."

"Tomorrow's another day," she said blithely and sat up, pressing the icy glass to her swollen bosom.

I sat on the edge of the bed, hunched over, lacking the strength to straighten my spine. "Sylvia," I said, trying very hard to keep my voice from becoming a weak croak, "what's happening between you and Griswold? The last time we spoke you implied you were thinking of leaving him."

"Not now," she said cheerfully. "We've come to an understanding. Soon after we married I realized my husband was a victim of the seven-week itch. That's how long it took him to stray. And guess who he picked."

"I have no idea," I said, one of my easier falsehoods since she could have had no idea of how much prying I had done.

"Sheila Hayworth!" she cried. "Can you believe it? Our maid! I do believe El Jerko is hooked. But that's okay; it's his problem. Anyway we've come to an arrangement. We're going to stay married. He'll go his way and I'll go mine. Naturally we'll have a financial agreement."

"Naturally," I said.

"It's best for everyone," she said, and I thought she was trying to convince herself as much as me. "Lucy will still have a momma and a poppa, and Griswold and I will have complete freedom to live the way we want to live. Don't you think that makes sense?"

"It does," I said, trying not to reveal my doubts.

She began stroking my bare back with drink-chilled fingers. *Then* my spine straightened. The woman *dabbled* with me. I can think of no other word that better describes her actions. I had the insane notion that she saw me as a human harpsichord and was playing me. Vivaldi? It felt more like Scott Joplin.

"Sylvia," I said hoarsely while this noodling was going on, "I'd like to ask you a personal question and if you wish to tell me to go to blazes you'll be entirely within your right."

"Okay," she said. "What's the question?"

"Did you ever make it with Tony Bledsoe?"

"Once," she said ruefully. "It was a rainy afternoon and I was bored. But then he got serious and I can't stand that. He had this crazy idea of our running away together. Rubbish! You probably think me a fluffhead but I do have a keen instinct for the bottom line. I mean what did he have to offer? Love? You can't pay your Neiman-Marcus charge with that."

"Indeed you can't," I agreed. "And is Tony still lovesick?"

She shrugged. "I suppose. He keeps giving me these moony looks. He'll get over it."

I wasn't so sure. A lark on a rainy afternoon for her might well have been an epiphany for poor Tony. He had caught a glimpse of how glorious life could be. I suspected it had given focus to all his inchoate longings. Now, suddenly, he knew what he wanted: he wanted *her*.

"It was Fern Bancroft, wasn't it?" I asked.

"What?" she said sharply.

"It was Fern Bancroft, the other maid, who tried to throttle you."

She looked at me, first puzzled then wry. "You're a busy busybody, aren't you? How did you guess that?"

"Elementary, as Mr. Holmes said to Mr. Watson. I put two and two together and came up with five. Fern is slightly off the wall and not a lady to be trifled with. She has hot eyes for Tony Bledsoe, he is enamored of you, and she attempted to remove the competition. Is that the way you see it?"

She nodded.

"Sylvia, why didn't you report her to the police?"

"Give me a break, Archy! I didn't want to put that silly girl behind bars. I had a long talk with her and convinced her that Tony is all hers; I have absolutely no interest in him."

"You're very forgiving," I said admiringly. "She could have done you in."

That earned a laugh. "But she didn't, did she? It's all water under the bridge or over the dam or whatever. Now come here."

I rolled back onto the bed and we nuzzled a moment. Why do so many nice things begin with an "n"? Nuzzling, nestling, nibbling, necking. Even noshing.

"Now that you're in a confessional mood," I said, "tell me about Timothy Cussack."

"You mean am I bedding him? No. Have I ever? No. You asked me that before, Archy."

"So I did. But I've since learned what a lecher he is."

"I suppose," she acknowledged. "I admit I was willing but I'm just not Tim's type. Too young."

"And not enough money?"

"That too," she agreed. "I don't always make a grand slam, you know."

"It didn't bother you?"

"His turning me down? Of course not. Why should it? There's no shortage of studs. You, for instance," she added, giggling. "You know what I'd like to do now?"

"Yes," I said.

I was right. We parted an hour later, having showered (à deux), dressed, and pledged to each other mock declarations of undying love. We both snickered. She was not a serious woman but then I am not a serious man. I suppose that's why we hit it off so splendidly.

"Sylvia," I said before we went our separate ways, "I want you to know that everything we talked about today, everything you told me, is strictly confidential." What a whopper! Connie Garcia is right: my nose gets longer by the minute.

"I don't care," she said carelessly. "You can't hurt me. No one can hurt me."

I thought that was a very brave and very foolish thing to say.

It was too late for an ocean swim even if I had the energy for it, which I didn't. Instead, before sprucing up for the family cocktail hour, I phoned Sgt. Al Rogoff and found him at his office. He was in a spleeny mood.

"Now what?" he demanded irritably.

"What did you have for lunch?" I asked him.

"Tortillas with onions and peppers. With black coffee."

"Ah," I said, "the surly-bird special. Listen, Al, I'd like to get together with you tomorrow."

"You've found a new disco? I don't enjoy dancing with you, Archy; you always want to lead."

"Oh, shut up. There have been developments in the Forsythe case you should know about."

He was silent for a tick or two. "Something good?" he said.

"I think so. I'll spell it all out for you."

"*All?*" he repeated. "Including the homicide?"

"Yes," I said firmly. "The whole shebang."

"You wouldn't be diddling me, would you, old buddy?"

"Not me. But it's going to take some work on your part to prove it out."

He sighed. "Hell, I'm still stuck in square one so I might as well listen to you. I really have no choice."

"That's right, Al. As the French say, when there's no alternative a man must sleep with his wife."

He laughed and we agreed to meet at ten o'clock on Saturday morning. "Come over here," I urged. "We can talk in the kitchen while you have your fourth cup of black coffee."

"I'll be there," he promised. "This better be good."

"It is," I said and rapped knuckles on my noodle for luck.

Ursi served saltimbocca that evening: a hearty dish of veal, ham, and cheese in a wine sauce. It was just what I needed after that exhausting day. I had intended to spend several hours working on my journal but when I retired to my chambers and undressed I saw the bed inviting me with fresh linen and plumped pillows.

This will shock you, I know, but despite my sybaritic tendencies—a fondness for good food, good wine, good love—I truly believe one of life's greatest pleasures is a good night's sleep.

"Go for it, McNally," I said aloud and slid gratefully between the sheets.

23

Rogoff was latish but I had no objections; before he arrived my father had departed for his Saturday golf game, mother and the Olsons had taken the station wagon into town for a spot of weekend shopping, and I had the McNally wickiup to myself.

I also had time to phone Connie Garcia. She wasn't at home so I took a chance and called her office.

"Lady Cynthia Horowitz's residence," she recited.

"Working on a Saturday?" I said. "You must really love your job."

"Bite your tongue," she said tartly. "I was planning to have a relaxed day, just futzing around my apartment, doing laundry, washing my hair. Then Lady C. decided she wanted to go over budgets and accounts today, so here I am. Hey, Archy, when are we going to the Bahamas?"

"Next weekend."

"You promise?"

"Of course. I'll provide an affidavit if you insist. Connie, how are you coming along on that matter I asked you to investigate?"

"I've got an answer for you. Actually, I've got half an answer."

"Better than none at all. Can you have dinner with me tonight?"

"Can I ever!" she cried. "Listen, Archibald, I'm going to be stuck here till late and won't have time to go home to change. I'm wearing scruffy jeans and a T, so I think we better meet at the Pelican Club. Okay?"

"Fine. Sevenish?"

"Around there. I warn you, after spending eight hours crunching numbers with the Lady, I'll be in need of a powerful transfusion. One, at least."

"Only one?"

"I'm driving and the roads are full of troopers. But we can always go back to my place and continue the festivities."

"What a marvelous idea," I said. "Shall I bring my tarot cards?"

"That's not exactly what I have in mind," quoth she, and disconnected.

Just in time, for through the kitchen window I saw Al Rogoff drive his pickup into our turnaround, and I went out to greet him. He was wearing khaki slacks and a Hawaiian shirt President Truman would have admired.

"Al," I said, "you shouldn't have dressed so formally."

"Go to hell," he said amiably. "It's Saturday, I'm off duty, and my dinner jacket is at the cleaners. Sue me."

Ursi had left a pot of coffee; all I had to do was heat it up and put out cups and saucers. I also piled a platter with her homemade chocolate chip cookies. They're chewy and rich enough to tempt a chocoholic to overdose.

We sipped our steaming java, wolfed down calories, and I began my recital. I started by advising Al to F & F (File and Forget) the attempted strangling of Sylvia Forsythe. I explained the circumstances: the assault was committed by

Fern Bancroft, Ms. Non Compos Mentis herself, in an effort to kill the woman she feared had stolen the heart of the man Fern coveted. Namely, Anthony Bledsoe.

"Beautiful," the sergeant said. "I love it. I also love 'Tillie's Punctured Romance.' Do you think Sylvia wants to bring charges against the Bancroft dame?"

"Nope."

"Will she sign a statement attesting to the identity of her assailant?"

"I doubt that very much."

"Good," Rogoff said happily. "I'll deep-six the whole schmear. Now what about the homicide."

"Here's where the wicket gets sticky," I said.

I explained what I thought had happened. I was careful to differentiate between hard evidence—of which there was precious little—and my own suppositions and blue-sky guesses. I told him of the thefts of property from Griswold Forsythe II, but I made no mention of the disappearance of Geraldine Forsythe's jewelry.

I finished my discourse. Rogoff's expression had not changed one bit during the telling. But in the brief silence that followed he rose to fetch the coffeepot and refill our cups.

"You know," he said finally, "sometimes you act like a mental dumpling. And sometimes I think you've got more than matzo balls between your ears."

"Thank you," I said humbly.

"Why didn't you tell me about the thefts before this?"

"Because our client would not allow it. That's why I was assigned to make discreet inquiries. Forsythe wouldn't even go to the police immediately after receiving that threatening note. Al, the rich are firmly convinced they're more intelligent than poorer folks."

"I know," he said mournfully, "but you could have told me after the guy was chilled."

"I didn't realize how closely the thefts were connected to the homicide until last Thursday. Then little bits and pieces of evidence accumulated until I had enough to fill a sporran."

He looked at me. "What in God's name is a sporran?"

"A Scotch fanny pack but worn in front of the kilt."

"You have more useless information than anyone I know."

"True enough," I agreed.

"Let's get back to business. Where do we go from here on the Forsythe kill, assuming your theory is on target?"

"Here's what I suggest," I said and detailed the things I could do and the things he might do. "It may turn out to be a blind alley," I admitted. "No guarantees."

"I realize that, Archy, but I like it. You know why?"

"Sure. You've got nothing better."

"I've got nothing, period. There's not much I can do today or tomorrow but I'll get cracking on Monday. With any luck we should have this thing wrapped up by mid-week."

"We better," I said. "I'm planning a jaunt to Freeport next weekend."

"Alone, of course."

"Of course."

He laughed. "When pigs whistle. Thanks for the coffee and cookies. Hit the spot. I'll be in touch."

He left and I cleaned up the kitchen. Then I debated what my next move should be. I decided it was time I made good on at least one of the promises I scattered about so freely. I phoned.

"The Forsythe residence." A young woman's voice.

"This is Archy McNally. May I speak to Miss Lucy Forsythe, please."

She giggled and I knew it was Fern Bancroft. "Just a moment, sir," she said.

I waited patiently and eventually I heard a piping voice: "This is Lucy Forsythe. To whom am I speaking?"

What a grammatical treasure the child was!

"Lucy, this is Archy."

"Hi!"

"Hi! Listen, dear, it looks like a lovely day and I was hoping we could have that picnic we talked about."

"Oh yes!" she said, suddenly excited. "I was afraid you forgot all about it."

"No chance. Now I'm going to bring our lunch; you don't have to do a thing but be there. Suppose we meet at your Secret Place at noon."

"Okay," she said happily. "This is the first date I've ever had."

"You'll have plenty more," I assured her.

"Archy, I've finished my poem."

"Wonderful! I can't wait to hear it."

After we hung up I went back upstairs to don a costume suitable for a picnic. Actually, all I did was change to black denim jeans, hoping they wouldn't show grass stains. I knew where I'd be sitting.

I returned to our utility room and rummaged a moment before I found what I sought: a small insulated tote bag designed to keep things hot or cold.

I breezed over to West Palm to a takeout joint I had patronized in the past. Not great but fast. I bought a large pizza, half-cheese and half-pepperoni; four cold cans of Coke; a pint of pistachio ice cream; paper napkins and plastic spoons. I had the pizza tightly wrapped in aluminum foil. The cola and ice cream went into my insulated tote. I can be practical when the occasion demands.

By the time I arrived at Lucy's Secret Place she was already seated on the grass and clapped her hands when I uncovered all the goodies I had brought. I flopped down beside her and we started our picnic, trying to eat delicately and making an enjoyable mess of it.

As we gobbled, she chattered—if one can chatter with a mouthful of cheese and sausage—about activities at school, what the teacher had said, a project being planned that would require Lucy and her schoolmates to write personal letters to the world's leaders. Listening to her jabber, I realized this child was telling me things she should rightfully be relating to her parents. I could only conclude they lacked the interest to listen, and Lucy knew it.

We had begun working on our ice cream when she said, shyly, "Would you like me to read my poem now?"

"I surely would."

She dug a much-creased sheet of notepaper from the pocket of her cotton pinafore, unfolded it, and began reading.

"'To my Grandfather,'" she said, then looked up. "That's the title."

I nodded and she continued reading.

I wish with all my heart I could tell you it was a wonderful poem: simple, heartfelt, and touching. In all honesty I cannot. I wasn't expecting Alfred, Lord Tennyson, you understand, but it was an awful poem. Just awful. Wasn't it Oscar who said, "When it comes to sincerity, style is everything"? Well, someone said it.

She finished and looked at me expectantly.

"Lucy," I said warmly, "it's a marvelous poem. Absolutely marvelous."

She ignited with happiness. "You really think so?"

"I certainly do."

"I read it to Mrs. Bledsoe, and she said it was a beautiful poem, and then she started crying. Why did she do that?"

I could guess but didn't answer. "Did you show it to your mother and father, Lucy?"

"No," she said shortly, and we finished our ice cream in silence. I could see my mention of her parents had saddened her. She sat slumped over, cobwebby hair hiding her face. Finally she said, "I can't come live with you, Archy."

"Oh?" I said. "Why is that?"

"Mom and dad aren't going to make a divorce. They're going to stay married and we're going to stay here. They told me so."

"I'm happy to hear it. That's good news."

"I guess," she said forlornly. "But I can come visit you, can't I?"

"Of course. Whenever you wish."

"Do you have a Secret Place, Archy?"

"Sort of. I have my own apartment at the top of our house."

"Gee," she said, "I wish I had like an apartment. I've just got this one little bitty room."

I was beginning to be infected by her mournfulness and determined to wrench us out of it. "Would you like to hear another funny poem, Lucy?"

She brightened. "Oh yes!"

I recited, " 'Twas brillig and the slithy toves/ Did gyre and gimble in the wabe . . ." By the time I finished she was rocking with merriment, her face alight, and I reminded God to give me a Merit Badge for good intentions.

I gathered up the refuse from our picnic, shoved all the trash into my tote, and rose to depart.

"Be happy, darling," I said to her. "Will you try?"

"Okay," she said with a smile as sweet as halvah.

What I planned next shriveled my heart. But I had promised Sgt. Al Rogoff I would attempt it, and I admit my incurable nosiness overcame my misgivings. Still, I knew it was going to be a touch-and-go confrontation, and I've never been much good at playing the inquisitor.

I found Mrs. Nora Bledsoe in the Forsythe pantry, working on her accounts. She looked up when I entered and gave me a wan smile. "I can't believe you're going to spend a lovely Saturday afternoon cataloging books, Mr. McNally."

"Not quite," I said. "May I speak to you in private, Mrs. Bledsoe? I suggest we adjourn to the library."

Her expression of alarm was fleeting—or perhaps I merely imagined it. "If you wish," she said warily.

She rose and preceded me through that maze of hallways. I finally decided why Mr. Forsythe's grandmother had committed suicide: the poor dear was lost and couldn't find her way out.

I closed the library door carefully and ushered Mrs. Bledsoe to the leather armchair alongside the desk. I took the swivel chair but wheeled it out so we were facing each other closely, no barrier of clunky furniture between us. I hoped it might help create a mood of intimacy. I didn't intend to browbeat the woman.

"Mrs. Bledsoe," I started, "as you're probably aware I have been assisting the police in their investigation of Mr. Forsythe's murder. He was an old and valued client of McNally and Son, and we want to do everything we can to help solve this horrible crime."

She nodded. She sat upright, face set, hands clutched

tightly on her lap. I knew she feared what was coming—
almost as much as I did.

"The police have a number of suspects," I continued. "I
must tell you that your son is one of them. They've been
unable to pinpoint his exact whereabouts at the time of Mr.
Forsythe's death."

If she was shocked her expression didn't reveal it. I think
she had been expecting to hear her son accused.

"Tony is innocent, Mr. McNally," she said, her voice low
but steady.

"I hope he is," I said. "But apparently the authorities are
basing their suspicion on rumors that he is a heavy
drinker."

"That's rubbish!" she said, flaring. "My son has a single
glass of wine or one beer at the most. He is not a boozer.
I can testify to that, and so can everyone else in this house."

"Glad to hear it," I said, leaning toward her. "But it's
also been reported he is prone to violence, has an ungov-
ernable temper. Is that also false?"

That shook her, I could see. She bit her lower lip, twisted
her linked fingers.

"Tony does get angry at times," she finally admitted.
"But it never lasts long. He says things he doesn't really
mean and sometimes he does things he's sorry for later. But
my son is a good boy, Mr. McNally."

That last was a plea. She wouldn't be, I reflected, the
first mother who didn't know her own son and whose opinion was in direct conflict with the judgment of others. You
may think me a wimp, for instance, but my mother believes
me to be an admirable combination of Tom Swift, Robert
E. Lee, and Noel Coward.

The first portion of my interrogation was finished and I

was convinced Mrs. Bledsoe had answered my questions honestly; nothing she had said was irreconcilable with what I had already learned. But the most difficult part of my discreet inquiry remained.

"Mrs. Bledsoe," I said softly, "I must also tell you the police are aware of your relationship with Griswold Forsythe. Your past relationship. Need I say more?"

Then she began weeping. Not noisily, not sobbing, but quietly and steadily, tears wet on her cheeks. I was not proud of what I was doing, you understand, but it was necessary. And I had more pain to administer.

"I'm not surprised," she said, her voice suddenly thick. "After Griswold died I knew it would all come out eventually. Yes, it's true. Tony is Mr. Forsythe's son. But I won't hear a word said against the father. He saved me—*saved* me!—when I thought there was no future for me but walking into the sea. He was the dearest, sweetest, most gentle and most understanding man who ever lived."

I found that hard to believe. I've made it plain I thought Griswold Forsythe II had been a stuffed shirt, a long-winded bore, a skinflint, and a man so convinced of his own omniscience I'm sure he would offer advice to the surgeon about to perform a quadruple bypass on him.

But then who of us is one and complete? I mean we all present different faces to different people, do we not? And they react accordingly. A woman might be a saint to her lover and a devil to her husband, or vice versa. So it was not too surprising that Mrs. Bledsoe saw qualities in the father of her son to which I was totally blind.

"One more question, Mrs. Bledsoe," I said. "I would not dare ask if it were not so important. You may find it offensive and a gross invasion of your privacy, but I *must* ask it."

"What do you want to know, Mr. McNally?"

"Did you continue your intimacy with Griswold Forsythe after you came to work for him and lived in his
home?"

She lifted her chin. Eyes blazed. She was no longer the
defeated woman she had been moments before.

"Yes!" she said defiantly.

I rose and thanked her for speaking so frankly. We shook
hands and I resisted a desire to kiss her cheek. We separated in the hallway. I returned to the Miata, schlepping
my tote bag containing debris from the picnic with Lucy. I
don't wish to get fancy-schmancy about this but it seemed
to me I was also carrying the detritus of an entire family:
all their sins and wicked secrets.

On the drive home, to dispel my melancholy, I sang,
"Toot, Toot, Tootsie!"

It helped.

24

What a joy it was to see Connie Garcia that evening! After the Sturm and Drang of the Forsythe household, Connie came on vibrant, bubbly, and full of hope. As warned, she was clad in tight jeans and a snugger T-shirt. More importantly, she wore an elfin grin. My spirits ballooned.

The Pelican Club was filling rapidly with frenetic Saturday night merrymakers, so we hustled into the dining room to grab our favorite corner table. Priscilla told us the special that night was barbecued pork ribs with a Cajun sauce. Oh yes, we went for that, with garlicked shoestring potatoes and a Mt. Everest of coleslaw.

We nattered nonstop as we gluttonized, exchanging gossip about friends and acquaintances, and who was doing what to whom—and why. Connie told me an amusing story about my pal Ferdy Attenborough. It was rumored that he had been arrested, while somewhat in his cups, for attempting to create an obscene sand sculpture on the beach, complete with a turret shell planted in an upright position.

"Somewhere a mother's heart is breaking," I said sorrowfully.

While we dawdled over our sublime dessert—chunks of pineapple soaked in Captain Morgan's Coconut Rum—I asked Connie what she had learned about the breakup between Geraldine Forsythe and Timothy Cussack.

"As I told you, Archy, I was able to learn only half the answer. Everyone agrees he dumped her for another woman. But no one seems to know who the other woman was—or is. Sorry I couldn't do better."

"You did just fine," I assured her. "It's exactly what I need. You're becoming a real female shamus—called a shamusette."

"You made that up," she accused.

"I did indeed," I admitted. "May we leave now and have a quiet, thoughtful evening in your digs while we discuss Heisenberg's discovery of the uncertainty principle?"

"Is that really what you want to do?" she asked.

"Not quite," I said.

Less than an hour later we were lolling in her snug little condo on the shore of Lake Worth and there was no uncertainty about our actions. We discussed, while recuperating, our coming jaunt to Freeport on the following weekend. We both asserted, vowed, swore we would gamble a limit of a hundred dollars each in the casinos. Absolutely. No more than a hundred. Then we almost strangled with laughter, acknowledging what liars we were.

I departed, regretfully, shortly after midnight and wheeled home in a mellow mood. I did not sing during the drive, as was my wont, but questioned for the umpteenth time what my life might be like were I to be married to Consuela Garcia, that estimable woman.

Not idyllic; I was not such a dolt as to imagine that. Our wedlock would have its pluses and minuses I had no doubt. But the bottom line, I reckoned, would not be written in red ink. Still, there was that damnable cowardice of mine which I blamed on a faulty gene that caused me to break out in a rash at the thought of being shackled by the holy bonds of matrimony.

And if that were not enough, my discreet inquiry into the affairs of the Forsythe clan had given me fresh insight into the perils of conjugality. They had made unholy messes of their marriages. And even though I knew they were probably in the minority, their shocking example was enough to give second, third, and fourth thoughts to any young bachelor contemplating a lifetime commitment.

My mind is a Dumpster of remembered tunes; old films; ancient jokes; actors, poets, singers, and clowns long gone. That night before sleep whisked me away, I was still mulling the pros and cons of hubbyhood. I recalled a line from an Andy Hardy movie I had caught at a grungy rerun cinema. The son (Mickey Rooney) is asked by the judge (Lewis Stone), "Don't you ever intend to wed?" The reply: "Why should I marry and make one woman miserable when I can stay single and make so many women happy?"

Ah, yes.

I awoke the next morning with no firm determination of how I wished to spend the day. I peeked out the window and it looked okay: hazy sun, pallid sky, a few cumulus clouds that didn't seem to be going anywhere. One of the problems of living in South Florida is that you expect every day to be perfect. They aren't, of course, but even the ones categorized as "not half-bad" can be enjoyable. That Sunday appeared to be one of those.

By the time I arrived downstairs my parents had gone to their church and the Olsons had gone to theirs. I inspected the fridge for breakfast possibilities. After the pizza and barbecued ribs of the previous day I decided a little abstention might be in order so I limited my intake to a glass of cranberry juice, a toasted English muffin coated with Dundee grapefruit marmalade, and two cups of black decaf. I felt very virtuous. And very hungry.

Ordinarily I am a sociable bloke but occasionally I like to spend a few hours of selfish solitude, regarding my navel and reflecting on the absurdities of human existence. Actually, my activities on that quiet Sabbath were not quite so highfalutin.

I changed to cerise Speedo swimming trunks, pulled on a purple velour coverup, and shod myself in raffia flip-flops. I gathered up my Yogi Bear beach towel and returned to the kitchen. I mixed a thermos of vodka gimlets and constructed two sandwiches: turkey on wheat (mayo) and liverwurst on sour rye (mustard). I also added an apple to my tote. Then I went down to the beach, coated exposed hide with SPF 15, and reclined in the partial shade of a royal palm.

Time passed. What more can I tell you other than I drowsed, nibbled sandwiches, sipped gimlets, took an occasional dip in the warm sea, stretched my bones, and craftily kept my mind totally blank for five hours—although my father would assure you it required little effort on my part. I returned home to shower and dress for the cocktail hour and dinner. Then I retired to my mini-suite for a long evening of scribbling notes in my journal on everything that had happened since the last entry.

About ten o'clock I received a phone call: my first personal contact that day with the Forsythe hullabaloo.

"Archy?" she said. "This is Gerry."

"Hey!" I said. "I've been meaning to call. When are you leaving?"

"Wednesday afternoon. I just phoned to say goodbye."

That alarmed me; I wasn't certain Al Rogoff and I would have the package gift-wrapped and tied with a gold bow by Wednesday. And Gerry's presence was essential if justice was to triumph.

"Perhaps I'll have a chance to see you before you leave," I suggested.

"I doubt it," she said bluntly. "I have a million things to do; a lot of running around."

"I can imagine," I said and then, lying through my molars, I added, "I hope we can get together when you return."

"That would be nice," she said with all the effervescence of flat beer.

"Have a good trip, Gerry."

"I intend to," she said and hung up.

Not bloody likely, I thought, and mused on the role I imagined Geraldine Forsythe had played in the meshugass now drawing to its close. I could not forgive her for what I surmised she had done. But it seemed to me her transgressions had been more sleazy than cardinal. And probably more venal than either.

I did not believe her a corrupt woman. I theorized that all her offenses had stemmed from loneliness, weakness of will, and a crippled ego. There I go again, playing Dr. Sigmund F. What the hell do I know? Get too involved in psychoanalysis and you'll hesitate to eat a banana.

If my Sunday was unplanned, my schedule for Monday was rigidly structured—and of course it started to fall apart almost immediately.

I began by oversleeping shamefully. I had a solitary breakfast, dashed out to the Miata, and my pride and joy refused to start. A moment's inspection revealed the reason: the fuel indicator signaled an exhausted tank. I gave thanks to Vishnu for allowing me to make it home Saturday night before being stranded on a deserted road.

I went back into the house, phoned the West Palm garage I use, and explained my predicament to Susan, my favorite mechanic.

She laughed. "You're losing it, Archy," she said. "I'll get someone out there this morning to give your baby a bottle—enough to get you to a pump."

"When?" I insisted. "Soon?"

"Before noon is the best I can promise."

I moaned, went outside again, and found mother chatting to her begonias in the greenhouse. I reported my problem and she readily agreed to lend me her old wood-bodied Ford station wagon. And that was the vehicle I drove to the Trojan Stables.

I must admit that despite the minor annoyances and delays, I was enthralled by that splendid morning. God was not in His heaven; He was in South Florida, and we had the lucent sky, beaming sun, and balmy breeze to prove it. What a perfect day to solve a murder!

I found Mrs. Constance Forsythe at the fence in what was apparently her customary posture: one foot up on the bottom rung as she leaned on the top rail. She was watching a horse galloping on the track. The rider, a woman, wore a helmet, but the fluttering fringe of flaxen hair convinced me it was Sylvia Forsythe.

"Hallo, Archy," Mrs. Constance said genially as I approached. "Come to visit us again, have you?"

"A pleasure," I said. "What a lovely morning."

"Just perfect," she said in a dreamy voice. She gazed out over the neatly trimmed acres of her farm, everything trig and glowing in early light. "I can never get enough of this place, Archy. I've been thinking of changing the name to Paradise Stables. I mean the combination of Trojan and horses might imply deceit to some people—don't you think?"

"It might," I agreed, "and it has another connotation as well."

She laughed. "What a naughty boy you are!" She turned away to observe the galloping horse and rider.

"Is that Sylvia up?" I asked her.

She nodded. "She's becoming quite good. I may start her on dressage soon. She's a natural."

"Talking about naturals," I said casually, "is Timothy Cussack about?"

"Nope. It's his day off. Sundays and Mondays."

"Oh damn!" I said, snapping my fingers. "I knew that but forgot. Don't know how I can get in touch with him, do you?"

She took her foot from the rail and turned to face me. "Haven't the slightest," she said. "On his days off Timmy is here, there, and everywhere. Why do you want to find him—something important?"

"It may be," I said. "To him. Look, I trust your discretion, and if you hear from him you might relay this: I've been working with the police on the investigation of your husband's murder. They've narrowed the list of suspects to a half dozen names. Cussack is one of them. I like Tim—we've hoisted a few together—and I thought I should alert him. He's liable to be picked up for questioning."

Her expression didn't change. I told you from the start she had the face of a mastiff, heavy and somewhat droopy. But there was rugged strength. Mastiffs are great protectors. I reckoned she qualified.

"Why on earth would the cops suspect Timmy?" she

inquired, mildly enough. "He had nothing to gain from Griswold's death."

"Exactly," I said. "What could possibly be his motive—the theft of a couple of hundred bucks? I think that's a crock, but you know what the police are like. In this case I believe they're simply floundering. Just between you, me, and the lamppost, they have precious little hard evidence and so they're casting a wide net. I thought I'd mention it to Cussack so it won't come as a rude shock if he gets pulled in for interrogation."

She looked at me thoughtfully. "That's very decent of you, Archy. But Timmy has had run-ins with the law before; he knows how to handle himself."

"Glad to hear it," I said. "I'm sure the whole thing will just dissolve into thin air. But if you hear from Cussack today you might repeat what I've told you."

"I will," she said. "Thanks, Archy. You're true-blue."

I wasn't; I was just being my usual devious self. But she didn't know that, and I was pleased. I genuinely liked the woman. She was so strong, you see, so determined, with the resolve of a sergeant major. I wished I had half her assurance. I have trouble deciding whether or not argyle socks can tastefully be worn with a seersucker suit. Important choices like that stump me.

"Enjoy your paradise, Mrs. Constance," I said, giving her my 100-watt smile (the Supercharmer), and then I departed.

I tooled the station wagon back to the McNally Building, hoping to finagle an audience with m'lord. I felt it was time to brief the executor of the Forsythe estate on what had happened, was happening, and what I anticipated would happen. It would not, I knew, inspire him to leap exuberantly into the air and click his heels with glee.

I went directly to my office—a cubicle small enough to serve as a loo for pygmies—and found on my desk a message to phone Sgt. Al Rogoff as soon as possible. I did and found him in a fractious mood. He wasted no time on idle prattle.

"Did you get out to the horse farm?" he demanded.

"Just got back."

"Were they there?"

"Yep. Both women."

"Did you go into your song and dance?"

"A magnificent performance," I assured him.

"Uh-huh. Well, things are moving right along on this end. It's beginning to look good. We got a search warrant from a friendly judge and I'm leaving now."

"I'll be home all night. Will you phone me and bring me up to speed?"

"Sure, I'll call."

"Guaranteed?"

"I told you I'd call," he said aggrievedly. Al hates to be goosed—as who does not?

He hung up abruptly, leaving me to reflect on what an ass I'd be if my suspicions turned out to be just that—suspicions. But faint heart never condemned fair lady, and so I lighted and smoked an English Oval slowly (first of the day) before I phoned Mrs. Trelawney and asked if *Il Papa* might consent to grant his only son a brief hearing.

She put me on hold and then came back a few moments later to inform me I had been given the gift of fifteen minutes if I arrived at once. And so, hoping my flowered sport jacket (peonies) would not doom the interview from the start, I headed upstairs to my father's sanctum sanctorum dreading what his reaction might be to the news I was bringing. Why did I suddenly recall the ancient custom of killing the messenger with bad tidings?

But to my relief I found him in a benevolent mood. Not exactly cheery, you understand—he hated to have his daily routine interrupted—but not spleenish either. We sat at opposite ends of his bottle-green leather chesterfield, and I launched into my speech.

I told him the whole schmear: what I knew, intuited, and presumed. My report took longer than the allotted fifteen minutes but not once did he interrupt. As I spoke, his features became increasingly stern, darkened with an ineffable sadness. We sat in silence after I finished. I awaited his reaction with some trepidation.

Finally he stirred, shifted position on the couch, and crossed his legs, being careful not to crush the crease in his trousers. "If what you say proves to be correct, Archy," he said in his precise courtroom voice, "I cannot represent any family member in this affair. It would constitute an obvious conflict of interest. If they ask me to recommend competent counsel to represent them, I believe I could do that."

"Yes, sir."

He fell silent again. I have commented several times in these chronicles on what a champion muller my father is. But at that moment, from his expression and manner, I deduced he was not mulling but he was brooding. There is a difference, you know. One may mull over whether to request a two-minute or a three-minute boiled egg. But one broods on the existential meaning of boiled eggs.

"How fragile life is," he eventually observed, and I knew I was in for a short lecture in Philosophy 101. "We all know accidents happen, illnesses appear without warning, chance defeats us all. But the greatest danger surely must be human passions and follies. We look for reasons and meaning in human behavior and they simply don't exist. We are left with only awe or despair or foolish hope."

"Yes, father," I said, longing to be gone.

He must have sensed my impatience from the tone of my voice for he looked at me sharply. "Assuming your suppositions are substantiated, how long do you estimate it will take to resolve this mess?"

"By tomorrow," I said boldly. "If it hasn't unraveled by then, I'll be proved totally wrong and we'll start all over again."

He sighed. "Archy," he said somberly, "everyone knows death is inevitable. But that realization is not much consolation when a man's or woman's life is ended violently before its time. That is why I desire very strongly that the murderer of Griswold Forsythe be apprehended, convicted, and punished. I appreciate your efforts to make that desire a reality."

He was thanking me! My old man was thanking me! What a delightful surprise. And he hadn't even lifted a hairy eyebrow at my peony-patterned sport jacket. I left his office feeling like one of Hannibal's elephants. Having crossed the frozen Alps I had debouched into sunny Italy. It felt so *good!*

I trundled the station wagon home and switched to the Miata. Jamie Olson informed me it had been given a high-octane IV, as Susan had promised. I slid into the leather bucket with a groan of content and sped off to West Palm where I had the tank filled and the windshield washed free of mashed bugs—a constant South Florida vexation.

And then, being in the neighborhood so to speak, I headed for the Pelican Club. After that exhausting morning I was in dire need of refreshment, liquid and solid. What awaited me that afternoon, I knew, required that I be in tiptop physical and emotional condition, ready for a spot of derring-do. And so I had a double cheeseburger with chips and coleslaw at the bar, the cholesterol helped on its way by two bottles of Heineken.

Before I departed I used the public phone in the rear of the bar area and called the Forsythe home. Fern Bancroft answered.

"Fern," I said, "is Anthony Bledsoe there?"

"Sure," she said, "Tony's here. You want to talk to him?"

"No, no," I said hastily. "I just wanted to confirm his presence. I'll drive out and speak to him *mano a mano*."

"What?" she said.

I hung up and went back to the bar to pay my bill. "Mr. Pettibone," I said to our wise majordomo, "why do so many women fall in love with absolute rotters?"

He looked at me with mild astonishment. "Why does a chicken cross the road?" he asked—quite reasonably I thought.

25

Fern had evidently informed him of my impending arrival for when I scrunched to a stop on the Forsythes' driveway, the front door jerked open and Anthony Bledsoe stood glowering at me, completely lacking in the hospitable welcome department.

"Good afternoon, Tony," I said.

"You want to talk to me?" he said truculently.

I decided it would be wise to establish the tone of our interview immediately. After all, I came not as a supplicant but as a succor. And I had had quite enough of his petulance.

"Yes, I want to talk to you," I said stiffly. "But not if you persist in acting like a wounded child. There's already one in this house. If you feel you can converse like a thinking adult, then we'll talk. If not, I want nothing more to do with you."

He backed off at once. "Well, yeah, okay," he said grudgingly. "Come on in."

We went into the library. This time I took the swivel chair and kept the wide desk between us. It gave me the superior position, you see: the magistrate deciding the fate of the accused in the dock. He was not comfortable in the armchair and I was happy to see it.

"Let's get to it," I said briskly. "First of all, my relationship with Mrs. Sylvia Forsythe is none of your damned business."

"It's got nothing to do with me," he said sullenly.

"It shouldn't," I said, "but apparently it does. Mrs. Sylvia is a free spirit, utterly independent. She selects her friends and will continue to do so as her whims dictate. I have been fortunate. You have not. Do I make myself clear?"

"Yeah," he said, "I know where you're coming from."

"Tony," I said, softening my voice, "give up this impossible dream. Or endure endless misery."

He was silent, head bowed.

"And besides," I added, "you have a young lady madly in love with you."

He raised his eyes to look at me. "Who?" he said.

"Fern Bancroft."

"She's a fruitcake," he said scornfully.

"She may or may not be," I said, "but don't take her love lightly. She thinks you a man of value."

His laugh was a snort. "Oh sure," he said, "after she heard I'm going to get a bundle from Forsythe's will."

It angered me. "That's a lie," I said hotly, "and you know it. Fern had a yen for you long before Mr. Forsythe was killed. That's why she tried to strangle Mrs. Sylvia. She wanted to remove her rival."

His eyes widened. "How do you know all this?" he asked, and I found his awe gratifying.

"I see all and I know all," I said—a slight exaggeration. "But please, try to forget your infatuation with Mrs. Sylvia—it can only lead to tragedy—and try to make a new life. With or without Fern Bancroft. The choice is yours, and I wouldn't have the temerity to advise you."

"Without," he said. "I have plans and she's not part of them."

"I think that's regrettable," I told him, "but it's your decision to make. Which leads me into the second topic I want to discuss. Your mother said you and Timothy Cussack are planning to open a restaurant-bar, a disco kind of place."

He stared at me, startled. "She shouldn't have told you that," he said wrathfully.

"Why not, Tony? Your mother's main concern—perhaps her only concern—is your welfare. She doesn't want to see you risking your bequest with a man whose reputation is somewhat flimsy, to say the least. He does have a police record, you know. All I'm asking is that you consider very, very carefully before investing all your legacy in an enterprise with a man of doubtful probity who apparently doesn't have a nickel to his name."

That lit the fuse. He lurched to his feet and leaned far over the desk, face twisted with fury. For one awful moment I feared he might launch himself at me with designs on my jugular. I arose hastily to my feet and retreated a step.

"You don't know a thing about it, you lousy snoop," he said, voice crackling. "For your information, we're going in as equal partners. I'm putting up half the money and Tim is putting up the other half. So don't tell me he's tapped out. And don't try to scare me with that police record stuff. Sure, he's been picked up for some piddling little things but he's never done time. You make him sound like a master criminal."

"No," I said, "he's not that." But my irony was wasted.

He straightened up and drew a deep breath. His rage was fading but there was cold venom in his stare. "Just butt out of my life," he said harshly. "I don't need you giving me advice—or my mother or anyone else. Now I don't have to answer to anyone."

"I wish you the best of luck, Tony," I said and I meant it, knowing he was doomed. It was presumptuous of me, I know, but I had him pegged as a loser.

"Yeah," he said, whirled around, and stalked out.

It had been a ticklish confrontation but it had served its purpose: I had connected another pair of those unnumbered dots. The final picture was almost complete. Not obscene but nasty, definitely nasty.

I drove home wondering how many more times I'd be required to visit the Forsythe fun house. Once, I reckoned, or perhaps twice. Then I intended never again to set foot in that mausoleum. If I wanted to see Lucy—and I hoped our friendship would not languish—I could always find her in the Secret Place. I now appreciated what a refuge that was for the poor lass.

I skipped an ocean swim and went directly to my aerie, thinking Sgt. Al Rogoff might phone. He didn't and I had no wish to bug him; I was certain he was carrying out his part of our scheme. I could have worked on my journal but postponed that chore, praying my next entry would be the last in the Forsythe epic.

Instead I sat at my battered desk and neither smoked nor imbibed strong drink. Proud of me? I was. But I did ruminate heavily, reviewing all the tangles of greed and passion that were finally being unraveled and the role I had played in their unsnarling.

I make no claims to being a Great Brain, mind you. Ask me what a quark is, for instance, and I'll probably reply it's the quack of a ruptured duck. No, it was not sharp intelligence, reason, and logic that enabled me to discover what the dotty Forsythes were up to.

If the truth be told—and I *must* tell it—the only reason I have achieved a modicum of success in my discreet inquiries is that I am just as loopy as the miscreants I investigate. There's an affinity, no doubt about it. I think, feel, and act as they do. And so I'm one step ahead of the gendarmes who have studied human behavior in such scholarly tomes as *Practical Homicide Scene Procedure*.

What I'm trying to say is that I'm just as guilty of daffiness as the Forsythes or any other crackpots. Are not my emotional entanglements, outré dress, and my inordinate fondness for frog legs meunière proof of that? But who's complaining? Not I, since my outlandish conduct may well be an essential aid in the profession to which I have been relegated.

The cream of the jest: I began this narrative with a few snide comments on how goofiness is engulfing the world. I end with the rueful realization that I suffer from the same disorder. Oh well, you told me it takes one to know one.

I was dressing for the family cocktail hour when finally my phone rang and I grabbed it up immediately.

Rogoff was exultant. "It worked!" he shouted. "He's running!"

"Banzai!" I cried. "Running where?"

"South. Right now he's on I-95. I've got an unmarked car on his tail. Two good men. They won't lose him."

"Where do you figure he's heading?"

"Who the hell knows? Maybe the Keys eventually. It's easy to hole up down there. Anyway we've alerted Broward and Dade. I don't think he'll keep going all night. He's driving a pearly blue Taurus wagon, easy to spot."

"What set him off, Al?"

"As soon as we got the warrant we tossed Suite 309 at the Michelangelo Motel. What a lush layout that place is! We found the book right where you said it'd be. What's the name?"

"Poe's *Tamerlane*," I said.

"Yeah. Listen, Archy, can we prove it was stolen from Forsythe?"

"It was on the list of missing property he gave my father. If we can't locate the original list I'm sure pops will testify Griswold Forsythe told him the book had been taken."

"Good enough. We checked the partial prints on Forsythe's wallet against the guy's file. The match is a good possibility but not enough to convict."

"Al, the man has so much at stake, why would he lift the wallet for a measly couple of hundred dollars and endanger himself?"

"Because he's a cheap crook, that's why. Probably figured that since he was croaking Forsythe he might as well glom on to a few easy bucks. Stupid, stupid, stupid!"

"All right, you found the book in his bedroom and grabbed it. When did he start running?"

"We made certain we left the place looking like it had been searched. And besides, I'm sure the desk clerk told him we had been there. Naturally I put a stakeout on the motel. He showed up about three o'clock in a helluva hurry. Went inside and the stakeout alerted me. I scrambled over there in time to see him come out with luggage: a duffel bag, valise, and what looked like a rifle or shotgun case."

"Oh-oh," I said.

"Yeah," Rogoff said. "My exact words. Anyway, he took off like the proverbial bat outta hell with my tail car right behind him. I'm back in the palace now, listening to radio reports, marking his progress on a map, and trying to figure when and where we can take him."

"Do you have an arrest warrant?"

"Come on, Archy, talk sense. We've got probable cause coming out our ears."

"Did you have a chance to check the pawnbroker?"

"Yep," he said happily. "The pawner was just who you figured. Tomorrow we'll start covering all the local hock-shops. Maybe we can find the other loot. Something I need to know: will the three Forsythe women be available tomorrow?"

"As far as I know. Geraldine is leaving for Europe on Wednesday, but the other two haven't mentioned anything about getting out of town. Al, I'm going to be in all night. Will you phone me when you catch up with the fugitive? I don't care what hour it is. Wake me up if you have to."

"My pleasure," Sgt. Rogoff said and hung up.

I was late getting to the cocktail hour and father raised an eyebrow but made no comment. Mother was in a bub-bly mood because one of her begonias had just won second prize at a garden show, and she had the framed certificate to prove it. We congratulated her and the family went down to a fine dinner of broiled red snapper.

After coffee and dessert (pecan pie with coconut ice cream) I started upstairs but was stopped in the hallway by my father.

"Developments?" he asked tersely.

"Yes, sir," I said and gave him an abbreviated account of what I had just learned from Al Rogoff. The news seemed to depress him.

"It appears your presumptions were correct, Archy," he said sadly.

I didn't reply.

"Keep me informed," was all he added, went into his study and closed the door. He would, I guessed, have a glass of port, smoke a pipe, and resume doughtily working his way through the six zillion words of Charles Dickens. I wished him well. I often thought he read those plump volumes not so much for enjoyment as from a sense of duty. One of these days I'm going to introduce him to Thorne Smith.

I continued upstairs, and since I did not expect an uninterrupted night's slumber I decided a short nap would be in order. I kicked off my loafers and lay down atop the coverlet. It had scarcely been a half-hour since dinner, and I know doctors advise against sleeping on a full stomach. So I slept on my back.

I had intended it to be a brief doze but when the phone shrilled, I roused, glanced at the bedside clock, and was shocked to see it was almost one A.M.

"I hope I woke you up," Rogoff said.

"You did," I admitted.

"Good," he said. "Our pigeon's gone to roost. Went east at Deerfield. Got onto A1A and turned south along the beach. Checked into a sleazebag motel across the Hillsboro Inlet. I'm on my way, phoning from Boca. When I get there I'm going to call in the locals for backup. I figure we'll take him around four or five in the morning. He should be smoggy with sleep by then."

"What's the address of the motel?" I asked.

"Archy!" he said sharply. "Stay home. This is cops' work."

I uttered a rude expletive. "Al, he's *my* pigeon. I did most of the work; I want to be in on the kill."

"Well, yeah," he said gruffly, "I guess you rate. Just keep out of the way. Agreed?"

"Positively," I said, and he gave me the address.

I looked out the window and it seemed to me a fine mist was falling. I pulled on a black nylon jacket and stepped downstairs as softly as I could. But not quietly enough. The door of my parents' bedroom opened and my father accosted me. He was wearing Irish linen pajamas but no matter what that man wore it looked like a three-piece suit.

"Where are you going?" he asked in a low voice.

"Father, they've got him cornered. In a motel south of Hillsboro."

He stared at me a long moment. I knew he wanted to say, "Be careful," but he didn't—which is why I love him. He just nodded and went back into the bedroom.

I was right about that mist; it wasn't heavy but it was persistent—and warm. I had a plaid golf cap stuffed in the pocket of my jacket. I donned that but it wasn't long before it was soaked through and flopped down on my ears.

The road south was slick and the infrequent street lamps were dimmed and haloed by the mist. I drove cautiously, having no desire to skid off the corniche onto the beach. Traffic at that hour was mercifully light, but it still took almost two hours to drive through the Hillsboro Mile and across the inlet.

I slowed, trying to glimpse numbers on motels and stores in the strip malls. I finally found the address Rogoff had given me: just your average single-level motel of perhaps twenty units. It looked like a hot-pillow joint to me, and I reckoned the neon sign outside showed VACANCY since the place opened.

I saw no evidence of police presence, but about a half

mile down A1A toward Pompano Beach I came upon a
parked collection of official vehicles that looked like a cops'
convention. There were squads from Pompano, Broward
County, an ambulance, a red fire rescue truck, and two cars
from Palm Beach. I pulled up near this jumble and got out
of the Miata slowly and warily. My approach had been
noted and immediately three uniformed heavies moved
toward me, hands on their holsters.

I was happy when Sgt. Al hustled up and waved them
away. He was as soaked as I but grinned when he saw the
sodden cap plastered to my skull.

"You look like you're wearing an unbaked pizza," he
said.

"Al, I passed the motel but I didn't see any police cars.
I'd have thought you'd have the place boxed in."

"And spook him?" he demanded indignantly. "You think
we're nuts? We pull up a fleet of cars, and the guy's liable
to hear the traffic and come out blasting with a rifle or
shotgun or whatever he's got in that violin case of his. Why
take the chance? He's not going anywhere; we've got guys
on foot covering the front and back."

"Well, what are you waiting for?"

"Tear gas grenades and launchers," he said. "It turned
out no one's equipped so we sent for them. They should be
here any minute now. Probably won't need them but as
you like to say, one never knows, do one?"

Rogoff and I joined a group of cops, all smoking and
chatting casually about the won-lost record of the Marlins,
Florida's new baseball team. Most of the officers, I noted,
were wearing bulky bulletproof vests, either under their
shirts or over. Al wasn't and I wasn't either. Not a comforting thought.

Finally a van from the Broward County sheriff's office arrived. Launchers, tear gas, and stun grenades were unloaded. Rogoff left me to confer with COs from other jurisdictions. All the officers present watched and waited. Then Al turned toward them, lifted his right fist and pumped it up and down twice.

The parade got under way, moving slowly, no sirens. I followed the last car. As we approached the target the units separated, apparently following a prearranged plan. The main road, A1A, was blocked north and south of the motel. The remaining cars coasted into the lighted parking area, forming a semicircular barrier around the front door.

Sgt. Rogoff got out, followed by two officers from the Palm Beach tail car. And after them came three Pompano Beach cops. No doors were slammed. The six men formed a wedge, Al leading. I watched from the misty distance, standing beside the Miata. I wondered if I had the courage to do what those men had to do. I decided I did not.

It seemed to me a well-planned operation, and it was. But who can prepare for the unpredictable? And that's what happened. As I watched, the motel's front door slammed open. Timothy Cussack strode out. He was holding a long double-barreled shotgun against his hip, muzzles pointed at the approaching men.

He fired. In that misted gloom it sounded like a cannon's roar. All six men crumpled as if an anarchist's bomb had been rolled into their midst. I didn't know—no one knew—if they were dead, wounded, or had hit the ground hoping to escape a blast from the second barrel.

There was a moment of shocked silence. Then I began running toward the motel entrance.

I insist it was not an act of heroism; it was an act of sheer idiocy. But the sight of Al Rogoff lying prone on wet concrete maddened me. At that moment I was irrational; I admit it.

An officer, guessing my intent, moved swiftly to block my way. "He's got a shotgun," he yelled. "What have you got?"

"The gift of gab," I yelled back, pushed him away, continued on.

I slowed as I walked into the lighted area, my arms raised high, palms frontward. I heard someone scream, "Hold your fire! Hold your fire!"

Cussack swung to face me, the shotgun still held against his hip. I am not an expert but I thought it a gun ordinarily used for trapshooting or potting doves. I am neither skeet nor dove, but I had no doubt that weapon could cause me grievous injury—if not instant quietus.

"You!" Cussack said. "I knew you were bad news the first time I met you. Just too damned slick."

I kept moving slowly toward him, arms still hoisted, until I was less than a yard away.

"Tim," I said quietly, "give it up. There's an army here. You can see that, can't you? You're an intelligent man. Take your chances with the law."

I didn't think him intelligent, of course. I thought him a thug—and a dangerous thug. He had expectations he could never gratify.

"My chances with the law?" he repeated scornfully. "Like the chair, you mean?"

He kept glancing at those six officers still lying quiescent. I don't believe he realized how close I had come to him.

"But what about the woman?" I pleaded. "You still have the power to get her a reduced sentence."

"Screw her!" he said furiously. "She's the one who got me into—"

That's when I made my move. You may think I have the muscle tone of linguine, but my sinews are not as flabby as you might expect.

I stepped in, chopped down, slapped the long-barreled gun aside, and grappled. I knew at once he was stronger than I—but then who isn't? We stood swaying a moment, locked in a lovers' embrace.

He finally flung me aside and, still holding the shotgun, swung the muzzles to point at my brisket.

I saw his eyes go vacant and thought sadly that my riotous weekend with Connie Garcia in the Bahamas was about to be put on hold—perhaps eternally.

It was at that moment that Sgt. Al Rogoff, still lying facedown, propped himself up on his elbows and, sighting his service revolver steadily in both hands, put four shots into Timothy Cussack's chest, firing rapidly. (Later it was discovered the four bullet holes were so close they could have been covered by a small saucer.)

Cussack was smashed back. I stepped in swiftly to snatch the shotgun from his grasp. He went down slowly. I leaned over him. He looked up at me with a dimming stare. I think he wanted to say something but it was too late.

Al Rogoff climbed shakily to his feet. I was expecting thanks for my intervention. But he glared at me.

"Moron!" he shouted.

26

Cleaning up that mess seemed to take forever. Three cops had been hit by the initial shotgun blast, two with minor wounds, one seriously. He was treated by paramedics and then taken away in the ambulance. The other two were given first aid before being assisted to a squad car for the trip to a hospital. The corpse of Timothy Cussack remained temporarily sprawled in a bloodied puddle.

While all this was going on, crime scene tape was strung and police photographers moved in to record everything. Rogoff and four other officers went into the motel to search Cussack's room. I remained outside, pacing up and down, smoking furiously and waiting for my flood of adrenaline to subside.

The sergeant finally returned. He was in a snarly mood.

"If you had done what you promised and stayed out of it, they'd have made Swiss cheese out of the guy. He was standing in a lighted area and there were plenty of shooters out there, including a couple of snipers."

"Al, I—"

"But, oh no, you had to interfere and almost got blown away. What in God's name were you thinking of?"

"Al, I—"

"How could I ever explain to your father why his son got

iced during a police shoot-out? Let alone what the newspapers and TV clowns would say. Did you stop to—"

"Oh, shut up," I said. "I admit I acted like an imbecile but at the moment it seemed the right thing to do. It turned out okay, didn't it?"

"No, it didn't," he said. "I was hoping to take the bozo alive. I figured he'd plea-bargain and implicate the woman. Too late now."

"Did you find anything in his room that could help?"

"Maybe. We found almost five thousand in cash. Fifty-dollar bills."

I was astonished. "Where do you suppose he got that?"

Al gave me his cynical cops' grin. "Down payment," he said. He paused a moment, then drew a deep breath. It was hard for him to say it but he did. "Thanks, Archy," he muttered.

"You're welcome," I said. "How long are you going to be tied up here?"

"Hours," he said. "Why don't you hang around and we'll grab breakfast somewhere. On me."

"Sounds good," I said.

It did take hours. It was past eight o'clock Tuesday morning before Al could break free. We breakfasted in a joint that looked like a Ptomaine Palace, but the food turned out to be excellent: fresh and flavorful. We were both famished and gorged on OJ, ham steaks, grits, home fries, toasted bagels, and enough black coffee to float the Staten Island ferry—if he's still around.

We finished that feast and Al picked up the tab, as promised. We went out to our cars.

"Look," the sergeant said, "you had a nice few hours' sleep. I didn't but I can keep going awhile. What say we pick her up before she learns about what happened to Cussack."

"Suits me," I said. "Just the two of us?"

"Sure. I really don't think we'll need a SWAT team, do you?"

As we drove northward the sun burned off a morning fog, and by the time we arrived at the Trojan Stables the sky was so clear you could glimpse a pale crescent moon in the west. The horse farm was bustling with several riders trying the low hurdles. I spotted Sylvia Forsythe, sans helmet, trying to coax an enormous gray nag to walk with a mincing gait. I was happy to see she had exchanged her harpsichord for a stallion.

Mrs. Constance Forsythe was nowhere to be seen. A stable lad was walking by lugging an English saddle and Rogoff stopped him.

"Is the owner around?" he asked.

The boy eyeballed Al's uniform with some alarm. "In the barn, sir," he said, jerking a thumb over his shoulder.

We headed there.

"Let me take it first," the sergeant said. "I want to shake her. Then you start with your charm routine."

"Bad cop–good cop," I observed.

"Something like that," he agreed.

Mrs. Constance was supervising the mucking out of several stalls. The air was choked with dust and the odor was pungent—to say the least. I know there are people who relish the scent of manure. There are also people who enjoy boiled cabbage. Include me out.

She was wearing jodhpurs and her usual stained riding jacket. But her white T-shirt was fresh, and I thought she had recently had her hair done. It appeared groomed and burnished in the speckled sunlight streaming through skylights. And she carried a crop as if it were a scepter.

She turned as we approached. "Well, well," she said, inspecting us, "two nonpaying visitors. I'm underwhelmed."

Rogoff wasted no time. "Mrs. Forsythe," he said stonily, "about five hours ago Timothy Cussack was shot to death while attempting to escape arrest for the murder of your husband."

If he intended that bald statement to shake her, he failed miserably; she was unshakable. I've told you she was a strong woman. Her only visible reaction was a tightening of the jaw, teeth clenched, a muscle ticking under her chin. She recovered quickly.

"Hard to believe," she said. "But Timmy was always a wild one."

"He was," Al said. "We also have evidence that you were implicated in the crime. That it was committed at your instigation, your urging, and that you, in fact, paid Cussack to murder your husband."

She picked up immediately on the key word. "Evidence?" she said sharply. "What evidence?"

"That you sold and pawned items of property removed from your home without the knowledge or permission of your late husband. That you used those funds to lure Timothy Cussack into joining your conspiracy. That he bought a new car with money you supplied. And that, finally, you gave him five thousand dollars as a down payment for the homicide. A withdrawal from your personal checking account attests to that."

Most of what Rogoff said was b.s., of course. He had not yet proved she had paid for Cussack's Taurus wagon nor had he uncovered a withdrawal from her checking account of five thousand dollars. He was running a bluff, and it didn't work.

"Are you wired?" she asked.

"Am I what, ma'am?" Al asked, startled.

"I watch TV crime shows," she said impatiently. "Are you equipped with a tape recorder?"

"No, I am not. Do you wish to search me?"

"No, thanks," she said. "I'll take your word for it. Now take my word. It is true I removed property from our home because I needed the money to keep the Trojan Stables operating. Expenses are horrendous, and I simply didn't want Griswold to know how much I was spending. Surely you don't expect to convict me of the theft of property owned by a married couple; it was as much mine as his. And it's true I paid Timmy Cussack extra from time to time because he was our most valuable instructor. The clients, mostly women and young girls, just loved him. But as for hiring him to kill my husband, that's garbage! Complete garbage!"

Rogoff sighed. "Will you be willing to accompany me to headquarters, Mrs. Forsythe, and sign a statement of what you have told us?"

"Is this an arrest?" she demanded.

"No, it is not," he said. "Just a voluntary action on your part to help us clear up this matter. You may have an attorney present if you wish."

"I don't need a lawyer," she said. "What I've told you is the truth, and I'm willing to swear to it. Now would you mind leaving me alone with Archy for a few moments? I'd like to speak to him privately."

The sergeant hesitated a moment, then nodded. "I'll wait outside for you," he said. "I have a car."

He glanced at me, turned, and marched out of the barn,

leaving me to face that redoubtable woman. She watched him go.

"Stupid man," she said.

I made no reply.

She moved closer to me. "I don't suppose your father would like to represent me," she said. It was more of a statement than a question.

"It's not what he'd *like* to do," I said tactfully. "It's a problem of conflict of interest. After all, he is the executor of your late husband's estate. But I'm sure if you have need of a reputable attorney, he could recommend someone."

"Yes," she said, staring at me thoughtfully, "ask him to do that, will you? In spite of what I told that odious cop, I may want to have a smart lawyer on my side."

The odor of manure in that vaulted space was so acrid that my eyes began to water. She noticed my discomfort and grinned. "The stink getting to you?" she inquired maliciously.

"Somewhat," I acknowledged.

"I happen to like it," she said. "Earthy. Primitive. God, what a stiff he was!"

At first I thought she was referring to Sgt. Al Rogoff. Then, to my horror, I realized she was speaking of Griswold Forsythe II, recently deceased.

"A stiff!" she repeated. "A mean, stingy old man. No juice in him."

I was offended. *De mortuis nil nisi bonum.*

"Others may think differently," I said.

She tried to appear amused but couldn't quite hide her hurt. "Nora Bledsoe, you mean?" she said. "He was screwing her from the day he moved her in. She could have him, with my blessings. He was a lousy lover."

I tried to be crafty. "Surely divorce would have been preferable to murder."

She laughed. "You *are* devious, aren't you? Archy, I'm not admitting a thing, to you or anyone else. Don't take it so hard. With Cussack's death, the cops can close out the case. Now my kids can live the way they want to, the Trojan Stables belongs to me, and everyone will live happily ever after."

"Not everyone," I said in a low voice. I don't believe she heard me.

We walked outside together. Al Rogoff was waiting. But before we joined him, she paused a moment to survey her domain: acres of greenery, jumping horses, the excited cries of young riders—all sun-spangled and glowing.

"Not bad, is it?" she said.

"No," I had to agree, "not bad at all."

"Paradise," she breathed.

She and Rogoff moved toward his car. I waited because Sylvia Forsythe was heading for the barn, on foot and leading her huge gray horse.

"Hiya, Archy," she said brightly. "Did you see me trying to make this monster behave?"

"I saw," I told her. "Have fun?"

"Loads," she said. "Busy this afternoon?"

"Afraid so," I said. "Besides, I suspect Suite 309 is closed down for the nonce. The police will want to conduct a more thorough search."

I told her what had happened to Timothy Cussack. She didn't seem shocked—or even interested. She shrugged.

"I knew he was a negative from the start," she said. "But you and I—we're positives, aren't we?"

"I'd like to think so," I said.

She gave me a flip of her hand. "We'll make it another time," she said lightly and continued leading her mount to the barn.

Not bloody likely, I thought. To be excruciatingly honest, she was just too frothy for me. I vaulted into the saddle of my mount and pointed the Miata eastward.

You know what I was wondering as I drove, don't you? Of course you do. You are questioning, as I was, whether or not Mrs. Constance Forsythe had an affair with Timothy Cussack, in addition to their conspiracy to murder her husband. Well, you know as much about their characters and motives as I do, and the choice is yours.

As for my opinion, berserk horses couldn't drag that from me—although an irascible Chihuahua might.

I arrived at the Forsythe aviary in a tempestuous mood, hoping both vultures would be present and strutting. There was really no rational reason for seeking this showdown; it would accomplish nothing. But I was stormy with resentment, determined to ruffle the feathers of those rapacious birds.

Anthony Bledsoe opened the door, and I could see he was stricken.

"Tim Cussack," he blurted. "Did you hear what happened? It was on TV."

"Yes," I said, "I heard."

"My God," he said, looking as if he might weep, "that's awful."

"Awful," I agreed. "Are Griswold and Geraldine Forsythe at home?"

"They're having lunch. Should I tell them you're here?"

"No," I said sternly. "Just direct me to where they're lunching."

I had never before entered the formal dining room. The

phrase "baronial hall" immediately sprang to mind. The enormous arched chamber was complete with tasseled velvet drapes at the windows and ghastly oil portraits of forebears hanging on oak-paneled walls. The long table could easily have accommodated a platoon of guests, and there was a carved walnut sideboard with a marble top that would have caused instant hernia if anyone ever tried to lift it.

Griswold Forsythe III was seated at the head of the plank, sister Geraldine on his right. They were both wearing crisp white linen and appeared to be sharing a gigantic wooden bowl of Caesar salad. Their glasses were filled with white wine, and the bottle was placed on a coaster between them. I caught a look at the label. Dreadful plonk.

They both looked up, startled, when I came barging in.

"Archy!" Griswold said without rising. "How nice to see you again."

I doubted that.

But I had no desire to exchange pleasantries. "You've probably heard," I said in the coldest voice I could muster, "Timothy Cussack was shot dead by the police while attempting to escape arrest for the murder of your father."

"We heard," Geraldine said. "A shock!"

"The man must have been demented," the Forsythe scion said, shaking his thick head. "What could he possibly have gained? It's just terrible."

"Oh, come off it," I said angrily. "I think both of you are secretly relieved."

They stared at me. "What a rotten thing to say!" he shouted, and then he rose to his feet.

"Is it?" I said. "How is this for a scenario: on the evening before the day he was killed, your father determined to his satisfaction that it was your mother who had been removing valuable items from your home and either selling or pawning them."

"I must ask you to leave at once," Griswold said. "You are no longer welcome in this house."

"Oh, stuff it," I said. "Your father reported what he had discovered, told you about the threatening note he had received and, I suspect, said he was convinced his wife had written it. He also announced his intention of taking the whole matter to the police the following day."

"You're hallucinating," he said. "Nothing of the sort ever occurred."

"No?" I said. "And neither did the Battle of Waterloo. The first thing you did, reckoning how you might profit from this state of affairs, was to run to mommy dearest and tell her what your father planned. That triggered his murder the following day before he could report his suspicions to the police."

"You're insane!" Geraldine cried. "Totally mad!"

I turned to her. "And you," I said, "what a dandy you turned out to be. I guessed almost from the start that the jewelry you claimed had disappeared had never been stolen; those were baubles you had *given* to Timothy Cussack to win his fidelity when you were having a thing with him. But he dumped you, and you suspected unjustly that he had taken up with your sister-in-law. And so you resolved to prove them thieves and asked me to provide proof. Then, when your brother eventually told you of your mother's involvement, you instructed me to end my investigation."

She gave me a scathing glare. "Louse!" she said.

I felt no contrition at all. "Congreve was right," I said. " 'Hell hath no fury . . .' And after you discovered it was your mother rather than Sylvia who supplanted you, you saw, like your brother, the profit that might result from that."

"Griswold!" she screamed. "Get this maniac out of here!"

I turned back to him. "Just as you called off my search for the stolen family property when you learned Constance was probably guilty. Neither of you acted from any filial loyalty. The two of you were not part of the murder conspiracy, I admit, but yours were sins of omission. You were hoping for your father's demise—visions of sugarplums were dancing in the shape of those grand bequests you'd receive—and so you did nothing to prevent your father's murder."

"Tony!" Griswold shouted at the top of his lungs. "Tony! Come here at once!"

"No need to have me forcibly ejected from the premises," I told him. "I'm leaving, happy to have had the opportunity to inform you that I and others are fully aware of your treachery."

I stalked to the door, then turned back to face them. "By the way," I said casually, "I forgot to mention that your mother is presently in police custody and is being questioned. Ta-ta."

I didn't tell them she had denied everything and was probably going to walk away scot-free.

Let them sweat.

27

My furies somewhat ameliorated, I drove back to the McNally Building on Royal Palm Way. I was eager for hours of dreamless slumber, but there was one more chore I had to perform: my father needed to be informed of what had transpired since I last reported.

I didn't have to phone for an appointment for as I pulled into our underground garage I saw him alight from his black Lexus and walk toward the elevator. I parked hurriedly, hopped out, and scurried to his side.

"Do you have a few minutes, sir?" I asked.

He frowned. "Very few. A client is arriving shortly. What is it, Archy?"

I told him what had happened to Timothy Cussack, omitting any mention of the part I had played in that sanguinary climax. Then I related a detailed account of Sgt. Rogoff's and my confrontation with Mrs. Constance Forsythe at the Trojan Stables. I concluded with a description of my most recent encounter with Griswold the Three and Geraldine.

The squire began to pace rapidly up and down the concrete floor of the garage. I had to hustle to keep at his side.

"Mrs. Forsythe admitted nothing?" he asked.

"Nothing," I replied. "She stonewalled. Seemed very

sure of herself although she did ask that you recommend an attorney she might retain."

"Do the police have any evidence other than what you've told me regarding her role in this affair? To wit, the pawning of property taken from her home, purchase of a car for Cussack, possible withdrawals from her bank account."

"No, sir. As far as I know that's all Rogoff has."

"Do you think it possible you or he may uncover additional evidence of her involvement?"

"Doubtful," I said. "Father, this woman may be perfidious but she is no dummy. I'm sure there were no witnesses to her plotting with Cussack, no letters written, nothing that might inculpate her."

I had never seen him so shaken. Because, I supposed, he admired Mrs. Constance as much as I did. Not, of course, for what she had done but for the woman she was, her awesome strength and resolve.

He wagged his head. "Not enough, Archy," he said. "Not nearly enough to charge her, let alone convict. The state attorney won't touch it. Prosecutors have no great love for lost causes. If she sticks to her denials she'll walk free."

I was indignant. "That's not right!" I cried. "I *know* the woman is guilty. I know it, Rogoff knows it, and *she* knows it. Whatever happened to justice?"

He gave me a tight smile. "Don't despair, Archy. Justice is a hope, not a certainty."

"Yes, sir," I said mournfully.

He stopped pacing to face me. "However," he added grimly, "I am the executor of the deceased Mr. Forsythe's estate. I don't believe you, or they, fully realize the powers of an executor. Almost unlimited. Obviously I cannot legally deny the widow and surviving children their inheritances. But there are two kinds of time, Archy: the ordinary of hours and days. And then there is legal time, measured in years and decades. There are many things I can lawfully do as an executor to delay the rewards Mrs. Constance Forsythe and her offspring so avidly anticipate.''

My father is not a vindictive man, you understand, but on occasion he fancies himself God's surrogate on earth. I was confident he had the power and resolution to do what he had stated. It would not be as satisfactory as seeing Mrs. Constance tried and convicted for conspiracy in the murder of her husband, but it provided a small soother to my outrage.

Father continued on to the elevator, and I returned to my velocipede. I drove directly home and asked Mrs. Olson to wake me in time for the cocktail hour. Then I went upstairs, disrobed, and flopped into bed. Fatigued? I felt as if I had just completed a triathlon while lugging a 150-lb. anvil.

I was awaken in time to shower, dress, and present a respectable appearance at family gatherings that evening. The preprandial martinis were especially welcome. The dinner of broiled butcher's steak completed my rejuvenation. Who was it who said, "I love to eat red meat but it must come from a cow that smoked"?

I went up to my digs afterward, beginning to feel I might live to play the kazoo again. I intended to complete the Forsythe saga in my journal, but Al Rogoff phoned before I could even start scribbling.

"Did Constance say anything while the two of you were alone?" he demanded.

"Nothing, Al," I told him. "Didn't admit a thing."

"She's one tough lady," he said. "We couldn't budge her. Did you tell your father about her?"

"I did."

"And?"

"He said she'll walk."

"He's so right," Rogoff said, sighing. "The state attorney's office laughed at us. It's a no-win. Well, what the hell, we got one of them, didn't we? Fifty percent. I'll settle for that."

"I won't," I said.

"Come on, Archy. You want everything nice and neat. You want the good rewarded and the evil punished. You know life's not like that."

"I guess," I said dolefully.

"Besides," he went on, "I'm not totally without clout, you know. There are a lot of inspectors in this town and county. Electrical, sewers and sanitation, environmental, labor, building codes, fire safety—all kinds of inspectors. I figure to drop a hint here and there. Mrs. Constance Forsythe is going to have more inspectors than customers. Not as satisfying as seeing her in the clink, I admit, but I can make her life miserable if I choose—and I do choose. It's not the solution I wanted but it'll give me a charge. How about you?"

"Better than nothing," I admitted, thinking that with the vengeful plans of my father and Rogoff, the Widow Forsythe might find her dream of paradise slightly tarnished.

"I'm off on a forty-eight," Al reported. "Nothing but sleep. So long, old buddy. Stay in touch."

He hung up and I was left staring at my open journal. It was dispiriting to consider completing the history of the Forsythe case. As Rogoff had said, it was a half-victory. But the half-defeat rankled. I craved solace and so I phoned Connie Garcia.

"What are you doing?" I asked her.

"Painting my toenails and watching TV."

"I yearn for you."

"You *yearn* for me?" she repeated incredulously. "Since when?"

"Since this minute," I told her. "If I rush over with a cold bottle of bubbles will you allow me entrance to your abode?"

"I might," she said.

That was good enough for me; I rushed. I think it must have been around midnight when, emboldened by champagne, I stood naked on her little balcony overlooking Lake Worth. I stretched my arms to the heavens and did an awful imitation of James Cagney in *White Heat*.

"Top of the world, ma!" I shouted joyously.